is waiting for George, her fiancé, to
return from the Navy.

THE BRETONS OF ELM STREET
is the story of a loving family who
stand by each other in the tough moments, from the time when Ed, the
father, finds that for the first time he
cannot fix things for his daughter, to
the moment when Freddie and Charles,
the young sons, try to sell a snake by
mail and run afoul of the U. S. Post
Office. The story also reveals the de-
velopment of the Bretons' little granddaughter who is the very heart of the
household and whose preparation for
life is its dearest concern; and touches
understandingly on the difference in
points of view of a grandmother and
her daughter-in-law.

But above all THE BRETONS OF
ELM STREET takes us back to a consideration of the ethics to which Americans are bred, of what is meant by love,
by family life, and to the strength of
our past, the fundamentals of our present and future.

Here is a book that lovingly reveals
the intimate relationships in an American family whose members are the de-
lightful sort of people you want to
know. To read THE BRETONS OF
ELM STREET is to gain new respect
and understanding for a way of life
that is good—and very American.

THE BRETONS OF ELM STREET

By Henrietta Ripperger

112 ELM STREET

THE BRETONS OF ELM STREET

The Bretons
OF ELM STREET

by

HENRIETTA RIPPERGER

G. P. PUTNAM'S SONS

New York

This novel is based on a series published
in *Redbook* under the title "U. S. Today."

Manufactured in the United States of America
VAN REES PRESS • NEW YORK

To

ROBBIE STEPHEN

The Author wishes to thank the copyright owner, Williamson Music, Inc., for permission to use some lines from "Oh, What a Beautiful Mornin'" from *Oklahoma!* by Richard Rodgers and Oscar Hammerstein, 2d. She also wishes to thank the copyright owner, T. B. Harms Company, for permission to use some lines from "Make Believe" from *Show Boat* by Jerome Kern and Oscar Hammerstein, 2d.

THE BRETONS OF ELM STREET

THE MAN ACROSS FROM ME was tall, even sitting down. His face was heavy, yet sensitive, as a dancer may have considerable weight yet be very light on his feet. There was a perpetual little frown of care above his nose. It went away as he spoke but returned the minute his face was still again. His eyes were a serious gray blue with a light in them which was often humorous but never mocking. From an armchair marked, invisibly, it is true, as his own, he dominated the pleasant room.

On the mahogany-top table beside him stood photographs of his family. The one in the dark blue leather frame was his eldest son Dick, a responsible-looking young man in uniform, and, at that time, a lieutenant with the Army. The girl whose picture was held between sheets of transparent plastic (the holder had been selected by her) was his daughter Babs. She had sleek dark hair, fine eyes, and wide lips, made even more generous with lipstick. From the parts of a small red leather folder two boys of thirteen and fourteen faced each other, scowling self-consciously out from under football helmets. These were his son Freddie, and Charles, a boy he had adopted informally when the latter was evacuated from England. Finally, there was a largish portrait of Eileen, Dick's wife, with their little girl sitting small and erect beside her; Eileen, thin, wistful, with a mass of blond hair; Barbara Elizabeth, sturdy-looking with great round gray eyes and a topknot of curls with a bow. There was no picture of his wife. "Why should I want one?" he had been known to say. "I have the original and that's a whole lot better." The man was my husband.

3

The room where we were was the center of our home. A hall ran through the house, dividing it. The living room lay to the left running the whole length of the house, with a sun porch off from it to the south. To the right was the dining room and beyond, the pantry, kitchen, and back piazza. The main stairway of the house fanned out into the middle of the hall with handrails on either side. It reached the second floor just outside Ed's and my bedroom. Babs's door was just across from ours and beyond that was a large room that had been Dick's and that had been occupied ever since he went to war by his wife and, subsequently, by his small daughter as well. The third floor consisted of a storeroom across the floor of which were strewn the tracks for an electric train, a dilapidated doll carriage, an old doll house, a broken-down typewriter, and many, many other things. There were also two bedrooms up there. One was shared by Freddie and Charles. The other, a big bare sunny room, belonged to Norah. She had been with us since Freddie was a baby and was indispensable not only to our household routine but also to our hearts.

Within this house we lived in a large but definitely drawn circle. True, the children ran in and out with their friends and the milk and cookies set out after school were for the whole neighborhood. But we did not do any formal entertaining; our household was far too busy for that. Our hospitality, when it was offered at all, was for old friends; we added them on special occasions, on birthdays or anniversaries, as a kind of loving audience to our family happiness. We did not meet strangers with their different outlooks, their varied experiences, their ideals at odds with our own. We did not do anything much for the outside world, nor did we worry about it. Our minds were comfortable, or had been. Only our eager anxiety for our son Dick led our minds outward. . . .

Such was the setting to which our children habitually came home.

As I entered the living room Babs's voice came from the depths of the couch. "You know, Moms, Daddy's awfully selfish in a nice way. It's all right—" she waved a pair of green-shod feet over the sofa arm, "they aren't on the pillows."

4

"Selfish? How?" I sat down across the room from her, eying the upraised sandals. I thought, unexpectedly, of our pony at home, when I was small, rolling in a grassy hollow, hoofs in air.

"Oh, I'm not picking on your darling," she went on, "but when you're grown up you notice things; things like how *you* run the house, *you* struggle with Freddie and Charles. *You* worry about the baby and help Eileen with her. And what does Daddy do? Sits in his big chair. And now *you've* got to cope with the decorating."

"Daddy's department is the office where the money comes from," I told her. "The house is mine."

"All the same, he could help. I heard him tell you you could do the house and he'd come back from the office when it was all over. Well, I wouldn't stand for that."

I tried to explain. "He didn't mean it literally. You and Eileen and I are home all the time; we like to stir things up. We love changing the furniture around and putting a different color on the walls. But men hate upsets; they get plenty of that in business." When she did not comment, I went on, "They want to be able to count on peace at home. This is where Daddy relaxes."

"I'll say he does." Babs's voice ran contemptuously down the minor scale as she disposed of her father.

Sooner or later I tell Ed everything. That night I quoted Babs, adding, "This is strictly for laughs."

He did laugh but rather shortly. I realized suddenly that he cared a good deal what his eighteen-year-old daughter thought. It was evident from the almost angry way he came back.

"And what is Babs doing to help on this job, may I ask?"

I shuddered. "Nothing, I hope."

"Well, make her handle the painters. She can do it."

"And find my home painted chartreuse-green with pink spots?" I said. "Not me!"

"Babs has good taste," Ed said, "and I bet she knows a lot about decorating, too. Kids pick up these things; they get around. Besides," he added, "you made some mistakes, don't forget, when you were her age or even older."

I laughed. "Remember the time I ordered pink for our first

5

bedroom and it came out that awful orchid? I almost cried myself sick."

"I sure do." Ed grinned. "It looked exactly like a—a harem. But we managed to survive in it for a whole year."

"Maybe this *is* the age for Babs to learn that a wrong color isn't one of the major tragedies of life," I said, slowly. The thought of Babs pouring her great energy into the harassing task ahead was beginning to give me a sense of relief.

"My bet is she won't make mistakes," Ed said. "I'll tell her she's got to do it, first thing in the morning."

Babs received the news with a thoughtfulness that for some reason I felt to be vaguely ominous. Was she going to object, or take Ed himself to task? I didn't want her to do that.

"Stop *hovering*." Babs looked up from a scrap of paper on which she was writing. "Daddy's giving me all the dope. What did you say Mr. Brix's house number was, Daddy?"

Ed told her. Mr. Brix is the painter who has done our work for years. Once he had half a dozen helpers; now he came alone. We'd probably have to wait weeks to get him.

"Well, that's everything," Ed said. "I don't want to be asked for advice and I won't look at samples. From now on, count me out." He left for the office.

Babs and Eileen preceded me into the living room.

"Personally," Babs said, "I'd like to do over the downstairs instead of up. I was thinking maybe the whole hall could be covered with mirrors, you know; small ones, like tiles. It makes a place look larger. Then I'd love to get a table and chair of that stuff that looks like glass. I think it would cheer up the front of the house as you came in."

Eileen glanced at me, half shutting her blue eyes understandingly, then opening them wide. "Furnishing is pretty expensive," she said. "That time I tried to do the one room Dick and I had down near the camp, before he was sent overseas; the prices were ghastly."

"Then I wish I could fix up this room so it wasn't so dreary," Babs went on.

"Dreary?" I looked about me at the composite of books, armchairs, pictures, rugs—"Why, I love it."

"I'm sure you do, dear." Babs sat down on the middle of

6

the couch and put her toes together, as another might touch his fingertips, in thought. "But it doesn't have to look quite so much like Lincoln's birthplace. I'd throw out half this stuff, beginning with the rugs."

"But these rugs are priceless." I was indignant. "They're old Orientals, vegetable dyes...."

"Also, they're dark, they're fussy, they do nothing for you." She gazed dourly at the pink design in the blue background at her feet. "I'd put a great big white woolly rug in here. You'd be surprised at the difference it would make."

"I'm sure I would."

The sarcasm passed unnoticed. Babs's glance had shifted to an etching in a gilt frame on the opposite wall. "There's another Civil War touch," she said. " 'Nymphs at Play.' Honestly!"

"It was one of the first things Daddy and I bought," I said. "We got it at an auction."

"Well, anyway." Some awareness made her suppress what passed through her mind at that point. "I'd like to put a great big photographic panel across that whole side of the room. I saw just the one, with clouds and telephone-pole tops. It made you feel you were right up in the air. It would just open out that whole side of the room."

"Daddy likes things closed in; sort of cozy," I said.

"But, darling," Babs's tone was patient, "coziness went out with bustles."

"Whatever *they* were," Eileen put in. "Wait—" She was listening for something.

"And I was thinking about *your* room, Moms. I don't know *why* you always have it painted ivory," Babs went on. "Even with that awful old green rug you could use any one of a lot of colors; lemon, orange, pistache—"

I tried a weak joke. "Daddy and I like vanilla." It passed unnoticed.

"It *is* Barbara Elizabeth," Eileen jumped up. "She wakes up and doesn't like being alone." She started for the porch.

"Listen, crumbbun, why don't we do our baby-pushing now and go around and see if we can get Mr. Brix? Want to, huh?" She followed Eileen.

I sat down at my desk. They went by in the hall, Barbie in a yellow sprigged muslin, sitting up very straight, full of importance. I heard the gocart jounce down the steps. I had already begun my weekly letter to Dick, somewhere in Italy. Through the window I saw them, Eileen, my daughter-in-law, leaning slightly forward, watching the crossing, not looking at the baby, Babs sauntering along, a hand on the side of the gocart. For the moment, slurs on my taste and forebodings over Babs's decorative activities were forgotten. "They look so adorable." I wrote, "I wish you could see them."

Negotiations between Mr. Brix and myself are always prolonged. It was a distinct surprise therefore to be aroused next morning by Norah calling up, "The painter's come!" and to hear the accompanying rattle of stepladder and boards in the back yard.

I came down later to find Babs, in gray slacks and a red shirt, astride the porch rail. Mr. Brix was working the cover off a five-gallon can. A radio the size of a cigarette box stood on the flat top of the post and gave out with "Oh, What a Beautiful Morning."

From the window of the pantry where I was making my own coffee—Norah was downstairs doing her washing—I could see and hear them.

"We'll do my room first," Babs was saying. "It's going to be green."

"White's the best color," Mr. Brix said. He looked down at the yellow, oily surface of the contents of the can. "White repays you. I did my whole house a glossy white paint; it washes like a dish. My wife wanted blue but I told her better." He poked with a wooden stirrer.

"It's my own room," Babs explained, "and I like green."

"Blue, green, yellow, everybody's got different ideas," Mr. Brix said. "White's my choice. Oh, not *dead* white, you understand," for Babs had moved impatiently, leaning forward, her dark hair falling unchecked across her face, "just a good clear ivory."

"Listen, Mr. Brix." Babs snapped the cover down, shutting off the music on high. "Did you bring the blue and yellow pigment, the way you promised?"

"I got 'em." Reluctantly, I thought, he pulled out two small

8

cans. "Of course I can mix green all right, if that's what you want. I done it last week up at Morcisson's. Kind of a hard, light bluey shade."

Babs leaned back, rocking on the rail, her eye roving the lawn. "Mr. Brix," she asked dreamily, "did you ever notice the very first little leaves on an apple tree, the tiny, baby ones? Well, that's the shade I mean."

Mr. Brix stopped stirring and stood up. "I ain't agonna waste no mornin' matchin' hues made by the Almighty," he said.

"All right, then," Babs swung a leg to the floor, "I'll do it myself." Her voice shook a little. "After all, it just happens to be my room and I'm going to have it the way I want it."

"You are, huh?" Mr. Brix looked hard at the vivid girl before him. He looked at the red shirt and the gray slacks. He was a spare man, not old, but thin, as if his thinness were the abrasive effect of time. "This country's being ruined by girls in pants," he said, "usin' up good seed, gardenin', workin' like men in shops. They'll be painters, too, first thing you know."

Babs stopped, caught by something outraged in his tone. Her understanding of how a man feels is instinctive. Her manner changed. "Please, Mr. Brix," she said, "*you* mix it for me. What do you say, huh? I bet you've got a wonderful eye for color."

"Well," he turned, somewhat mollified, to the paint pots, "I'll try fixin' up a sample for you."

He poured a little of the white paint into an empty can. They bent over the process, thick as thieves.

"Oh, and another thing, I forgot; I want the ceiling pale yellow."

Mr. Brix straightened. "Ceilin's has *gotta* be white." he said. Then he went to stirring again. I heard a sound, half grunt, half groan. Mr. Brix knew when he was beaten and at his own game.

Encouraged by Babs, Mr. Brix kept briskly at work, and in due time her room was completed. He parked his paint pots and brushes at the end of the upper hall for the night. Babs summoned us all by shouts.

The yellow ceiling hung like a colored umbrella above the green. It was a bright but soft yellow. The effect was engaging,

The boys and I crowded through the door. Eileen poked her head in. "Hey, what's the cover charge?—I'm just being silly." She had seen the anxious look on Babs's face. She stepped in and gazed admiringly about her. "It's lovely."

"*I* like it." Babs studied the effect. "I mean, personally, I was sure the green and yellow would set each other off. I mean, I hope so. I *think* it's going to be all right—" Her voice trailed off uncertainly.

Charles mounted the footboard of the bed and looked about him, eying the enveloping color. "It's like being up in the horse-chestnut tree," he announced, "only the sky ought to be blue."

"Don't you get up there, too," I checked Freddie. Bingo Brown was behind him; the footboard certainly wouldn't stand up under them all.

"Our room's goin' to be sort of a navy color." Freddie countered my words with another topic.

"What color's that?" Bingo said it with his fierce manner as if it was all-important for him to understand.

"It's what sailors use."

"Oh, I didn't tell you about that, Moms." Babs sat down on the edge of the bed and clasped her hands. "I got the idea from some kids at college; they painted their room dead black with a white ceiling. It was simply *outstanding*."

"It must have been," I said dryly. "Well, don't do it here."

"I'm not going to." Babs's voice was serene. "Relax. The boys' room is going to be navy blue with a scarlet trim. Mr. Brix thought of the red. He remembered a room he saw in a store window with a red line around the doors and baseboard. Wasn't that bright of him?"

"I thought at first he was going to win out and get his old ivory after all," Eileen put in, "but you—"

"The guy's all right, after you get to know him," Babs said earnestly. "It's just he feels kind of—kind of *defeated,* having women tell him what to do, every house he works in."

"That Mr. Brix knows what he wants." Norah stood in the doorway eying the walls and ceiling. It was plain she and Mr. Brix saw eye to eye in the matter of decoration. She voiced her experience of life. "In the end things have got to be done a man's way."

"Now, Norah," Babs's voice was eager, "Mr. Brix is all right and please don't say anything against men. I love them all."

The boys' room was a success; more immediate, perhaps, than Babs's own. The double-decker maple bed stood out smartly against the dark, clean color. I almost trusted her to go ahead in my bedroom. Almost. Anyway, I would let her use some light, pretty shade. Perhaps I could get Ed to express a preference. When we were all at supper I asked him.

He smiled tolerantly. "Do it fireman's red so long as you don't bother me." It was at this moment that the phone rang. Norah came in to summon Babs. We could hear her voice in the hall.

"But you can't do that to me." It was just a wail. "You don't have to go now; not right away. It won't take you all day." There was silence. Evidently the person at the other end had finished and hung up.

Babs came back to the table, sagging her shoulders to indicate despair.

"It was Mr. Brix," she said. "The draft board's got him. He's all in a lather. He has to go for a physical examination. He says he has all sorts of things to attend to. He just won't come back and do your room, not now, maybe never." She sat down and reached for a cinnamon bun. "He has broken my heart," she said.

Before I could answer, the phone rang again. It was the head of volunteers at the hospital calling me. I'm available, theoretically, for emergencies. Would I come early tomorrow and take care of the receptionist's desk till six o'clock? If the painter were coming I would have found some excuse to stay at home and supervise the decorating of my own bedroom, but I had none now. I promised to go.

I drank my breakfast coffee hurriedly. Ed lingered with Barbara Elizabeth. I could hear the boys in the kitchen running the water as they filled their canteens—they were going on a scout hike—while Norah urged them to get through and out of her kitchen.

I refused Ed's offer to drive me to the hospital en route to the factory. They were having such a good time together, Ed and the girls. War is awful, I thought, as I rode down the street in the bus, but it does give the men Ed's age the center of the stage again. Ed was so happy with them.

The hospital always makes me sad; I left for home at six almost eagerly. There was no one around when I came in. I found Norah giving my small granddaughter her supper, which in itself was unusual.

"Have a cup of tea, Mrs. Breton." Norah spoke almost anxiously. She seemed to wish to detain me.

But I had heard faint sounds from overhead, like something being dragged across the floor. "I'll have my tea later—"

I ran up. Our room is at the top of the stairs. Eileen stood in the doorway wielding a paintbrush. "Oh, hello." She drew back to let me enter.

The room has two windows facing south. A French window to the west opens onto the sleeping porch. Now, the late sun beamed through it.

My first impression was a shock of repellent color. The walls were a livid, orchidy pink.

"You *would* come home like food shot out of guns." Ed turned under the ceiling and sat down on the top of the stepladder. "We just barely got through."

"I'll say we did." Babs was wiping paint spots from the floor in the corner. Now she stood up, her hands full of rags. There was a smear of rose under one brown eye. It gave her a distracted look. "Like it?"

I stood for a moment speechless, as the walls smote my eyes.

"It's—it's *outstanding*." Babs's own word came to my rescue.

"We were just dying to surprise you and Daddy said to go ahead. I mixed the color myself." Babs looked critically but not unfavorably on her work. "I meant it to be a sort of bluey violet, but then it went kind of pink on me; and trying to fix it I kept getting it darker—" Her voice hung in air. "But it'll dry lighter, won't it?"

"It was a continuous operation," Eileen explained. "Everybody but Barbara Elizabeth swung a brush. Norah painted that baseboard while we ate lunch." She pointed to the near wall.

"Even then we'd never have finished if Daddy hadn't come home and helped. Eileen and I were just about shooting our cookies from the paint fumes, when he blew in and took over the hard part, up top. I was never so glad to see a man in all my life."

Ed's eyes met mine. They were very gray and very deep. Try to understand this, dear, they begged me. The important thing is that the youngsters wanted to do this for you, not that the color of the room is all wrong—

"Daddy's a good man to have along," I said.

"I think the room is up to date now; modern," Ed said, stoutly. "I like it; but then I'm no old stick-in-the-mud."

His eyes moved to Babs. He was telling me. From now on *he* was going with them, whether he agreed with their taste or not. And he was giving me my chance; I could come too if I wanted to. I made my decision.

"Cat got your tongue?" Babs asked. "Or how's for a few words of appreciation?"

"You did a wonderful painting job," I said. "I never dreamed my room could look like this. It—it was darling of you."

Ed watched me. "I said you'd be tickled *pink.*"

No one paid any attention to this terrible pun but me. *I* grinned up at him.

"Thanks." His warm glance swept mine. No one would ever take away from me my place as end man in the old team, it told me; that place was mine to keep.

I swallowed hard; I must think of something more to say to the girls. I backed up to the wall behind me for support.

"Hey; look out; watch it, you little dumbbell!" Ed sprang from the ladder.

But he was too late. My hands and dress were pressed into wet pink paint.

13

CHAPTER

2

"ASLEEP?" Ed's hand touched my cheek.

I opened one eye. "Hello! What time is it? How was the bridge game?"

"A little after one." Ed turned on the light and came and stood by the bed. The hairy wool of his suit gave off tiny currents of night air. "It was one of the nicest games we ever had," he said. "I don't know why."

I yawned and sat up. Ed was plainly in the mood in which he craved companionship. "How about something to eat?" I suggested.

"I could go for some scrambled eggs. I thought I'd come home and have 'em with you."

We went down together to the kitchen, shining and orderly at this hour. A clock on the shelf ticked loudly as if waiting just for us. While I cooked, Ed made toast; after which we sat down around the corner from each other at the enamel-topped table.

"Now tell me about everything," I began.

It was then we heard the voice. It came down the dark well of the back stairs and asked anxiously, "Is somebody sick? Can I do anything?"

"Come on down, Sarah, and join us," Ed called into the dark. My sister Sarah appeared in the doorway. One hand clasped the neck of her navy silk bathrobe, the other held up a small bottle of pills. Her eyes, blue where mine are brown, and very big, blinked at the sudden glare. "Oh! I heard you moving around and I thought perhaps someone was ill."

"I never felt better in my life." Ed smiled up into Sarah's

troubled face. His feeling for my older sister is one of affectionate respect, tinged with amusement. "I made Elizabeth get up. She's no fun when she's asleep," he added, cheerfully.

Sarah eyed him doubtfully and a little shyly. I sprang to her rescue. "Let me fix *you* something to eat."

"Not at this hour, thank you." Sarah's tone regained its normal note of assurance as she spoke to me. "If you *do* have an upset," she went on, "these are simply wonderful." She studied the label on the bottle. "It says, 'Reduce dose for elderly persons,' but *I* take all I want." She put the bottle in her pocket. "You'd better come up soon, Elizabeth. We're not as young as we were, you know," she added seriously, looking at Ed.

"I suppose not." Ed sighed. "Well, we'll all turn in shortly."

Sarah had arrived for a visit the day before. "You'll all love her," I told the children. "She's just a brick." As a matter of fact, they already loved her. Ever since I had married and had children, Sarah had lavished a long-distance affection on us all.

She came in with her large eyes shining and both arms wide. Ed, behind her, was carrying a suitcase which she could hardly wait to open. It proved to be full of presents; a baseball mitt for Freddie and a catcher's mask for Charles, red bedroom boots, ankle high and lined with lamb's wool, for Babs ("I remember how cold the corridors were at night when I was in college"), records for our daughter-in-law, Eileen, and a billfold for Dick ("When he comes home from Italy, and I think Hitler will give in pretty soon, don't you?"), and for Barbara Elizabeth a tiny music box with three angels that revolved on the top.

"Aunt Sarah is so good to us," I told them all, my arm around my sister's familiar figure. "This is like Christmas when you used to send the children a big box. Remember the time you cried, Freddie, because the box was late? And you thought Santa Claus had come again and brought you only four presents?"

"Not me," Freddie said, "I'm not that dumb. I bet that was Babs." Freddie biffed the mitt with his right fist. "Gee, this is some glove."

15

"I miss Babs." Sarah looked around the circle of five.

"She'll show up," Freddie said, "she never misses a good thing.

"She will?" Sarah asked.

"Yes. She'll be back Saturday. College is so near by she almost always spends her week ends at home; we count on that."

Sarah spoke gently. "I should think it would be much better for her to stay at college and not interrupt her academic life."

"I suppose it would." I considered this. "But Babs is a girl who loves her home. I never thought of telling her not to come. On the few times when she doesn't come, it's because there's a better engagement. Usually it's with George."

"George? I must hear about him—later. Now, I want to see Barbara Elizabeth."

As if sent on by the coach, Barbara Elizabeth came straddling down the hall from the kitchen. She wore a crew-necked sweater over her rompers. Clutched in her right arm, like a football, was an egg. Behind her was Norah. As she heard Norah's steps she slid the egg under her sweater.

"The old Carlisle Indian play," Ed observed. "They invented that play back in 1903. It's been barred for years."

"Oops! Touchdown!" Charlie jumped forward as the baby took a nose dive.

All arms and legs, Barbara Elizabeth got up. There was a brief moment of uncertainty, but as everyone else smiled, she did, too. Miraculously, the egg appeared to be unbroken, but as she lurched onward toward her mother it slipped from under her sweater. Freddie caught it deftly in his mitt.

"Let's get out of this shambles." Ed put one arm through Sarah's and one through mine.

"Babs always says it's a relief to go back Sunday nights to a nice quiet college dormitory with only seventy girls in it, where everybody isn't in everybody else's hair." I laughed as I said it because to me, and I knew to Babs as well, all this riot is homelike.

Sarah made no comment and just momentarily I had an uneasy feeling, nothing more, a cloud no bigger than a man's hand, that she was going to see much in our house that could be improved; and Sarah is not one to leave any wrong uncorrected.

On the morning following Sarah's arrival, and the bridge game, the two of us went into the living room for a good talk. "Lie down on the sofa," Sarah urged. "You ought to rest whenever you can." Perhaps she had got me to thinking of myself, for as I stretched out it occurred to me how seldom, in a big family, the living room couch was available to me. Eileen had joked about it once, asking as she came in, "Is there a small uncomfortable chair for mother?" Sarah chose a large, straight seat. "Want a cigarette?" she asked. "Let me get you one."

"They're right here if I do," I told her. "Remember the first ones we ever smoked?" I went on. "It was on the side steps at home. Mother made them for us out of sweet fern and tissue paper."

Sarah smiled. "And she thought using tobacco was a sin."

"I know. I suppose there are things about each other that people even in the same household just never can understand," I said.

A warm current of family feeling ran between us. "And remember the horse-chestnut tree outside our window?" I asked. "And the night you were saying your prayers and a bee flew in and stung the bottom of your foot? The way you shrieked, I thought the Indians had come."

"I'd forgotten that," Sarah said. "But I do remember the birds in that tree just after dark and the different little sounds they made settling down at night. They weren't at all like the ones they made in the daytime."

"That's the way Barbara Elizabeth does," I remarked. "She lies in her crib, just making interesting little sounds to herself. They get louder as she gets older."

"And I suppose *you* run up to see if she's all right." Sarah shifted in her chair and her finely formed hands followed the contour of the wooden arm as if molding it. "I've been watching you, Beth." She used the childhood name I hadn't heard for years. "You wear yourself out running after your family."

Silly as it was, it was by no means unpleasant to hear oneself

17

discussed in such favorable terms. But all I said was, "Oh, I don't think I do."

"You don't realize it." Sarah's serious blue eyes were fixed on my face. "I made up my mind before coming not to say a *word,* but—Ed's a dear, of course—but honestly, Beth, making you get up at two in the morning to cook for him and saying you're no fun when you're asleep—"

"That was just his little joke," I put in.

"But we're not as young as we used to be, Beth," Sarah said, "and you need your rest. I *do* think that if you had your own room or at least your own—" She hesitated.

I suppressed a smile. Sarah frowns on double beds, which I consider, among other things, cosy. Sarah, who is a sensitive person, changed her ground. "Freddie and Charles could be far more considerate of you than they are. They could stay away from the house more than they do and let you have a little quiet."

"But I *try* to keep them around home," I told her.

"A person coming in from the outside has a little more perspective," she went on as if she had not heard me. "And I've been wondering if it wouldn't be better for everyone concerned if Eileen took a little home of her own, even if it was just a room or two somewhere. She herself might really be happier that way."

I moved restlessly. I do not like fingers, even loving ones, poking about the roots of my life. I could laugh off comments on Ed and the boys but this remark about Eileen upset me because I wasn't completely sure of my ground. Eileen is reserved; with Dick far away and in danger she has often seemed sad. But I have never thought she was not happy here. Yet Sarah might be right.

"I think she likes being just one of us," I said. Sarah smiled.

"Are you sure that isn't just wishful thinking?" she asked. "Don't you think it's possible that she might like to manage her own little home? Any psychologist would say so. Of course, the pattern of your life is so different from mine," she went on slowly, "but you do seem to be all on top of each other here."

"I guess that's our trouble," I admitted, glad to shift to a

18

more general theme. "We just live along, kind of naturally, taking things the way they come."

"But you *could* plan," Sarah said. "You could have *much* more quiet and rest and time to yourself. And while I'm here," she finished, "I'm going to give it to you.

"And now, tell me about this George."

"Well, where shall I begin?" I thought a moment. "He is twenty-one. He just got his B. S. at the university; the accelerated course. He has just been put in the reserve, or deferred, or something, to study medicine. He's about five feet eight, with brown hair and dark hazel eyes, and a nice fresh skin. And he's a lot of fun." I paused.

"You haven't told me anything about him, actually; his background and so on. Is he really our kind?"

"I don't know what you mean, exactly," I said. But I did know. Sarah and I had been the only children of a grand doctor and a spare, sensitive woman whom, although she was our mother, we had never known completely. "I've never met his family. They're a little more sophisticated than we are, I suppose. Babs rooms with George's sister, you know. Patty's the kind that spends her holidays at Sun Valley or Sea Island. Apparently they have a lot of this world's goods, or, as Mother used to put it, 'an abundance of means.'"

"People with money have to justify themselves to me," Sarah said. "I hope it hasn't ruined him. Is Babs really in love, do you think?"

"How can you tell?" I parried. "But when they are together, I feel they belong there; that it's the right thing."

"That's important," Sarah agreed. But she looked dubious and did not continue the conversation. After a few moments she went to her room.

It would be hard to say at what point during the days that followed we began definitely to feel Sarah's influence. Norah was the first to comment on it. "Mrs. Hayes was asking why I didn't use a tray, clearing away after meals," she told me over the morning ordering. "She's gone down to buy a big one for us. She's a very brainy woman, your sister," Norah said.

"Look at the darling little fork and spoon Aunt Sarah bought you," Eileen told the baby over her supper cereal. "She

19

says Barbara Elizabetn is much too old to use a pusher and a spoon with a ring handle. Oh, dear, I guess she'll have to get used to it gradually," she said as Barbara Elizabeth flung the unfamiliar tool from the tray of her high chair to the floor.

"If I were you, Eileen," Sarah said, "I'd try feeding her alone for a while."

She bought blue daylight bulbs for Ed's reading lamp, moving his big armchair on the other side of the table so that the light would be on his left, a fact he noted with immediate disfavor and had to be nudged to keep still about. The boys no longer roared in and out of the house like trucks with their fellow Bearcats. Consulted at breakfast about their daily after-school plans they exchanged glances. No comments were forthcoming but it soon became evident, even to me, in fact especially to me, that Freddie and Charles were deliberately trying to keep out of my way. As for Ed, his tone toward me took on a tinge of affectionate concern that made me feel a thousand. But it was all well meant. I could be amused and even grateful.

And then it was Saturday; the day Babs was due home and the last one of Sarah's visit. Just before lunch I made ready to send the boys downtown. "Nothing good ever comes in until late in the morning," I said, "butter and meat and things like that." Sarah heard me calling Freddie and Charles and came downstairs. "Let *me* go for you," she offered. "The boys have gone out for the day."

"They have?" I was surprised.

"I sent them downtown for lunch for a treat and then to the movies," she said. "I thought they'd like to go to a restaurant by themselves. I remember when I was thirteen making Mother go in first somewhere because I was afraid the waitress would think I was too young to go out to lunch alone."

I sighed inwardly. But aloud I said, "That'll be fun for them. And don't worry about the errands. I'll do them."

But after lunch Sarah urged me to my room to take a nap. She put a quilt over me, opened the windows, and drew the shades. She leaned down and kissed me. "I've had such a lovely visit."

"I always leave the door open," I said anxiously.

"I know you do, but you'll rest better with it closed." She shut it and went away.

I awakened a good deal later to find Ed tiptoeing around the room. "I didn't mean to disturb you."

"Come back, you goon." I sat up. "It's awfully quiet! Where *is* everybody?"

"Darned if I know. I couldn't even find Barbara Elizabeth. By the way, I just took Sarah to the train."

"You did?" I sat up, startled. "For heaven's sake! She didn't say she was leaving; she wasn't going until tonight. And you just let me sleep—"

"She found she had to leave earlier to make her connection in Chicago. She wouldn't let me disturb you. You know how considerate Sarah is."

So that was why she had kissed me good-by. I sat thinking lovingly of her.

"Why don't you lie down again?" Ed asked.

"I feel wonderful." I stretched luxuriously.

"I know." Ed's face looked sad and drooping, the way a dog's sometimes does. "But we're not as young as we were. We're getting on, you know." He went out.

Time passed. Eventually I got up and dressed, hoping I was not too late to buy at least a quarter of a pound of butter. I had just snapped on my pearls when I heard Babs's voice loud and gay in the lower hall, and other sounds too. I ran down. Coming in at the front door was Ed, in his arms an enormous brown paper bag with celery sticking out at the top. "I never heard such nonsense," he said. "Why don't they sell you the week's butter at once and be done with it?"

"Daddy!" Babs stood gaping at him. "Do you feel all right?"

"Hello, Toots. Here, somebody take this." He thrust his package forward. "I'm just trying to save your mother, that's all."

"What are you saving her for?" Babs's eyes were innocently round.

I ran down the stairs. "If you weren't bigger than I am I'd spank you," I began, then, "Hello, sweetie." I reached up and kissed her cool cheek. Suddenly, wonderfully, like a ball bouncing into air, I felt just about Babs's age again.

"Hi!" She hugged me for a moment. Then she pivoted like one who has just driven a golf ball a hundred yards or so and peered into the empty living room. "Hey, Eileen? Pretty dead around here, isn't it?" she said. "Somebody sick or sump'n? First I meet Freddie and Charles hanging around downtown so you can be quiet, and then Daddy comes in off the street with his arms full of vegetables. And where in heck is Barbie?"

"She was upstairs all day." Norah appeared from the back hall to take the groceries. "And her mother wouldn't bring her down either," she added darkly. "Not even to the kitchen."

"I'll get her." Babs ran up the stairs. In a moment she came down again. The look on her face, usually half teasing, was now wholly serious.

"She isn't there," she said. "And neither is Eileen. And the funny thing is there's a suitcase there all packed. And you know that old red felt school banner Dick won at track? Well, it's folded on top."

"That banner—" Eileen had made me tell her just how Dick looked coming home from the meet that day, his face drained of color. We had thought, both of us, that he must often look the same way now, under the strain of war.

"The gocart is gone." Ed opened the front door. The early fall night had begun and the trees on the lawn were only a tangle of black against a blacker sky. "It must be long after the baby's suppertime."

I joined him, "She should have been in bed an hour ago."

"Of course, there's nothing to worry about—" He watched a bus roll by. It looked huge and senseless.

"It isn't that—" I stopped. Now I was remembering what Sarah had said about Eileen, that she might prefer to live by herself. I felt rather than reasoned that her absence had something to do with a change of plans for herself and for our baby and something akin to terror took hold of my heart. You get things together, I thought, all meshed, just right, and then an invisible force pulls them apart. I said nervously, "I do wish the boys would come in."

Then suddenly close at hand we could hear them; the boys *and* Eileen; the scuffle of Fred and Charlie's heavy shoes, the sound of the gocart bumping against the gate. Charles's high, in-

22

nocent voice (it has the quality of a choirboy's) said, "I bet Bee's out like a light." Bee is a name Charles concocted from the baby's initials. Together the three of them lifted Barbara Elizabeth and all up the steps and pushed her in. And there they were. The baby's head drooped sideways in the complete exhaustion of one who has been jounced over half the town. Freddie looked at me with eyes that were indignant and scared, too. "We met 'em way down on Congress Street. Eileen was looking at a room in a boardinghouse."

"Yeah. She was, honest." Charles, too, sounded frightened.

Above the bottle green of her wool dress, Eileen's face was colorless. She did not look up.

"That's all right, dear," I said. "It's natural for you to want some little place that is all your own. It was bound to come sometime. I'd thought you might be happy here until Dick got back, but I understand; I understand it perfectly."

"But Mother B.," Eileen raised her eyes. There was a stricken look in them.

"What's been going on here?" Ed stood unsmiling before us.

"I was just looking for a room for Bee and me," Eileen said. "I think we'd better—I mean, I thought we all—"

"Do you want to go away?" Ed's head was on one side as though he were listening for her reply.

"Of course I don't. I'd die—but—" Eileen looked to me for help.

"What do you mean 'want to'—" Babs put a protective arm around Eileen. "How could anyone want to go live in an old boardinghouse with a rubber plant?" Suddenly she whirled on me eying me suspiciously. "I bet it was something you said. You must have done something. A nice mother-in-law *you* turned out to be."

"It wasn't. It wasn't that!" Eileen came back eagerly. "It was Aunt Sarah. We got to talking, I don't know how it started; at first she said it would be better for Barbie if I moved out, and after that she talked about you and Dad." For the first time a hint of a smile brought a quirk to Eileen's lips. "She said you weren't getting any younger."

"She did, did she? I like that!" Babs's voice made Sarah's

statement sound like the silliest thing in the world. "I wish *I'd* been there."

I moved closer to Eileen. There was no need to say anything further. I had seen her eyes and she mine. I slid my arm through hers and said, "And now we'd better get this tired child to bed."

"I thought there was something phony about this." Babs started cheerfully toward the living room beside her father. "I go away to college leaving a perfectly normal family and I come back and find everybody being considerate of everybody else, and the place like a—like a morgue. What becomes of the old Struggle for Existence?"

"Your Aunt Sarah is all right," I heard Ed say. "In fact, she's one of the nicest people in the world. Trouble is, she thinks we ought to think and feel just as she does. Well, I guess I can move my own chair back now, where it belongs." There was a grating sound as he pushed it back into its old place and then a creak as he sat down. "I like it this way," he said.

SARAH'S COMMENTS had stirred up something in my mind. In the manner of mothers, I began to worry. My concern was the status of my daughter's love affair. At the age of seventeen Babs had met George Litchfield, the brother of her college roommate, and gone to Junior Prom with him at the university. Ever since then they had been a good deal together. Now, each week end when she came home from college, there were long-distance telephone conversations, if in fact he did not arrive in person. My mind was on the two of them.

I found Eileen in the dining room giving her diminutive daughter a dish of cereal. Barbara Elizabeth sat in her high chair, a blue bib over her daffodil-yellow sweater, and whenever Eileen's attention strayed she waved her spoon. She waved it now, for Eileen was trying to read a letter spread on the table before her.

"Let me help." I adjusted the dish before Barbara Elizabeth. I took the spoon and started to feed her. "Good news?" I asked Eileen as she smiled over the contents of the envelope.

"My old boss has landed a commission in the Army," she told me. She used to work in Manhattan. "The office is giving him a farewell party. They want me to come down to New York for it, Friday. Little do they know," she sighed.

I glanced thoughtfully at my curly-headed daughter-in-law. Though she was never husky-looking, there had been nevertheless a kind of glow about her after the baby came. Now it was gone. Her face was thin and angular. Eileen has never allowed anyone to take over the care of the baby. Then there had been the constant strain of anxiety over Dick. She hadn't had a chance to relax since Barbara Elizabeth's birth. She was fun-starved. It would do her good to get away, if only for a few hours.

I ran over the coming weekend in my mind. Babs was expecting a visit from George. I sensed some sort of emotional impasse or crisis ahead. I wanted to be on deck at home.

"Write them you'll come, dear," I told Eileen. She had been so faithful to her special responsibility that I had fallen into an almost masculine habit of thinking there was nothing to it. Without a shadow of premonition, I added, looking down at Barbie, "I guess we won't have any trouble, will we, sweetie?"

Rather than move the baby in with us, Friday night, I slept in Eileen's room. I took a last look at the hump under the pink blanket and pulled the quilt up under my chin, thinking how utterly cozy it was to have a child in the crib next to my bed, her little round head exactly opposite my own. It was half dark and cold and far from cozy when I woke. There was a small noise going on near by. I rolled over, bewildered. Oh, yes; Barbara Elizabeth. She was sitting up, her fat little legs uncovered and one small foot sticking out between the bars.

I carried her to the bathroom and brought her back. Then I offered her a drink but she shook her head away from the glass and, putting her hands out pawlike on either side of her face, fell instantly into sleep again.

By now, however, I was thoroughly awake and needed coffee. I went down and made some. There is nothing so lonesome as being up ahead of the rest of the family. As I took a cup into the dining room, however, I ran into Babs, hugging a bright green bathrobe around her.

"I heard you on the prowl." She yawned. "Can I have some, too?" She settled sideways into a chair at the table, her brown eyes still half shut. It was not a propitious moment to invite confidences but the opportunity might not arise again. I took the plunge.

"Babs, I want to ask you something. Are you really engaged to George?"

"Now, Mother," Babs got up and went for a cigarette, "we know what we're doing."

"I don't," I said, "and I wish I did."

26

She lit the cigarette carefully. "You always want everything to be so—so definite."

"Being engaged *is* definite," I answered. "I don't mean to crowd you, dear, but I just worry because I love you and—well, I wondered how things stood."

"That's just it, Moms, I don't *know* how things stand." She put down the cigarette and looked directly into my eyes. Her own were stricken. "That time last summer, when we wanted to get married and didn't; well, I supposed we were at least engaged and he'd give me a ring or sump'n, even if it was just a little one. But he's never mentioned it. And now—ever since he graduated—he's been, well, funny. I know he's worried about the future—he'd like to know where he goes next—but it isn't that, I'm sure. And it isn't another girl either," she finished.

It could be you. I thought it but I didn't say it. I looked at the girl before me. Her shoulders under the green wool were easy and strong. Her hair was dark and soft around the face that had an inner warmth. She gave off a sense of untapped power. A girl like that could spell trouble for any man and I knew that a boy just graduating from college, out on his own for the first time, is pretty apt to start thinking seriously about his attachments. It seemed quite probable that George had "frozen" himself, pending some decision that he would make, and that, no matter how closely it involved Babs, he would make it alone.

"So try to let me have him to myself as much as you can, will you?" Bab's voice was pleading. "Much as I love Barbara Elizabeth, I'll never get anywhere with George if every time we start talking I have to agitate and see if she's O. K."

"Is he here?" I asked. When Babs said he was I went on, "Then he'll be coming down soon for breakfast." The difficulties of the day began to take shape before me. "We'd better dress."

Babs followed me along the hall, studying me sideways. "You look positively *haggish*," she commented. "Given up lipstick for the duration? Come on in with me." Her voice dropped to a whisper. "I want to see how mine is on you—"

It was perhaps an hour later, however, when George joined us. The family breakfast was almost over; Freddie and Charles had in fact been excused and were out in the yard where we could see them practicing drop kicks. Ed was glancing at the paper when a very pleased masculine voice said, "Good morning. We woke up and everybody had gone off and left us."

George was carrying Barbie on his right hand and forearm. Her pink bathrobe was trailing and her blue eyes were staring delightedly at the small world before her; hers, all hers.

George's face was alive with amusement. Some boys are youthful in a callow way, with tawny faces and expressions youthfully indefinite. George was different. His athletic figure was hard rather than lithe; his skin was fresh looking; his dark eyes were keen; his mouth, although sensitive, was a firm line. George was brightly, sharply young.

"Be careful, you goon, you'll drop her." Babs was holding out an anxious hand. George brushed it aside.

"Listen, I know a lot more about it than you do." He demonstrated his hold by raising his right arm. "You carry 'em exactly the way you do a football, grip firm and well under." He popped the child on the floor. "You stay there," he told her, "while your uncle George has his K ration."

"Here, pull on this." Babs dropped to her knees and bent her head so that her hair swung into the baby's grasp. "Ouch, have a heart!" George turned his attention to a plate of corn bread. "I've had plenty of experience with little kids," he explained. "In fact, the professor I take my seminar course with has a baby." George was doing graduate work in medicine at the university. "The nights we meet, his wife goes to the movies. He lives on the ground floor of one of the men's halls," he went on. "The university sort of shut its eyes to his getting married and so on and let him stay there. Makes quite a stir, though," he added, putting a second spoonful of sugar into his coffee, "having the diaper service drive up to the dorm."

I retrieved the honey and passed it to him. Ed got up and said good-by. George rose and, sitting down again, continued as if we two were alone in the room. He did not seem to notice Babs. I saw very clearly what she meant.

A moment or two later, I followed Ed. I found him in the garage.

"Listen, dear," I began, "would it be all right if you had your bridge game at our house instead of at the Smith's this afternoon? I've had a phone from the hospital. You know, I'm on call for emergency duty. Well, they need me a couple of hours this afternoon, and somebody has to stay with the baby."

"And I'm to worry about her while I'm trying to play a hand?" He climbed in under the wheel. Ed resists any change in the routine of the historic Saturday afternoon session. "Why can't Babs do it?"

"She won't bother you," I urged. "She's such a *good* little thing." I put my hand on the door. "Babs just can't—she and George are at some sort of crisis again."

"Listen," Ed said, "I'm tired of hearing about them and their crisises."

"Get rid of them." This was the moment to strike out for Babs. "George intends going to see a friend who lives a couple of miles out of here. Let him have the car; then Babs can go along. You have enough gas for that distance," I pleaded.

Ed looked down at me. "It's about time they thought about *you* for a change," he said. "You look like a wreck," he added, candidly. "And *where'd* you get the purple lipstick?" But he leaned forward and kissed my head. "O. K." he said, "we'll play here. If Barbie cries, though, I won't promise to leave the game."

"You're a darling." I drew back so he could shut the door.

I followed an early lunch with a tray for Barbie. Babs and George had gone out and hadn't returned. I couldn't ask Norah to feed her; it wasn't her job. She is always in a hurry, Saturday afternoons, to get out to confession; and anyway, I couldn't quite trust her not to add to it a few sips of tea from her own spoon. I went up the stairs with the boys around me. Charles was climbing up the outside of the stair rail and Freddie was going over the one on the other side. Some sort of game, of course. It seemed just a short time before that Barbie's father was playing cops and robbers all over the house and yard.

As I fed the baby behind the closed door and in hasty silence, I studied her face. I could see Dick in the shape of her tiny nose and the way her eyes were set. She was laughably like him. The kiss I gave her was for them both.

I came back from the hospital at perhaps half past four. I opened the door on a room that was like a train shed with an engine in it. Black, acid-laden smoke moved visibly about the

29

four men at the table and hung in the corners under the ceiling. Beyond them, in a high chair, sat Barbie. Her little face was hot with perspiration. She was way past crying now, however. She looked out haggard-eyed at the four men; she was licked and she knew it.

"Hello, Elizabeth." Bill Gray, who was dummy, looked up and smiled. A bachelor, Bill is nevertheless familiar with what's expected by small children. From time to time he looked over at Barbara Elizabeth. "Kootchy, kootchy?" he inquired solemnly.

I waited, staring over Ed's shoulder. I was preparing a few well-chosen remarks for somebody. Fred Beard, being a doctor, should know better, but, easygoing in most things, Fred is rather touchy about his professional prestige. I did not dare to scold him. Ben Smith has brought up a child of his own; he would only laugh. I would have to tackle Ed.

"Oh, *hello,* dear—" Ed had finished the hand. "Barbie's been sitting right here with us." His manner was relaxed and easy. "Try one of these cigars, Fred," he said. "I think you'll like them." He sat back while Ben dealt.

"Listen," I began, "all this smoke and that *poor* child..."

"You leave us alone; we're doing all right. She's been a great help to me." Ed arranged his cards and held them in front of Barbie's face. "What would *you* bid on this, hmm?" He snuggled his head over nearer hers. "Four spades? O. K., four spades it is."

I lifted Barbie out of her chair and took her upstairs. Babs was just coming from her room. "Run down and get the orange juice," I ordered.

"Hey, why can't Norah do it?" Babs was indignant. "George is in the car, waiting."

"She's out and so are the boys." My voice sounded querulous.

"O. K., relax," she said. "I'll get it." She eyed me for a moment. "Moms, you look awful. Listen, I'll take care of her. You go down to the beauty parlor and let them fix you up. Good for the old morale. Come, kitten." She took Barbara Elizabeth's hand. "Tell George to drive you down there and come back for me. By then I'll have her all orange-juiced and in her crib. Any questions?" In spite of myself, I laughed. "Maybe you're wrecking my whole future," she told Barbie, "but what the heck. It doesn't look like I've got one anyway."

The bit of bravado didn't fool me; Babs was sick at heart. It was hard for me to see how anyone could turn to stone against her. I rode the few blocks with George in a silence which he did not try to break.

Babs was right; I came home feeling made over. In retrospect, the episode of the bridge game seemed almost ludicrous. It hadn't done the baby any harm; she was all right. I told Norah about it, gaily, as I fixed the baby's supper and took it upstairs. I opened the door of Eileen's room softly. Barbara Elizabeth has a favorite tune—"The Campbells Are Coming." She puts her head sideways and peers through the crib bars when she hears it. It means us and fun. I hummed it as I opened the door.

The window was up and the curtains were blowing softly into the room. The side of the crib had been let down—the baby was not there!

Deep inside of me everything stood still. I must keep hold of myself. "She's fallen out of bed; she's somewhere, here, in this room." Getting down, I looked under the big bed, in the closet, behind the armchair. But the window was open and the baby was gone.

She had been taken while I was sitting in the beauty shop, thinking it mattered whether my hair was curled or not. I got up and stood stiffly, every muscle contracted. Then I turned to the only person in the world at that moment.

"Ed!" My voice was a loud croak. "Ed!"

"What's the matter?" Ed appeared from our room. "Good Lord, you scared the wits out of me. Don't shout like that!" Then, "What is it?"

"Ed," I could hardly speak, "it's—Barbie—she isn't here!"

"What do you mean she isn't here? Somebody's got her—Norah—Babs!"

"But they haven't. I just left Norah, and the kids are all out. I tell you somebody's stolen the baby."

Ed walked rapidly to the crib, the closet, the window.

"Nonsense," his voice was harsh. "She couldn't have fallen out the window—"

"Somebody's stolen her—the house is always open—anybody

31

could get in—I tell you somebody's taken her away—" My voice came out thinly, squeezed through my throat.

"Norah!" Now Ed was shouting over the stair rail. "Norah, where's Barbara Elizabeth?"

"The baby?" Norah appeared in the lower hall. "I—sure, I don't know. Mr. Breton. She should be sleeping in her crib—"

"We'll have to tell the police," Ed said. Suddenly, his voice was grim. "We're responsible, you know. She isn't *our* child— she's Dick's—and Eileen's away"—his voice sank. He started down the stairs. Close behind him, I saw his hand groping along the banister. He motioned Norah back. "Not now, don't ask me anything now—"

"What it is, Mrs. Breton? Sure, his looks is a knife in my heart," Norah whispered, her hands working under her apron.

The front door opened and Babs came in with George behind her. Her face was set and the air of bravado was there, unchanged. "We ran out of gas and had to leave the car a few blocks down the street," she began. Her glance took in Norah, standing behind me, and Ed at the phone beyond us. "What's biting everybody? Mother! What's happened? What's the matter?" For now she had seen my face.

"The baby," I said, "she's gone—she isn't here." I dropped my head on her shoulder and began to sob hysterically. "And Eileen coming home tonight!"

"Barbie? Oh, my gosh—" Babs dumped me off her shoulder, fell on the front doorknob, and was gone.

"Don't cry, *please* don't." Both of George's arms were around me "She's all right, I'm *sure*. Let's go—"

"What's *this* now?" Ed dropped the phone. I could hear the operator's voice nagging at air through the dangling instrument.

"We took her along, sir." George freed me and faced my husband. "I thought you knew. We put her in a little seat arrangement we found in the garage." That seat—Ed had bought it the week before, just in case. . . . "She was sound asleep—and we— we just forgot her."

"Well, where is she now?" Ed stood opposite him, strangely stern.

"I'm sure she's there all right; in the car." The words were reassuring but his voice was anxious. "Come on." He opened the

32

door and stood back to let us out. "I'm not trying to alibi out of it, sir, but I wasn't thinking about the baby—I was thinking about your daughter."

Ed did not answer. We hurried the length of the block and turned. Now, ahead of us, we could see Babs, opening the door of the car.

"Find her? Is she all right?" Ed called ahead as we came up with her.

"She was *just* starting to cry!" Babs said remorsefully. She sat down on the running board and held Barbie in her strong, awkward young arms. Barbie turned her head, felt the softness of Babs's white sheepskin coat. She yawned, opened her eyes, and then glancing up, she saw Babs. She smiled happily in recognition.

"She likes you, funnyface." George's eyes were on Babs's dark, bent head. But Babs did not notice him.

"Aw, cherub," she was saying softly, "I didn't mean to leave you alone, honest I didn't. I wouldn't scare you for the world—I just forgot you for a little *minute*. Oh, Barbie—sweetie... She dropped her head and kissed the top of the little blue bonnet.

I stepped forward, and it was then I saw it: something was happening to George. Relief—tenderness—they ran over his face like little waves across a bright sand bar. After them came a wave of something very deep. It broke.

"Give her to your mother." His voice was husky. "I want to talk to you."

Babs's lifted eyes held his. Hers were clear, resolute—and grateful. "O. K., Coach."

She stood up. George took her hand and bent his arm around it. They wandered off, diagonally, across the street. It was empty. Had it been full of fire trucks, they would not have known.

4

IF IT HAD BEEN just before Christmas instead of just before my birthday, I might have seen a connection between the extraordinary behavior of Freddie and Charles and the need for ready cash. Somehow, with the war, my birthday hadn't loomed very large. In fact, when I made the remark that set things rolling I wasn't even thinking of it.

"You know what I wish I had?" I had said. No one had asked but I was in a chatty mood. "I wish I had an electric gadget like one I saw the other day. You put in two carrots and a chunk of pineapple and out comes something yummy to drink."

"Sounds terrible." Of us all, Ed was the only one not reading the Sunday paper. This was because he had finished it before we began. Attempts to refold it as it was are always unsatisfactory to him; I get the sheets out of order, the girls put the sections they take down somewhere and forget where, and Freddie and Charles, even if there isn't a scuffle, always manage somehow to tear the comics. So it is understood that Daddy, who is fussy about a certain pristine freshness, is to have the papers first.

"It isn't terrible; it's wonderful. It blends all kinds of drinks. You put in whatever you like—it doesn't *have* to be carrots."

"It's an idea, at that," Ed said, idly.

"Well, by the time *we* get around to buying one, probably they won't be manufactured any more." I sighed. "But they *are* something."

Freddie and Charles were stretched out on the rug, reading. Charles always picks the comics with animals in them but Freddie dives directly for the story of a baleful-looking villain pictured in indigo blue. He was solemnly studying it now. As I finished talking, he looked up, fixedly, at me. He's so like Ed. I thought. When he's busy with his paper he simply can't bear it if you interrupt him. I watched, affectionately, his round, brown head. The gadget sank forgotten to the bottom of my mind.

Certainly I saw no connection between it and the conversation I overheard that night. I went to the linen closet to find an extra blanket. The door of the boys' room stood half open and from the cool darkness beyond I heard Freddie's voice, muted but clear.

"Aw, it's a cinch" he said. "You just take 'em back of the ears and squeeze so the poison squirts out. You just let it drop into the bottle. Nothin' to it. Venom's very valuable," he finished.

"What for?" Charles wanted to know.

"For sick people, stupid. It said so in the paper." There was a jouncing sound as they thrashed about in bed in the throes of the idea.

Then Charles asked, "How can you tell this one's poisonous?" I dropped the blanket on the shelf. Had those boys . . . ?

Freddie's voice registered extreme exasperation. "Listen, dimwit, you hold its mouth open and see if it's got fangs."

"Well, I dunno. Seems as if you could make nine dollars easier someway else," Charles said slowly.

"Awright, you think of one. I gotta think of everything around here. I thought up the paper. That's where the ten dollars we got so far came from, isn't it? Suppose you think of sump'n then!"

I picked up the blanket again with a sigh of relief. At least there was no captive reptile in the house. It was just an idea in their heads. I laughed at myself as I stole away.

"Mrs. Breton," Norah said a couple of days later, "If breakfast is to be earlier, you'd a right to tell me the night before."

"Earlier?" I was sitting at my desk; Norah stood in the dining-room doorway. We had finished planning the meals for a couple of days and I was copying the items she had written on a bit of brown paper. Norah's list always contains an element of surprise; today it read, "tea, rasons, 4 Lion chops." I looked

35

up. "I haven't changed the breakfast hour," I told her. "Breakfast is always at half past seven."

"Well, the boys has been coming down at seven for four days now wanting their breakfast," she said. "They're going somewhere before school and this morning Freddie had somethin' buttoned under his coat; he wouldn't tell what. They'd ought to stay home and eat their food, but, of course, it's not for me to say." Norah looked at me with the relief in her blue eyes of one who had eased her conscience.

"Thank you, Norah," I said, "I'll see what's going on."

The next morning I went early to the dining room.

"Gee, Norah, step on it, will ya?" Freddie was saying as I entered. "We gotta get outa here." Charles was busy emptying his glass of milk into a small wide-mouthed bottle which he slid under the table when he saw me. With his right hand he lifted the almost empty glass to his lips as if he had been drinking the milk all the time.

"*Good* morning." I sat down. "How does it happen you boys are having breakfast so early? Going somewhere?"

"Aw, Moms," Freddie's voice sounded cross, "you always want to know everything."

"I want to know what's happening before school," I said, "and no fooling." Charlie looked quickly at me. He is always polite—he never joins in the give and take between parents and children. Perhaps it is the English reserve which he has never lost in spite of the years in our family, but he doesn't go in for confidence to his elders. Freddie, on the other hand, always has difficulty in not telling us everything he knows.

Now, however, he hedged. "If we tell, you'll say we can't go."

"I probably won't." I poured myself a cup of coffee, eying it slowly as it blended with the cream.

Again Freddie's eyes watched my face. They are onion-green. They are not gorgeous like Babs's brown ones or wistful like Charles's and Eileen's, which are the color of sea haze. But they are good eyes; like trustworthy instruments they betray the smallest deviation from the truth. They were wavering a little now; I was going to hear the story but only part of it.

"And you can put that bottle on the table. I saw it. Who's the milk for, anyway?"

36

Charles squirmed down and brought it up. "It's for a poor hungry animal," he said. "It's in Bingo's woodshed and Bingo doesn't dare ask his mother for anything for it to eat."

"Why don't you bring it here?" I asked. "I'd certainly rather have another pet in the house than have you boys rushing off every morning with your breakfast half eaten."

Charles brightened. "Gee, could we..."

"Aw, shut up, will ya?" Freddie glowered across the table. "What's the matter with it where it is? It's—it's all right there. Come on, we gotta get goin'." He reached for the bottle and screwed on the cap.

"Get home right after school," I called, but they were already out of the house.

I sat thinking of Bingo's mother; a fierce little woman driven by hard work. There wouldn't be any extra food in that house. Well, I was glad that Freddie and Charles could help out. No wonder I hadn't known what the boys were up to; I had, I told myself, rather neglected them of late. In a family your mind can't focus on everybody at once. You get around to each in turn. It was the boys' turn now. I would go down to school this very week and see how they were coming along.

"You know, Ed," I began, a few nights later, "maybe Freddie isn't as dumb as we think. I went down today and had a talk with the boys' teachers. Mr. Cutter, the science teacher, was really enthusiastic about Freddie. He says he isn't strong on books, but he has a genuine curiosity about science. 'Inquiring' was the word he used."

"Wouldn't surprise me," Ed said. "Getting teacher to talk is the oldest little-boy trick in the world."

"This wasn't in class," I defended Freddie. "He says the boys came in after school Monday and asked so many interesting questions that today he devoted a whole period to a lecture on how venom is used commercially. Mr. Cutter got some printed material for them from a laboratory in New York." I laughed reminiscently. "He said Freddie ought to make a good businessman; he asked at once whether you'd get more for the venom or the whole snake."

"I'll bite," Ed said. "What's the answer?"

"I didn't inquire." When I looked up Ed's tired face had an almost sad little smile on it. "What's the matter?"

"Oh, I was thinking—" he said. "When I was a kid you didn't have to *read* about snakes and listen to lectures. You caught 'em and kept 'em. Sometimes," he finished, "I think the way kids grow up nowadays, their life is awfully tame."

I did not answer. For once I wasn't sure he was right.

That afternoon I managed to be in the dining room pouring out chocolate milk when the boys came in from school. I learned long ago, when Dick and Babs were little, that if you want to share in the children's lives, you'd better be there when they first come home, full of the day's happenings, to register enthusiasm at their successes or to try to help them understand why things sometimes go wrong; what, if anything, can be done about it; how it should be taken, if taken it must be. It is at this time, too, that they usually make their plans, and if you are there you can keep the children on the beam. This was what I actually thought.

"Moms, can I have that shoe box, the one your old black evening slippers are in?" Freddie asked between gulps of the dark brown liquid. "I saw one on the shelf in your closet."

"Why, yes, I guess so," I answered. "What do you want it for?"

Charles nudged Freddie, his watchful eyes on my face. "Oh, nothin' special."

Freddie changed the subject. "Say, Moms, where's my old flashlight, the one I had in camp?"

"It's on a shelf in the pantry where I keep my flower holders and garden scissors. Take good care of it," I warned him. "They say it isn't going to be easy to buy them any more."

"It's my own all the same." Freddie's tone was questioning. "I can do anything I want to with it." It was in his hand.

"Of course, I didn't say it wasn't."

"Well!" Freddie rammed it into his pocket. "Have we got any heavy brown paper?" he went on.

"Yes, up in the sewing-room closet." I took the glasses into the pantry. When I came back, Freddie was rummaging at my desk. *"Now* what?" I asked.

"Listen, Moms, could I have a piece of your writing paper,

38

the kind with your name and address on top? Just one sheet and an envelope?" he added plaintively, as if he feared I would refuse.

"Of course you can. Here." I found it for him. "And now upstairs, both of you, and get your homework done." Because there was no comeback, I looked up. Charles was staring at me in a kind of dumb despair and Freddie's brows were simply furrowed with anxiety.

"Listen, Moms," he said, "I *can't* do my homework now. There's no use your saying we gotta, either."

"By the way," I went on, "I want this going to see your rabbit before school stopped. I thought you understood that, the other morning."

"What rabbit?" Charles's voice was full of surprise.

"O. K., Moms, forget it," Freddie said, unexpectedly. "We won't, not after today. Then can we go now?" I looked at his round face. I felt sorry for him; he had a thwarted expression. Here we were right back where we started—at homework versus going to Bingo's. The confidence and guidance system which used to be so successful with Dick somehow never worked out with Freddie and his gang.

"All right, but don't be late," I said, weakly. I had meant to add, "And I want you to take baths before supper." The last time they were at Bingo's after school they went frogging in a scummy pond beyond his house and fell in. Oh, well, I could chalk up one victory for my side. They weren't going around to Bingo's at breakfasttime any more. That, at least, was something.

True to their word, the boys made no attempt the following morning to leave early. They pushed off at the normal time. Ed kissed me good-by and went for his hat. Just then the phone rang. At eight-thirty in the morning it is usually for me; a friend asking what I'm going to wear Saturday night or what'll we serve at the bridge benefit. I lifted the receiver negligently. But the voice I heard was strange to me. It asked if F. Breton lived here. I called Ed back from the door.

"It's some man," I said, "at the post office. I can't understand him very well. It's about a package." I handed Ed the instrument.

39

"Why, yes, there is." Ed's voice was unguarded. "It's Freddie, my twelve-year-old son. But he has left for school now. Can I help you?" Presently he put his hand over the receiver and turned to me. "Did you mail anything yesterday?" he asked. "Nothing to Babs, for instance?" His voice was grave.

"Not a thing." I came and faced him. "Why?"

"They've got something down there with our name in the corner. A package. He says there's a little sound inside." He hesitated, then, "sounds crazy, doesn't it? But we're at war and —well—I'm in the munitions business. It could be sabotage. I'll be right down," he said into the phone.

"But Ed." I followed him. "It's not addressed *to* us. It's *from* us."

"Sure. So we're responsible for what's in it." I saw Ed's concern was real. "It's addressed to a laboratory in New York. They've sent for a man from the police station who knows about those things."

"You don't mean it's—you don't think it could be a bomb?" I ran to the back closet and took my coat. "No use saying no," I told him as I climbed into the car. "If you get blown up, I do, too!"

The rear door of the post office opens onto a plot of grass that runs into rank weeds at the far end. We found the postmaster awaiting us there. Two policemen were leaning over a parcel wrapped in brown paper lying on the grass. It was about the size of a shoebox.

"Oughtn't we to look at the writing?" I said.

Instead of answering the policeman jumped up suddenly. "Get back," he said. "Watch it!"

The package was resting on its side. Now it moved. With no hand near it, the box turned slowly over.

"Ed." I was almost sick with fear and excitement. "Do something. Why don't they douse it with a pail of water?"

"Same of them babies go off when the water touches them," the policeman said. "It's probably some sort of spring-type mechanism and it must of worked loose and uncoiled some. Well, we'll have a look at it." Slowly and carefully he made a slit around the top of the paper. The cord had already been removed, and he lifted the top section. Under it was a shoebox. With infinite caution he raised the lid.

"Look out, everybody!"

Something long and thin slid like liquid from the aperture and wriggled off across the grass. In less than a minute it had disappeared into the tall weeds.

The man from headquarters stood up and took off his cap. He ran a hand across his forehead, wiping off beads of sweat.

"It's—that was a rattlesnake," I shivered.

"No, lady." The postmaster turned to me, relieved to talk. "First off, it looked like one. But there's a lot more brown in the diamond pattern on the back and the tail is just a plain pointed one. It's what we boys used to call a pasture snake."

"How did you discover it?" Ed was getting hold of himself.

"It was held for insufficient postage," the clerk joined in. "I was heftin' it and it felt like somethin' was movin' inside. I set it away to show to the chief here first thing this morning."

"I detected a sort of rustling sound," the postmaster added, "and I thought best, Mr. Breton, to call the police. Here," he reached in his pocket. "There was a letter in the same mailbox with your address on the back. I saved it for evidence, but I guess we won't need it now." He held out an envelope. My writing paper! I took it from his hand and tore it open.

To whom it may concern: [I read]

We are mailing you at this date one venomous reptil. Please send ten dollars for the same to the above. If you need any more snakes, we are in a position to supply some.

Yours truly,
Frederick Breton
Charles Heather

P. S. What it likes to eat is milk.

P. P. S. If you cannot use, please send by return mail.

"Ain't there a law against shipping live critters by mail, Chief?" The postal clerk was not asking, he was telling us.

Ed put his hand on the man's shoulder. He said, "You people were pretty smart; it didn't get by *you*."

We walked out to the car escorted by the group. Ed slammed the door and lifted his hand in a salute. He tossed the empty box and the wrapping paper with the address on it into the back seat. He climbed in. "Good-by Captain." He waved to the officer. "And except for the snake," he said as we drove off, "that takes care of the evidence." Suddenly, his face grew serious. "By the way, I wouldn't say anything about all this. It—it comes under the head of unfinished business, and I'd rather handle it myself."

And then it was Saturday morning, my birthday. I came downstairs into the dining room to find the whole family around the table. Eileen sat holding the baby. The boys were hopping up and down behind their chairs. Ed was waiting for me at mine. Everybody began to sing, "Happy birthday to you." With Eileen's hands beneath them, the baby's arms moved rhythmically up and down; she stared gravely at us. The voices petered out—Ed always pitches a tune so low no one can stay with him.

"You darlings." I sat down. And there in front of me was the gadget that mixed the drinks, the carrots and pineapple.

"It's from us," Freddie and Charles said.

"But, boys," I went on after we had all marveled at it, "how in the *world* did you ever get the money?"

"We sold the snake," Freddie was fairly shouting. "Lookit, we got a letter from the company—it's from the president. Want to hear what he says? 'We are in receipt,'" he read, sounding the "p," " 'of your valuable animal for which we are glad to send you the enclosed ten dollars. We shall not be in the market, however, for any more snakes by mail.' It's something about legal," Freddie explained.

"Ed," I said as soon as we were left alone, "I've got to know —I can't wait. You did it somehow—but how?"

Ed filled his pipe deliberately. "It wasn't as simple as you might think. In fact, the whole thing was a pretty complicated bit of business." He sat back, thinking how to put it. "You see, the snake was Bingo's. I did a little snooping and found that out. It was his—his only attraction. It put him on the map and made people want to come to his house. I guess they never had before."

I didn't comment. Presently Ed went on, "After he'd caught it down by the pond, he got the idea of giving it a great build-up. He knew it wasn't poisonous—I'm pretty sure of that; but he made the other boys believe it was. You can't blame him. It was his big moment."

"I know."

"The boys couldn't give him money for it because money was what they were after. He held out for roller skates. He'd never had any before."

I was silent, thinking of what fun our youngsters had on theirs. Funny, I'd never noticed—now I remembered how Bingo always ran along with them, on foot.

"So they gave him a pair," I said. "I see." Freddie and Charles practically live on wheels.

"That's right. They'll share the pair that's left," Ed said.

I cleared my throat. "And what about the laboratory people?"

"Oh, them? I called them up long-distance, got the head of the concern, and told him the story. At first he thought I was crazy—really crazy, I mean. But I managed to put it to him so he understood in the end. He wrote the check and the letter. All I did was send him ten dollars to cover it."

"So that was all you did!" I went over and put my arms around him. Suddenly, outside there was a swirl of noise as Bingo, on roller skates, brought himself up short against the wall of the house by grabbing the blind. He peered in at the window.

"Freddie home?" he mouthed.

There was an answering yell from behind him as Freddie and Charles came scooting along the asphalt. Each was wearing one skate. Bingo turned, gathered speed, and zoomed magnificently past them down the street. He did not look back.

"It's all so hard when you're little," I said.

"Think so?" Ed asked. "I don't know; I don't know."

5

IN THE LIFE OF ALL people over, let us say, forty, moments come that make them realize they are in the upper age brackets. Sometimes the event is a child's remark, overheard. Sometimes it is a genuine tribute from someone younger. Always, it is a shock and means a mental readjustment.

My sister Sarah's visit had dealt us a mild blow of that sort. We made a family slogan of her line, "We aren't as young as we were," trying to laugh it off, but the suggestion remained. She left us vulnerable, especially Ed. He had been a shade quieter ever since.

Babs's return to college always left him a shade quieter, too. Blake, the lovely little coeducational school where Ed and I had met and from which he had graduated, was not too far away and it was familiar, like an extension of home, to both of us. But it took Babs with all her nonsense out of the house.

I awoke one night to find Ed's pillow pushed into a lump. He wasn't there. When he did not come back I got up to investigate.

I found him in the living room. His head was high-lighted by a reading lamp. He did not hear me coming and for a moment I stood watching him. Suddenly he seemed almost old. Subconsciously I think of him as about twenty-two, the age he was when he came out of the last war, his face thin and eager above his uniform. Tonight he looked his years. His cheeks sagged, making squares at the jaw, and his hair lay flat instead of curling debonairly from his forehead. His eyelids drooped sharply, forming triangles. He glanced up.

"Hello," he said. "What are you doing around at this time of night?"

44

Usually there is a light behind Ed's gray eyes. "Don't you love the way Daddy looks at you?" one of the children once said. "It's so, so—magnanimous!" Now his gaze was stern, almost empty. His expression was hardening, I thought, from some fear or knowledge that I did not share.

"I came to see where you were. Is anything the matter? Listen Ed," I said, when he did not speak, "you haven't heard anything and not told me? It isn't anything about Dick?"

"No, I wasn't thinking about Dick, except indirectly, perhaps." It was almost as if I were not there.

I am a fool, of course, but I assume that any situation is bettered by having the person you love around. I took my knitting out of its bag and sat down. I measured the body of the sweater, holding it against myself.

"If that's for a sailor"—Ed glanced at the navy-blue wool—"remember, he *could* be bigger than you."

I had his attention now, so I asked, "Did anything go wrong today at the plant?"

"No; no wronger than always," he said. "Why?"

"I thought something might be worrying you."

He got up and put his hand on my shoulder, but he faced away from me. "Don't bother about me," he said at last. "I guess I'm just kind of low and tired. I think I'll go back up to bed."

I did not follow him immediately. Instead, I sat thinking. I had been troubled about Ed lately. For several weeks now he had been restless, even irritable, which wasn't like him. But Ed never puts a burden on anyone else. I would have to find out for myself what was wrong.

It might easily be that he was worrying about Dick, even if he had no news; perhaps for that very reason. When Dick left the country with his Army outfit, we both had had our intolerable moments. He was sent out so suddenly. For the first time in my life, I cried and cried and cried, with no power or will to stop. It was only when, next morning, I woke to find Ed pacing the room and to hear him say, "It's hard on me, too," that I pulled myself together. Soon after that, Eileen, Dick's bride of a few months, came to live with us and eventually gave us our first grandchild, and I could feel that in caring for them I was doing something at least for my eldest son. Sometimes Dick would end a family letter with "Love to the home front," or, when he heard I was taking the nurse's aide course, "Glad to hear you're in there pitching. Keep up the good work"; well-worn phrases that gained significance as the fighting went on and on. The few hours I spent each week as a volunteer in the hospital gave me great satisfaction too. Although I never told anyone, I felt I was putting my very slight weight against the wheel; that in helping to release a nurse for the fighting front I was doing at least a little toward the winning of the war. I realized Ed had nothing like that as an outlet, yet I did not connect this with his present unease. Well, I would have to wait; that was all.

Ed's regular bimonthly stag bridge met the next night and since it was his turn to be host they were due at our house. I came into the living room soon after supper and set up the bridge table. Ed had gone down to the corner for extra cigars and cigarettes. Eileen had already turned in; her day begins at about six o'clock and she takes every chance to catch a good night's sleep. I put the younger children, Freddie and Charles, at the dining-room table with their homework. I had just shut the door on them when Bill Gray came in.

Bill is a bachelor. The men are tolerantly fond of him but he is one of those people against whom wives are always struggling. He drinks too much and wants to play too late. He had had too much already. He sat down and said, "Why don't you stop running around? Why don't you relax?"

I took a chair beside him. "How is everything, Bill?" He tried to focus his mild blue eyes on me and then looked down at his hands, one after the other, as if they might explain something he did not understand.

"Terrible, since you ask," he said. "They turned me down again today."

"You were a flier in the last war, weren't you, Bill?"

"Sure I was. That's what I tell 'em. They say, 'You're just about ten years too late.' Been drowning my sorrows ever since."

He moved restlessly in his chair, sitting on the edge of it and leaning forward. I looked at the flabby figure, the kindly but subtly disintegrated face, and I felt an immense pity. I guessed

46

that ever since the First World War ended, Bill had been looking for excitement and had tried to find it in drink. Now there
was a chance to recapture the old thrills and they would not let
him do it.

"How about a cup of coffee?" I asked. "I think Norah has
some left."

He did not answer. When I came back with two cups, Ed and
Dr. Beard had come in together.

"Hello, Elizabeth." Fred Beard patted my shoulder. "Haven't
seen you helping us down at the hospital lately."

"Look tomorrow," I told him, "between two and six."

Ed pulled out his watch. "Where's Herb?" He sounded irritable. "I know he hasn't forgotten because he was in my office
yesterday. Had to come around and show off his gold braid."

"Gold braid?" I looked at him in surprise.

"Didn't you hear about Herb?" Fred lit a cigarette a little too
casually. "He got a commission in the Army at last. He's a
major or lieutenant colonel or something. Going to Washington
in a few days."

"I certainly didn't know." I really was astonished.

The door bell rang. Ed followed me into the hall so that when
I turned I looked directly into his face. But first I opened the
door. It was Herb, complete in khaki with gold emblems on his
shoulder. He strode in, tossing a greatcoat onto a chair, a dark,
well-fed man, with enterprising eyes and a hearty handshake.

"Sorry to be late." His voice was unnecessarily loud. "Been
packing. Alice didn't want me to come at all. Leaving tomorrow, you know."

It was then I turned and saw Ed's eyes. What I found there
shook and startled me. They were fixed on the insignia on
Herb's cap. They were sad; yes, sad and deeply envious.

Herb paced into the living room. Bill Gray did not rise. He
was sobering up fast and his eyes had a dreary look in them.
Fred Beard was standing, but instead of shaking hands he
walked around, studying the almost portly figure in the snugly
fitting uniform. He prodded Herb in the ribs.

"Army'll sweat that off you," he said.

"Yeah." The monotone was Bill's. "Understand they get all
the heat they want in Washington."

"You look simply gorgeous, Herb," I said. "It's just terribly becoming." It seemed to me somebody had to say it.

Ed turned abruptly away from me and stood over the bridge table. He said, "Well, let's get going."

The four of them sat down.

So this was the thing. Herb was showing them it could be done, by the right man. Herb was in the pink of physical condition; Herb had hung on somehow; he had got back; he had found a place in a young man's war. Herb was in it and they were out. It made you want to cry, looking at them. Three such nice men. My heart ached.

I went to bed while they were still playing. I woke hours later. Ed was feeling for the light.

"Hello, dear." I looked at my watch. "You played late."

"Matter of fact, we stopped early." Ed sat down in the armchair rather heavily. "Herb had to go home so Bill and Fred and I just sat around talking. You know," he went on, slowly, "there are things about this war that are kind of hard to take."

"Taxes, eh? Where have I heard that one before?" I tried to be funny.

"I'm not talking about that." Ed pulled off a shoe. "It's that— well, us older men seem to be kind of on the shelf."

I didn't want to mention Herb but it was an obvious reply to say that *he* had managed to get in.

"Herb's an exception. He's always kept up his connections. But take Bill, for example—used to be a crack flier. Oh, I know he was tight tonight. But give him responsibility and he'd snap right out of it."

I shouldn't have said it, but I did.

"You don't snap into the war effort by just sitting around, highball in hand. I mean, I don't think opportunity comes knocking at the bridge table and the club."

Ed sat up suddenly. "That's not fair." His tone was almost angry. "I know any number of guys my age who've moved heaven and earth to find something they could do to help; men with experience and ability. But I tell you, they don't want us." Ed's voice rose. He walked across the bedroom and back. "Oh, they'll let us give out ration books down at the schoolhouse; but

48

all we've learned—all we know—it doesn't count. This is a boy's war and we're out of it."

"Seems to me it's a kind of universal war," I answered. "And your plant is working entirely on government contracts—"

Ed twisted his shoulders impatiently. "I don't kid myself," he said. "I'm making a living by running a business which is exactly what I'd be doing if we weren't at war and we were turning out the old product." He repeated it. "I don't kid myself.

"You see," he went on after a pause, "everybody's got some special equipment. Bill's a born flier; I have business experience and connections—"

"And nobody in town has more friends," I said.

"And then your country's in a jam and what you've got to offer isn't needed." He spread out his hands and looked at them exactly as Bill had done.

I sat hunched under the quilt, watching him. Ordinarily when Ed was bothered, he'd finish by saying, "Well, I guess it'll all work itself out somehow," or "We'll fix it." But this was something he could not fix. This went deep. He was suffering from frustration of the feeling that, next to his family affection, ran swiftest through his being, the feeling of loyalty to a sunny-hearted people facing the powers of darkness. Ed's heart was so warm. He wouldn't any more be satisfied after a while, I thought to myself, sitting at a desk, even if he were in uniform; Ed needed to be doing something that gave his emotions a chance. I've always thought he'd have made a wonderful doctor. A good doctor does so much more than merely effect a physical cure. A good doctor tells you what to do about your troubles. A doctor! The word gave me the answer. I sat up suddenly. I'd get Fred Beard to talk to Ed. He is not only our physician, he is one of Ed's closest friends. I would fix it up tomorrow when Ed picked me up at the hospital. But first I'd have to find a chance to speak to Fred alone—

The next afternoon was busy beyond belief. The supply of trained nurses had been drained off into the service so fast that now there was a ratio of only one nurse to twenty patients. We aides were kept on the run. I had no opportunity to see Fred,

49

but I left a note asking him to meet me in the front hall, if possible, just before I left for home.

I waited for him inside the main entrance. I passed the time by talking to the receptionist, a Mrs. Green, who, like myself, was a volunteer.

"What gets me down," she said, "is having to turn away the wives of servicemen that follow the boys here." We have an enormous camp only a few miles out of town.

"You don't turn them away!" I protested.

"Listen, Mrs. Breton, this hospital is so understaffed and so in the red, they don't even dare fill it to capacity. Haven't got the nurses, haven't got the help in the kitchens, haven't got the money."

She saw Dr. Beard coming toward me and gave her attention to a man in uniform and a woman in a shabby coat who had just come in.

"What's on your mind, Elizabeth?" Fred asked.

I led him a few steps away. "It's Ed," I said. "He's been terribly sunk lately. And somehow seeing Herb in uniform—I think he's grieving because he isn't actively at work helping the service."

"Yeah, Herb was kinda hard to take." A shadow passed over his face. He studied the couple at the desk absent-mindedly. "You know, I thought *I* was going to get back into uniform. I was a natural for it, a doctor, age O. K., no family ties. But then they found out I'd once had ulcers of the stomach and it was all off. Now I'm stuck with twice as many private patients and about ten times as much work here in the hospital."

"I know."

"Of course! You can see it for yourself. We're snowed under. We've just lost the president of our board but nobody cares about working for a hospital. Everybody's got to have a label on what he does, to show it's a war effort. They're all looking for sleeve badges and uniforms. And *your* husband's just as bad as anybody." He shifted his position and looked down at me. His hand sawed the air. "I could fix it up in a minute for him to head the executive committee here. I've talked to him. He could help us raise money; help us get organized so we'd have enough volunteers; help us try to find the necessary labor; but he can't see that a hospital like this has anything to do with winning the war." He shrugged his shoulders in a tired way and looked off into space. He jerked his head sideways toward the desk. "And there's another poor little war bride we can't do our duty by," he finished.

I turned to look. The receptionist sat calmly, her hands clasped on the desk, looking up at a young soldier. The boy had clear-cut features and bright color and a nervous and resolute gaze. His mouth was fine but inflexible looking. He was capable, I felt at once, of making a desperate decision and sticking to it. Beside him was a short, red-headed girl in a cheap plaid coat which didn't quite button over her dark blue dress. The baby must be coming very soon.

"I'm sorry," Mrs. Green was saying, "but we simply can't accept another maternity case. Why don't you have the baby at home?"

"Listen, ma'am," the boy said patiently, "we ain't got any home. She come on here with me from Texas. She's boarding and they won't keep her unless we can show she'll be accommodated in a hospital when her time comes."

"Why don't you try somewhere else?" Mrs. Green asked.

"We been to 'em all. They're full up."

"We made the acquaintance of a nurse that works here," the girl put in, pleadingly. "She said you had vacant beds."

"We have, but we're not equipped to handle any more patients at present." Mrs. Green's voice was kind but firm. "Why don't you look around during the next week or so? You'll have plenty of time before the baby comes."

"All right." The boy's voice was hard. "I ain't supposed to say it, but I got my reasons for thinking we're going out. I want to know she's took care of and I want to know it before tomorrow."

"What *is* this?" It was Ed's voice. Standing with my back to the door, I had not seen him come in. Now he was speaking almost crossly to Fred. "You know you can't let a boy in uniform be shipped out of the country not knowing his wife and child will be taken care of."

"Don't you worry, sir." The boy looked directly at us, one after another, with a level, hostile gaze. He had reached his desperate decision. "If they don't take care of Belle and my kid, I don't *go* out, that's all." He took the girl's hand and turned to go. She, however, stood staring down at the receptionist as if hoping that Mrs. Green would change her mind.

"It's tough, but it happens all the time." Fred spoke into air in his impersonal, professional way.

"But look here, Fred." Ed's eyes were troubled. "This laddie may go AWOL; and if he doesn't, what kind of a fighter is he going to make, knowing we won't take care of his wife for him?"

Fred Beard parried. "What are we going to do? There's a limit to the human capacity for work and we've pretty near reached it, down at this hospital."

Now the man was watching us. The girl tugged at his elbow. Her thin face was a triangle of white between her red hair and her ungainly figure. She was conscious of Ed's gaze on her. "Come on, Andy," she said. "We better try someplace else."

"Wait a minute." Ed's hand fell on her arm. He faced Fred, still retaining her with his hold. "We must be able to do something. I believe there's government money available, or going to be, for soldiers' wives—how about that?"

"I don't know. It's a rumor; we haven't time to find out. I tell you, we're shorthanded and it's not only nurses and cleaning women; it's office force, too—so I really wouldn't know."

"That's absurd. You doctors shouldn't have administrative worries. If I were ready to take it, Fred," Ed paused, "is that job heading the executive committee still open?"

"That's right. I only told them last night you'd turned it down."

"Then I'm going to take it. We'll fix things up. Mrs. Green," he faced the desk, "would you be good enough to make a reservation for these people?"

Oddly, the boy made no sign of hearing. But as Ed removed his hand from the girl's sleeve, she looked up at him and said, "Oh, thank you. Thank you so much."

"Quite all right." Ed did not smile back but his face warmed with pleasure. As we walked briskly out under the porch light I saw his lips moving.

"It will be a lot of overtime, you know," Dr. Beard said as we stood ready to part at the hospital gate. "Using your own office force and all that sort of thing. Sure you want to take it on?"

Ed's eyes followed the small pair disappearing into the shadows of the somber street. "I'm sure," he said.

Ed had not been connected with the hospital a couple of months before some of its greatest problems took shape before his mind. The girl we had encountered there had her baby. It was born prematurely, at less than seven months, the day after the soldier husband shoved off.

It was a tiny baby and the nurses called it Tarzan. It then appeared that the hospital did not own an incubator; they had to rush one from some other place. "They just saved it by sheer devotion," Ed said.

He discovered other shortages. One Sunday when he dropped in down there—the hospital became a sort of second office for him—he saw a load of clean diapers going into the linen room with a penciled note on top. The head nurse showed it to him. "Go easy with these, girls," the note said, "you know who had to launder them, don't you?" It was signed by the superintent. "Who?" Ed asked. The nurse told him they had been put through the washing machine by the superintendent himself— who would not let his staff down even on diapers if *he* could help it.

"Those people," Ed said, "they deserve the best, and they are going to get it." He began to send for the reports of other hospitals, in order to study their methods; and he tried to make friends with more of the doctors. "I'm ready to work on this," he told Dr. Beard, "but you fellows are the doctors. You've got to tell me what you want." In the meantime he was getting ready to tell them. Ed's work was cut out for him for months, indeed for years ahead.

"No LETTER—for me, I mean?" Eileen came into the dining room where Babs, Freddie, Charles, Ed, and I were having breakfast. In her arms was the baby, a solid little figure in a pink sun suit. "I thought I'd hear from Dick today. He hasn't written for just ages. I dreamed he—" She paused.

Freddie looked up from the business of snowing under each particular corn flake with sugar. "Some daddy you got, Barbara Elizabeth."

I opened my mouth in defense of my son as Eileen opened hers in defense of her husband. Both of us closed them just in time. We had caught watchful and delighted glances from both Freddie and Charles.

"No bites?" Freddie asked. He resumed the snowing business.

"Not even a nibble." I gave my young son a warning glance. With Dick in Italy, pretty certainly in danger, mail is serious business. In a way, of course, the healthy give-and-take in a family relieves the tension, but Eileen was an only child; she can never quite take it; certainly she shouldn't be asked to just now.

"Look out, dear!"

The baby's gaze had fallen on a slender, shiny pitcher. Her arm swung in mid-air and came down, palm open, on it. The cream, only top milk in these times, ran in a thin stream to the edge of the table. Barbie turned to her mother, plainly pleased with her prowess.

"Oh, darling!" Eileen stopped the stream with a napkin. "I suppose I ought to scold you."

54

"Don't," I said. "Upsetting pitchers is a habit she's bound to outgrow. The less fuss we make about it, the better."

Ed put down the morning paper. Seated behind it, he hears everything, yet it acts as a barrage against the family's chat. Now he asked, "When did you last hear from Dick?"

"It's been over two weeks," Eileen said slowly. "I wish I knew he was all right. It—it sort of haunts me."

Ed watched Eileen for a moment in silence without speaking. Her eyes dominate her thin, lovely face. They're gray-blue and are very large and now they held a haunted, even a hunted, look. Ed noticed it too.

"Oh, I meant to tell you," he said briskly, "I saw it in the paper last night. If a child was born after the father went overseas and is less than a year old, you can attach its picture to your V-mail letter. You know," he explained to Charles and Freddie. "they photograph them on tiny rolls of movie film to save shipping space."

Freddie looked up. "Can we all get taken?" he asked.

"*No.*" I turned to Eileen. "We'll take the baby downtown this morning," I told her. "I want to show you a hat I saw."

Charles came around the table and put his forefinger in Barbie's clutch. "I'd better go along," he said. "She always smiles for me."

"That's true, she does." I spoke before anyone could say he shouldn't. In some curious way Barbara Elizabeth is a spiritual anchor to windward to Charles. When he first came to us from England, a shy, nervous child with eyes as clear as lake water, he had nothing that was his own. Freddie was generous about sharing the dog, Rags, but once when they went to visit the camp they gave him to Dick's company as a mascot. Blimp, the dog Babs brought home later to take Rags's place, made an entertaining companion for both the boys, but he was very definitely Babs's dog. And then Eileen had her baby. Eileen was the first one to notice the bond between the two. She had found Charles patiently sitting in a chair next to the crib where the baby, a pink and brown bundle, lay fast asleep. "She might wake up and be lonely," Charles had told Eileen earnestly.

"If you can go right away I'll give you a lift," Ed broke in

55

on my thoughts. I smiled at him. It was like him to turn Eileen's mind to happier and more immediate affairs.

"Mother B., do you believe in dreams?" Eileen asked. It was late that afternoon. We were both sitting in her room, folding away the baby's freshly laundered clothes.

"I think they're a very good index to the state of mind of the person who *does* the dreaming," I said.

"I don't mean quite that." Eileen folded the sleeves of the small nightgown one over the other. "I was wondering if when you were asleep you could tell what was happening to somebody who was away from you."

"I don't know, dear." I spoke gently, careful not to startle Eileen out of a rare mood of confidence. "Do you dream very much?"

"I dream about the baby every night," she said. "Last night she got smaller and smaller, like a cake of soap. Then she dwindled away and disappeared."

"It's only natural to have those anxiety nightmares," I said. "A baby is a great responsibility, especially a first one."

Eileen laid aside the nightgowns and smoothed a little shirt on her lap. "But—remember when I went to New York," she asked, "how Babs and George left the baby out in the car alone?"

"Yes." Too bad we had ever told Eileen about that. You forget how anxious, how easily terrified the mother of a child can be—especially Eileen.

"Well, I was on the train coming home that afternoon. I fell asleep and dreamed I lost Barbara Elizabeth. I hunted the whole house over. Then all of a sudden I discovered a big round pipe. It went on and on across the fields, into the horizon. I got down and looked into it. And then I knew the baby had crawled off inside and I would never reach her." Eileen paused and looked at me darkly. "Well," she said, "you see at that very moment my baby was all alone, practically lost."

I did not know how to answer this. Instead I said, "But last night when you dreamed she dwindled, like a cake of soap, she was right here in the crib beside your bed."

"I know. All the same, that time on the train my dream was

56

true. Barbara Elizabeth had been deser— forgotten. She was all alone and I knew it."

I looked at her horrified at the impression Babs's carelessness had made. It concerned me more than the subject of nightmares for the moment. But Eileen brought me back.

"You see," she finished, "I was way off in a train, asleep; but my baby needed me and I knew it." She got up so suddenly that a pile of tiny shirts fell like leaves to the floor. She took a cigarette from the table. "Sometimes they *are* true." She walked to the window and stood looking out. The moment of confidence was over.

I went about my work that day thinking again and again of Eileen and her nightmares. With Dick gone, she was so alone, even in the midst of a big and loving family, even with her baby. Was it true that in the quietness of sleep one's mind *could* reach out and know what was happening elsewhere? Plenty of stories came to my mind where this had seemed to be so. I said as much to Ed that night. He was taking off his shoes in a leisurely fashion, sitting in the low chair beside my dressing table. He put down a shoe and looked at me fixedly.

"Listen," he said, "just because you've got a son off fighting in the war you're not going nuts, are you?"

"No." I looked in the mirror and saw there my own sane and sensible face. (Too sensible. I'd love to have a real professional make-up sometime, I thought, just to see how different I could look.) I went on brushing my hair. Aloud I said, "Sometimes I think women know."

"You and Madam Futura." Ed put on his slippers.

"Who's she?"

"A dumb dame with a bony face at a restaurant out near the plant," he said. "She wears a long skirt and a gypsy headdress and reads fortunes. For two bits she'll tell you anything."

"Gypsies *are* supposed to have a kind of sixth sense or second sight or something," I remarked.

"Listen, just think of the millions Madam Futura could make today if she really had it," Ed said. "Think of what the RAF would give to know where Hitler and his gang were at any given moment." He put on his slippers with a decisive jerk. "That kind of nonsense makes me sick."

57

"Can I come in?" Freddie followed a little-boy habit of looking in first to see if it was all right to knock, then withdrawing and tapping on the door. Now his head came through the crack. Eileen was behind him. "I heard what you said about gypsies," he said accusingly. "Honestly, Moms; I bet you wouldn't walk under a ladder."

I did not look at him. "I do walk around them usually," I admitted.

Freddie squared off and studied me. "My Mom," he said.

I laughed but in the mirror Eileen's eyes met mine. He's too young, they told me. He doesn't know.

After that Eileen kept her thoughts to herself. The hunted look did not leave her eyes but she maintained her disciplined gaiety. That it was all on the surface, I knew. Once when I was a child I lived where a tiny river emptied into a harbor behind a reef and thence into the North Atlantic. The little river had cut itself a channel where even at low tide six or eight feet of water ran coldly between wide stretches of warm brown sand; sweeping about the base of seaweed-covered rocks and swirling into the deep tide holes. The ridged sand formed a beach along the border of the bay where small incoming waves broke brightly and evenly. Only in the channel were there no breakers. It would take a big storm to bring them there. I knew that the bright and even gaiety of Eileen's manner was like the sand, and beyond there were deep and level waters into which one could not see.

And then one night the deep waters broke. I was sleeping soundly when I felt a hand touch my ankle. (The children's way of waking me without disturbing their father was learned from the Pullman porter on the night train when they were small.) I sat up to see Freddie outlined against the stars—Ed and I were on the sleeping porch.

"Moms, get up, will you?" Freddie's voice was a whisper. "Something's happened to Eileen. She's crying and crying and crying and she doesn't answer when I knock."

I pulled on my bathrobe to follow him sleepily into the hall. I heard high, excited sobs. In an instant I was wide awake. I opened the door softly.

"May I come in?" I asked.

There was no answer. The sobs went fiercely on, and I

snapped on the bedside lamp. In the crib beyond, Barbie lifted her head and eyed us doubtfully; then in a single motion like the flop of a fish she turned away, face down, and went to sleep again. Eileen was lying on her back, her head rolling from side to side with a queer rhythmic motion. Her hands, the backs flat on the blanket cover, clenched and unclenched themselves, nervously doubling the beat of her head.

"Dickie," she said, "oh, Dickie, Dickie, Dickie, Dickie, Dickie!"

"Hey!" Freddie leaned over her, putting a hand on Eileen's arm. There was no response. I stood looking helplessly at the thin, shaking figure; a cold current swept around my heart.

"Go call Daddy," I said.

Ed came in, tying on his bathrobe. He stood beside Eileen, his eyes soberly inquiring. Then he put a hand on her twitching shoulder.

"Come, dear," he said matter-of-factly, "wake up. It's all right now. Come on," he urged, "tell us what's the matter."

Gradually the sobs ceased and Eileen lay quiet. Then a shudder ran through her. She opened her eyes and stared up at Ed.

"It was Dick," she said. "I was with him, somewhere out on the prairie. He wanted something and I went to get it and all of a sudden I was hurrying along a narrow board sidewalk into a town. I tried to go back but the walk turned into a steep uphill path with big rocks all across it, black and sharp like a picture in a fairy book. I had to crawl. I could hardly move. It was like—like being a diver with lead on your feet."

"I know," Ed stood up straight. "It's always that way in a dream. You can't move."

"But that wasn't all." Eileen went on talking in a low, hurried tone. "That wasn't the thing," she said. "It was what happened after that. At last I got back to the big open place but when I looked up the road had forked; I'd taken the wrong turn. Dick was miles and miles off; he was just a little dot in the distance now and an enormous river was swirling in between us. I stood looking at him. I kept saying, 'I can't, I can't!' And while he stood there, he—he just disappeared." She stopped. The muscles in her forehead knotted, distorting her face. "Something terrible has happened and I can't get to him."

59

I motioned Freddie to silence; it was no moment for his brand of common sense. To my relief, Ed made no attempt to dismiss the nightmare lightly. Instead he said, "Don't cry like this; Dick wouldn't want you to. You've got your baby to take care of, you know." He glanced at the clock under the lamp. "It's after four. The rest of us can sleep because it's Sunday," he said, "but you can't. Barbara Elizabeth'll be awake before you know it." He tightened the sheet awkwardly but firmly across her shoulders. Her eyes were closed. "All right, now, huh?" He turned off the lamp. "Good night." He turned away.

In bed once more, I pulled up the quilt and lay looking at a brilliant star beyond the pear tree. "You know," I said at last, "Eileen believes in dreams."

"Sure she does." Ed's voice came thoughtfully through the darkness. "It's bad business," he said, "very bad business."

It wasn't like Ed to do nothing further about such a matter, yet the days went by and he didn't refer to Eileen's anxiety or her nightmare. This time I told myself there was nothing that even Ed could do. Then came the night (it was Saturday) when he said, "Fellow was telling me the other day these Army planes practically commute around the globe. Seems his factory got word the Japs had hit a warehouse full of small parts out in the Pacific. That was a Friday morning. Tuesday they delivered replacements. And Italy—well, it's just a sort of suburb. Our Army freight planes shuttle to and fro all the time."

I looked inquiringly at him. I knew he was leading up to something. It couldn't be that Dick—no, even Ed wouldn't be so casual if Dick were coming home. But what?

"Yes?" I asked encouragingly.

"Well, a young fellow called me up today; came over on one of those converted planes that run freight to Italy. It seems he saw Dick only last Sunday. Sure, Dick's O. K., fine. This chap's coming out tomorrow for Sunday dinner; then Eileen can ask him everything she wants to."

After all it wasn't Eileen, it was the family who plied the young flier with questions. Was it true, Charles wanted to know, that the planes that landed on the desert had been camouflaged pink? Was it true about radar; could it really locate an object hundreds of miles off? And did the Germans have it? The pilot

60

was a big, blond boy, evidently quite used to being stared at by girls and questioned by small boys like Freddie and Charles. His manner was easy but his answers were brief. "Could be." "That's right." His information about Dick was equally scant. Words were something he used sparingly. Dick was O. K. He was fine.

I sat wondering how to get more satisfying information out of this lad. "It there anything more you can tell us about Dick?"

"I wish I could think of something." Plainly, he was trying to. He brought his hand down sideways through the air in a movement quick, like a snake's; a hand, I thought, deft at rolling dice. Perhaps that's what it would be doing if this war hadn't put it at the controls of a giant monster of the air. Young as he was, the responsibility he held made him careful. Danger shared with others had made him considerate, too, considerate of others; aware of how they felt. He knew he hadn't said enough to satisfy us.

"I wish I could tell you more, ma'am," he said. "Lieutenant Breton looked in top form. I guess that's about all there is to say."

Sitting opposite this god, Freddie heaved a deep sigh. He was too overwhelmed to speak. Eileen continued to look quietly at her plate. She was unable to square her experience, the nightmare of that early Sunday morning, with the meagerness of what this boy had to tell. I must try to see that she had a chance, later, to question him alone.

But now he was looking at the face of his watch inside his wrist.

"It's not very good manners, ma'am," he said, "but I'll have to be on my way in about five minutes." He did not explain.

Eileen looked up from her dessert. There was no time to arrive at what she wanted to know by indirection. There are moments one has to live through in front of everyone, like good-bys at trains. Eileen's arms tightened around Barbara Elizabeth, sitting solemn-eyed and sleepy in her lap. I saw her steel herself and step beyond our reach. She fixed the boy with great blue eyes and spoke as if they were alone.

"When it's four in the morning here it's nine o'clock in Rome. That's right, isn't it?" He nodded. "Well, then, do you by any chance know," she spoke slowly and exactly, "what my husband was doing at nine o'clock last Sunday morning?"

"Last Sunday, at nine in the morning, eh?" He set down his coffee cup and looked back at her almost wonderingly. "Funny your asking that, about the time, I mean."

"Why?" I saw Eileen stiffen.

"That was the morning we were together. I looked him up because I knew him back in camp, over here; we got to be pretty good friends. We were on the beach that morning. It was a swell day, and afterward we went swimming. It had been rugged; I reckon a lot of things had been pretty tough to take and that day out on the beach, the men were all like a bunch of kids out of school. At nine o'clock last Sunday morning, ma'am, your husband was lying on the beach, with his head in his arms. That was when he told me about you." His eyes ran over Eileen's head as if he were seeing her for the first time; the light hair curling back from her forehead, the full mouth half open, the great gray-blue eyes completely and unself-consciously aglow as they looked into his own.

"I see what he meant." Then he went on. "All of a sudden he stood up and began skipping the stones. He skipped a brute; he said he was sending you a message. That was when I told him I was leaving for home that afternoon and I'd sure call you. I guess most of what he wanted to say, ma'am, he couldn't tell a third party, so he said I was to say he'd already sent you a message. That was the way he put it."

Eileen sat very still. What was going through her mind I knew as if it were going through my own. At four that morning he really had been thinking of her. The nightmare scene in her dream, the fear, the frightening circumstances, all those were the machinations of her terror-stricken heart; of a mind that in sleep was out of control. She had conjured them up out of the dark, the loneliness, and her fears. She must remember after this that specific things, good *or* bad, were meaningless; she could never know what actually was happening. But that he loved her, that he wanted her, that was different. Like radar, his thoughts, his love had found their object, across hundreds and hundreds of miles of sea and air.

We were up now. The pilot was leaving.

"Could be I'd see your husband again sometime," he said. "Anything you want me to say?"

"Tell him I got his message," Eileen said slowly. "Tell him—there was a lot of static, at first. But then it came through all right. He'll know what I mean." She put her head firmly against Barbara Elizabeth.

"HEY, SIS, it's for you!" Freddie's thirteen-year-old curiosity often overcomes his very considerable inertia; it being the Friday of the Thanksgiving holidays, he might have slept late. Instead he answered an early ring at the front door. He padded up the stairs. "Registered package, special delivery, from George."

"Give it to me!" Babs's voice came back quick as a blow. Sounds of a brief scuffle soon died away.

I finished dressing and went to her bedroom. "May I come in? What d'you get—a present? Babs! *No!*" I dropped into the nearest chair.

She was lying back now on the pillows, her left hand raised. The blue nightgown with the white eyelet embroidery set off her skin—there was a lot of rose under that brown—and her dark hair and eyes. She looked warm and fresh and utterly blissful. She moved her hand. The sunlight caught a spark of fire.

"Look," she said, dreamily, "I'm an engaged woman."

Eileen, coming by with Barbara Elizabeth, stopped in the doorway. "Oh, Babs, how gorgeous!" She freed her hand to pick up Babs's. "Did you know it was coming?"

"George sent me a piece of cardboard to stick my finger through for size," Babs told us, "but I thought probably he'd take me along when he got it. They always do in the ads. I'm glad he picked it out alone, though," she added loyally. "I'd never have had the nerve to ask for a rock like this." She gave a delicious sigh.

Almost absent-mindedly Eileen looked down at her old-fashioned ring. "I did better too not picking out mine." She smiled

64

at me. Hers was left by my mother for my eldest son to give to his bride-to-be. I knew she was remembering the day when Dick had taken it to put on her finger, soon after he went into uniform. "I suppose George just couldn't wait to give it to you himself." She said it as if thinking aloud.

"Do they, usually?" The ring halted in mid-air. "I never thought of that, but now you mention it, it *is* kind of funny."

"Oh, no," I broke in. "George wanted you to enjoy it the first possible moment. There's Daddy going downstairs to breakfast." I hurried out.

As I went a tune from Babs's bedside radio followed me. It was a song from *Oklahoma!*

> Oh, what a beautiful mornin',
> Oh, what a beautiful day.
> I've got a beautiful feelin'
> Everything's goin' my way.

I hope so, dear, I thought. It really looked as if it was.

Since Babs did not come down before Ed was ready to go, I told him about the ring. "And now," I finished, "I suppose they'll be making plans to be married."

"But George is still in medical school under the Navy," Ed said.

"I know, but according to Patty that needn't matter. Babs said she never knew it till she discovered how much traveling Patty's done—one of the nice things about Blake is you never do know who has money and who hasn't—but the family must have oodles. Patty told Babs that they could easily live on the allowance their father gives him."

"Well," Ed said, "I'd like to see Babs married, too—maybe I'd get some sleep. But let's wait and see."

It was dinnertime before our family of six—seven with the baby and eight counting Norah—got together. Babs sat beside her father, her middle finger and thumb pressed to her cheek and her ring and little finger moving in a gesture that could only be called arch. Freddie saw it and rolled his eyes ceilingward, reaching for Charles under the table with his shoe and getting me with a well-placed blow on the ankle bone. Charles answered with a sideways and downward jerk of the head and suddenly I didn't want my soup. But Ed leaned seriously toward Babs's hand, pretending he had to squint.

"What's that stuck on your finger?" he asked.

Babs laughed and held it out. "Oh, Daddy, I thought you were never going to notice. Isn't it the biggest stone you ever saw?"

"Some Taj Mahal," Freddy said.

"Kohinoor, stupid," Charles prompted. "It used to be in the Tower of London before the blitz. I saw it."

"Oh, Moms, I forgot." Babs turned toward me. "Patty says her mother wants to know the date you're going to announce our engagement. She'd like to have a cocktail party for her friends the same day."

"Well, I think you can tell anyone you want to now," I said.

"But aren't you going to ask all your friends here to meet George and then surprise, surprise, Daddy announces we're engaged? You had one for the christening," she went on, accusingly. "I guess if you can give a party to launch Dick's baby you can give one for your own daughter."

I sighed. Dick is five years older than Babs, and Babs still feels a childhood rivalry for the family's attention. Yet she was entitled to her share.

But it was Ed who plunged in to back her up. "Why not?" he asked. "We'll have to fix a day when George can come. Look here." His gray eyes lit up and he let his hands rest on the table. "George deserves to know you got his ring. Why don't you go call him up?"

"Now? Long-distance? Oh, Daddy!" Babs was already on her way into the hall. It's hard not to overhear Babs at the phone but I made a determined attempt. After a few moments, however, she came back, picked up her napkin, and slipped into her seat. She looked limp and confused. "He wasn't there," she informed us. "At first the operator said they couldn't send for students so I told her to leave a message for him to call me. Then she came back and said there was no such person as George Litchfield in the medical school. She said," Babs's tone was baffled rather than alarmed, "his name was not on the enrollment list."

"You got it wrong somehow." Ed was impatient. "Let me

66

try." He went to the phone and now we listened frankly. At last he came back. His face had a squeezed look. The skin between his eyebrows was wrinkled; his lips were pushed out. "You're right." His voice was grave. "I made her put on one of the other men in the hall where he roomed. The guy wasn't very communicative. But I did get it out of him that George had left school. He checked out, bag and baggage, yesterday afternoon."

"Then he isn't hurt or anything," I tried to be comforting.

But as we gathered in the living room a current of apprehension ran coldly under our chatter. Babs, curled up on the sofa, looked half frightened, half angry. She kept silent, alarming in itself. Eileen, sitting down near her, began to talk about plans for the party. The endearing thing about Eileen, or one of them, is that she doesn't expect her constant anxiety about her own husband to make other people's lesser concerns seem unimportant; or as Ed once put it, "Let's just say she has imagination."

Suddenly Ed snapped off the radio beside him. "Why don't we call up George's family? His father will have the facts."

But Babs sat up stark and determined. "I don't want you to," she came back. "He may not have let on to them. I know my guy better than anybody. He'll tell me, next letter." Babs was stoutly putting herself on the inside and George's family and us on the out. I loved her for the spirit that made her do it, but the stark fact remained that George had walked out on the work to which he had been assigned, and she did not know where he had gone or why. She put the stone of her engagement ring to her lips and, gradually, between them, and held it there as if she was steadied by its very hardness and reassured by its reality.

The next afternoon Babs and I spent together, pushing the baby. It was Norah's day out. We had persuaded Eileen to go to a movie. She left, taking Freddie and Charles along. We put Barbara Elizabeth into her gocart and set out to market. The stores deliver large orders but odd lots of food we lug home. We met outside and piled the purchases in the foot of the carriage, a performance which Barbara Elizabeth fortunately thought was meant expressly to amuse her. "And now let's have something tall and cool," Babs suggested.

A big elm tree threw its bare-boughed shadow across the

diagonal doorway leading into the drugstore. A semi-circle of baby carriages was braked foot-first about it. In the interior was a row of young mothers while outside the babies stood up in their harnesses, leaning forward like laughable little charioteers gazing round-eyed into the place where their protectors had gone.

"Everybody seems to be having them." Babs watched a girl passing the window whose baby was apparently coming any day. "What I wonder is why dress designers tie a bow right in front."

"I think the maternity clothes are adorable this year," I told her, "and I just love the way all the girls push around, so perky and determined, in their flat heels and their cute clothes and their shiny little hair-does with bows on top."

"And the escorts in uniform looking so self-conscious," Babs said.

"It takes a second baby," I told her, "before most men really enter into the spirit and humor of the thing."

"Well," she finished, "I still think putting a bow right on top is overdoing it."

"Don't be too superior," I laughed. "First thing you know you'll be married and having one, too."

Babs twisted her face above the straw and stared at me with round, brown eyes. "Oh, Moms, do you suppose we really can get married soon?" She looked at her ring and then pulled in her shoulders as if she were hugging herself. "Then I won't take those old summer courses next year." She dug for ice-cream with a long spoon. Keeping step with the "acceleration" which would give her an A. B. degree in three years instead of four, she had taken courses the previous summer at a college here in the city. "I'd look cute," she giggled, "pushing down the aisle for my diploma with Junior six months along!"

"I'd keep going as you are for the present," I said, "until you have a chance to talk over plans for the future with George."

"Oh, gosh!" She slipped down from the high stool. "We'd better putt-putt. I didn't get a letter this morning so I think maybe's he going to call up." We went out to the gocart. Babs took Barbara Elizabeth and bounced her into it, fastening the strap. "Come on, small fry," she told her, "we've got to roar."

68

They jounced off up the street, Babs lifting and bending exaggeratedly, the baby grabbing the sides of the gocart delightedly for security. It's fun to be young with babies, I thought, fun for all concerned. It was evident that Barbara Elizabeth, for one, would have agreed with me.

But in spite of her speed, Babs missed her phone call. It was Ed who told her, after supper. George had tried to get Babs in the afternoon and when the operator failed to raise anyone at 112 Elm Street, he had called Ed's office. He had not said where he was or what he was doing, and Ed with typical consideration had not asked.

"Honestly, Daddy," Babs groaned, "I suppose you didn't even mention my ring or the party."

"Oh, yes; I told him it was a beauty," Ed said. "And I fixed it up for the party. It has to be day after tomorrow. I guess he's up to his ears in something," he went on, "because he said he probably wouldn't get a chance to call up again before he came and I was to take care of his girl and look out for his interests."

Babs's face, which had sobered pathetically at first, lit up. After all, he was coming in—she counted it up—in about forty-two hours. "Then we can make our plans and everything," she said happily.

The rest of the evening and all of the following day she went around in a dream. Details of living slipped past her like a fleeting landscape. It touched me to see her come in at breakfasttime, slip her arms around Ed's neck, and press her cheek against his hair with an ecstatic look. But half an hour later I came upon her sitting on the stairs hugging Blimp. His doggy eyes were squeezed shut in a contented way; her face, pressed against his shaggy head, wore exactly the same expression as before when Ed had been in her arms.

Babs's sole contribution to the hurried preparations for the party was always to be dreadfully in the way. However, Norah, who normally regards entertaining as an unnecessary interruption of the business of running a home, proved to be wholly behind this event. She popped in constantly from the kitchen to mention something I might have forgotten, the punch bowl to be taken down and polished, the shamrock-embroidered cloth with the wide Irish lace border to be pressed. Between times she

69

rubbed and scrubbed in what seemed to be an interminable and unnecessary attack on obscure spots which would never meet the visitors' eyes. But I have a compulsion myself about the linen closet, which I simply have to clean before any big event in the house, Norah's worries were therefore understandable and distinctly on the right side. I did not try to direct her energies.

At last the great day dawned. I walked about after lunch viewing my shining home. The makings of the punch were set out on the sideboard where Ed could review them. Norah, decked out in a new gray taffeta uniform with embroidered organdy, was arranging tiny sandwiches at the big kitchen table. The boys and Blimp were on the side porch. Babs and Eileen were still upstairs. House and household hung in air, waiting.

One of the most likable traits a man can have is that of entering wholeheartedly into the spirit of a company of close friends. George knew none of the people whose ups and downs we have shared over twenty-odd years and who feel any happiness of ours almost as deeply as if it were their own, but he made you feel he wanted to. He came in before them. His alert figure in the cool brown suit gave off an air of power under control. His eyes were eager. Babs was waiting for him at the front door. In a dark blue dress and something scarlet clipped at the top of her hair she looked like a radiant child. George's eyes shone as he took her in his arms, but all he said was, "My, my. Don't we look gorgeous!" Then together they bent over the ring.

"What'll I do with these, buddy?" Behind George a small boy had now descended from a bicycle and was bringing up a couple of small white florist's boxes. It was characteristic of George that it had not occurred to him to bring them himself.

"Oh." He handed the boy a quarter. "There you are, son. These are for my girls."

Mine was a corsage of tiny white rosebuds and something else that lay in frothy white around them.

"Oh, George!" Babs lifted out an exquisite spray of small white orchids. Then, "Where is he? Where is that wonderful man?" For he was gone.

I could hear George talking to Ed. "With Daddy," I told her. But Babs was already on her way to him.

70

People began to come—Dr. Howard, the minister who married Eileen and Dick, Fred Beard, our doctor, the three other couples in our bridge club, the wispy little old woman with the wide, humorless eyes who augments a tiny income by writing social notes for the paper. I heard her whispering up at me, "May I quote a tentative date and plans for the wedding?" I smiled absent-mindedly back. That was one of the things I would have liked to talk to Babs and George about before the announcement.

Well, it was too late now. Across the living room Ed was ringing his glass for silence. Beside him stood Babs and George, gay, excited, utterly at ease, completely at home in an atmosphere of high-pitched emotions. For just a moment I felt a twinge, not of envy, but of regret. It was as if I were not needed in the picture. It would be that way, too, when Babs was married. It would be Ed who would take her down the aisle. Acting as instinctively as a child, I worked my way through the crowd and took my place next to him. Now he was raising his glass.

"Has everyone something?" He waited while Norah and the boys went here and there with pitchers. Then, "I want to propose a toast. I want you to drink with me to the happiness of Barbara and George." He was going to say more but something choked off his voice. Instead he dipped his glass toward them in salute. He turned toward me and touched his cup to mine. The moment had come. Babs was to be married and now we had approved and confirmed it; we had told the world. One of the great events of our life was happening; now it had happened; was over.

At last it was dark and everyone was gone. The family had turned in. Only George was left, on the porch with Babs. I helped Ed with the garage doors as he put up the car and we walked back to the house together. A great wind rushed through the trees overhead. I took Ed's hand.

"I'm so happy," I told him. "Makes you think of when we were engaged." Ed did not reply but his fingers tightened on mine.

A few minutes later he came into our bedroom with two tall glasses in his hand. "I fixed one for you, too," he told me. "Do you good."

"Thanks, dear. I need something." I took mine.

We sat in silence sipping the icy liquid. We were marking time. Soon Babs would be up to tell us how wonderful it all had been. But the outside door shut, heavily and slowly, and still no footsteps came. And then I heard it, a queer thump, or knock, on the wall below. It was repeated. "What's that?" Ed shook his head, listening.

I went to the top of the stairs. The light from our floor reached down into the darkness.

On the bottom step sat Babs, crouched as if getting away from something that had struck her. She did not see or hear us and as I watched she hit her head against the wall in a fierce and desperately repeated motion.

"Sweetie!" I called. "What's the matter?" We were both beside her now. Ed put a firm hand on her shoulder. She looked up dry-eyed, staring into the semidarkness.

"George has joined up as a sailor," she said. "He told me just as he was leaving. He said he had got himself deferred for medical school just to please his father but now he wants to get in quick. He asked the Navy to transfer him. He starts boot training tomorrow. He's going to put in for sea duty. Now I don't know *when* he'll marry me." Suddenly Babs's face contracted, pulled this way and that as the muscles went out of control. Her big eyes asked Ed for help; then she threw herself against me and began to sob with all the reserve force of her young strength.

8

It's just that different things seem important to different people. It's a matter of age, perhaps, but children's tempers don't seem awfully vital any more; I don't live or die over every spoonful of cereal they do or do not eat. But there are other things that matter tremendously to me, things the younger people never think of at all.

On a certain Saturday, I went for a kind of shakedown cruise of the emotions and found out how to put across what I believed a child should be taught.

My nerves got their first jolt that day, at about ten in the morning. I came down the stairs and saw Barbara Elizabeth in the living room; at least I saw her brown curls and a bit of her red sweater and her stout brown boots sticking out straight before her.

"Hello, darling," I called. "What are you doing?"

Barbie did not answer, having a well-founded distrust of questions which so often prove to lead to bed or bathroom. Instead she turned about, slipped to the floor, and made off to another chair in a far corner. "Botch it, be ca'ful," she admonished herself in a soft and confiding voice. Once in the chair, she sat back again, never looking my way.

My eyes still on her, I stepped off the bottom stair. As I did so, the floor slid from under me. Grasping the rail and wrenching my right arm only slightly, I broke my fall. On the floor before me lay a tiny and particularly vicious-looking jeep whose inch-high wheels had moved from under my sole. I picked it up just as Eileen appeared at the end of the hall. She was wearing navy-blue slacks, a flowered shirt, and red rope-soled shoes, and her arms were full of mussy baby clothing.

I said, "We ought to teach Barbie to pick up her toys. This little jeep—I just stepped on it."

"Oh, Mother B., you *didn't!*"

Eileen hurried forward and peered, not at me, but at the little car, an anxious frown on her thin face. "It's her best toy. You can't get them any more. But I guess you didn't hurt it," she added matter-of-factly.

I refrained from comment and Eileen went on, "Well, I've got to get my washing done."

"I'll keep the baby with me," I offered.

Eileen hesitated. "Don't bother," she said. "She's better playing alone. You don't have to watch her all the time."

She went off, leaving a trail; a tiny red sock, the legs of some little pink pajamas. . . . I was on the way to the pantry where there would be coffee in the percolator. I did not like, however, to leave the baby alone. I had once been casual, too; but now I could remember things: the time Dick closed his soft little hand over a sharp kitchen knife, the day Babs pulled over a heavy lamp, hitting her temple dangerously near an artery. . . .

"Come along with me, darling," I said, and I added brightly, "Crackers!"

"C'ackers." Barbie got down, her eyes wide and happy.

I lifted her into her high chair—it makes me nervous the way Eileen lets her climb up and down—and brought my coffee and her crackers from the pantry. With only a slight feeling of guilt, I realized I was committing the error called feeding-her-between-meals. Oh, well, I said to myself, never mind. Nourishment is good for her no matter when she takes it. She began shoving crackers into her mouth. "Be careful!" she said through a shower of crumbs, and laughed sputteringly at her own joke. *I* could keep her quiet and happy.

And then I heard voices in the kitchen. I held my spoon in mid-air. "Listen!"

Babs must have come in the back way.

"Hello, Eileen!" I heard her over the sound of running water. "Gosh, do you have to wash all the time?"

"I certainly do." Eileen's tone was grim.

74

"Give me them small pieces!" Norah's voice joined in. "I'll be rubbing them out. I want to do my kitchen floor," she explained. Along with her quick temper, Norah has a ready acceptance of the inevitable and has long faced the fact that Eileen is going to wash a little every day and in Norah's kitchen, instead of a lot every now and then and in the laundry.

Babs swung into the dining room. She wore a soft box coat of gray, and there were gray rosettes over her ears, like a pony's, between which her eyes were big and brown. "Hi!" She kissed me and hugged the baby. "How come they let you stay inside this lovely day?" she asked Barbara Elizabeth. "I used to cry to come inside, but no. I had to play in the yard."

"Hello, sweetie," I said. "Why don't *you* take her out? And I wish you'd go to the store."

"I thought so. I should never have come home." Babs bit into a graham cracker. "Why can't they send the stuff?"

"No cartons, no delivery boys. You should have seen me yesterday, trying to bring home the vegetables in little paper bags. I did all right until an eggplant got away from me and rolled right out under the bus."

"And you after it, I bet." Babs patted my head. "Good old Moms. Well, come on, then." She gathered the baby up in her arms, Barbara Elizabeth grasping delightedly at Babs's hair as one who seizes the flying ring.

They did not get back until late; in fact, we were at the luncheon table. Eileen was mashing baked potato and mincing chicken when Babs popped Barbie into her high chair.

A silver mug stood on the table. The baby lunged toward it. "Milk," she said.

"Not yet." Eileen set the plate down before her. "String beans, first."

The baby's face began to cloud and then it puckered.

I shouldn't have said it but I did. "Oooh." I leaned forward. "Can't she have her milk?" I asked.

Encouraged by my tone Barbara Elizabeth lunged again. "Milk," she demanded.

Eileen stood beside her and spoke as one woman to another. "First you've got to eat something."

The baby fixed on me her large and sorrowful eyes and then,.

putting her head forward, she screamed. Eileen said nothing. Instead she slipped into her own place at the table. Barbara Elizabeth looked around the table and with what, had she been using a foot instead of a hand, would have been a kick, she sent the dish flying to the floor.

"All right. That settles it. Up to bed we go." Eileen took the little girl, all flailing arms and legs now, and went upstairs.

"I'm sorry, dear," I said when Eileen came down again, flushed but stern-eyed. "I guess I started that."

"I guess you did," Ed said. "Whose baby is she, anyway?"

I ignored this. "But I don't see what difference it makes," I persisted. "I mean it seems funny she can't have milk when she wants it. She's probably thirsty."

"It isn't funny," Eileen did not look at me. "If she fills up on milk first she doesn't eat her meat and vegetables."

"It seems funny that she hasn't more appetite," I said.

"Maybe she'd eat, out with me." It was Norah standing between us and looking from one to the other, feeling her way as a cautious bather feels the bottom under the water before him. "I've not much education," she went on, "but I've a good hand for mothering."

Usually Norah's warm voice comforts Eileen. This time it seemed only to bait her. "I'll bring her down myself," she told us shortly.

Ed cleared his throat but thought better of what he might have said. Babs eyed me speculatively. The returning child, subdued, ate with only an occasional gulp. Lunch ended in a rather somber silence.

Afterward, I rested a little. Later I went to the linen closet to put away some sheets I had mended. The door of Babs's room was open; I could see two pairs of feet opposite each other. The red rope-soled shoes were sticking out of an armchair; Babs's hung off the bed.

I heard Babs say, "You mustn't let Mom get you down."

"She doesn't get me down, she gets me scared." A curl of smoke blew over the feet.

"That awful vague way she has; don't I know it," Babs broke in. "She used to be that way with me before George and I got engaged. 'It seems funny.' It's that expression of hers that gets you down. She was always saying it seemed funny he didn't write, or something."

I thought it best to declare my presence. Both girls looked up at me. Eileen had been about to speak. Now she said nothing. In those few seconds of silence I had a sensation I had had only once before in my whole life. The other time was at college. A new girl, not knowing any better, I had stood in the doorway of an upperclassmen's room where three seniors had been talking together. Seeing me, they had stopped and watched me, not hostile, just waiting for me to go away.

"Well, here we are, smoking ourselves to death again." Babs spoke. "Have one. Do you good. And come on in." She moved over. "We're discussing baby care," she went on. "I saw this folder about babies. It says, 'Don't take the advice of relatives.'" She waved a cigarette. "I just told Eileen, if she worries about the way Barbie eats, why doesn't she zoom around this afternoon and let Dr. Beard see her?"

"I think I'll do just that." Eileen sat up.

"Lucky for you two dimwits you have an educated woman in the family. Oh, and the folder particularly says, 'Don't let grandma upset you.'" But to soften this remark Babs put an encircling arm around me.

"I guess I'll take the baby up now before she is really awake." Eileen eased herself out of the big chair.

"It seems kind of funny, waking her up, I mean," I said.

"It wouldn't," Eileen came back firmly. "Not if you had to do the laundry." She went out.

Without questioning, I accompanied Eileen and the baby to the doctor's. Fred Beard met us at the door.

"What are *you* doing here, Elizabeth?" he asked.

I was somewhat taken aback. A long-term friend of ours, Dr. Beard always manages, somehow, to make me feel immature. His deeply lined face tells you nothing nor do his dark but indefinitely colored eyes.

He took Barbie's hand. "Let's have a look at you."

I followed him into the white-tiled inner room and stood receiving the tiny garments as Eileen pulled them off. Presently I found myself sitting on a small hard chair in a corner while

Fred and Eileen, on either side of the big white table, bent over Barbara Elizabeth.

For a time the doctor said nothing. His lean deft hands ran over the child's round little body and his voice quieted yet amused her. He didn't even look in my direction when he said, "Grandma can dress her. You and I'll go into my office and talk."

I put a shirt over the baby's head. "Where's the baby? Oh, here she is!" Her small surprised face came laughing out of the shirt top. It was a routine as familiar as an old song. Yet suddenly I felt I had no place there; that I was like one of these "sitters" the girls hire, trusted to watch the baby, considered reliable but not fitted to do anything more.

That night a tired little girl went off early to bed and we sat down to our family dinner. We were entertained by Babs, who, perhaps with some idea of telling us how to get along together, described her struggles with a onetime roommate, a super-neat person who lived in a constant state of protest against Babs's carelessness about her clothes, her books, her shoes, and tennis rackets. "So finally I told her off," Babs explained, as Ed looked at her as if he were seeing things. "I said she'd come to college to learn to get along with people; that some people were tidy and some were not; that I was not and she'd better begin her education by trying to get along with me."

And so the supper passed. A few radio programs followed, and Babs and Freddie both went up to bed. Charles, however, hung around. He was trying to learn to play bridge. He and Ed and I and Eileen settled down with the cards before us.

It was almost eleven when we finished. We were talking over the last hand as we went upstairs when we heard crying, sleepy but recurring, the sort you associate with pain. It came from Barbara Elizabeth's room.

Eileen was there first. Through the open window the heavy mist glistened against the street light and moved like a fog into the room. Barbara Elizabeth lay uncovered, her little body hunched against the headboard. When Eileen started to put her back under the blankets she made a pitiful sharp sound; Eileen's touch made her scream sharply.

"What's the *matter?*" Eileen drew back, terrified.

78

"She was all right this afternoon." I bent over her too. "I mean it seems funny she could get sick in such a short time."

Ed leaned over the crib, laying his hand gently on her shoulder. Again came that short, sharp crying.

"Sit up," he said, almost sternly. But Barbara Elizabeth continued to lie huddled as if in pain.

"Better call Fred Beard. I'll do it." Ed went hurriedly downstairs.

Usually it cheers you up just to see Dr. Beard's big buoyant figure. Tonight, however, his appearance frightened me; it was so indicative of haste. He was dressed, of course, but his shirt was unbuttoned and one of his shoes was black while the other was brown.

"Can we have a better light?" he asked. As I removed a shade, he began tapping Barbara Elizabeth on the knee, then ran his fingers along her spine. When he reached the base of her neck she cried loudly.

He stopped and drew the blankets over her. "All right, sister," he said. "I won't hurt you any more." As he busied himself taking her temperature he went on, "She didn't have any fall today, nothing to cause that soreness? Because she was all right when I examined her this afternoon. But of course some things strike very quickly...."

Eileen shook her head. She simply could not speak.

Fred Beard read the thermometer without comment and then walked from the room. We gathered around him in the hall. Ed's eyes avoided mine. We were both thinking...Ed cleared his throat. Then he asked, "What about infantile? No danger of that, I suppose, Fred?"

"Polio? We can't exclude it, even in winter." The doctor's answer came back so quickly I knew it must have been the first thought in his mind. "I don't think this is it," he went on gravely, "but we can't be sure; not yet. In the meantime I think I'll run down to the Board of Health and see about some serum, just in case. Want to come along, Ed?" He looked down and saw Charles's white face at his shoulder. "You come too, Charlie," he said. "This fellow down there has some white mice and he lets them out at night. They have the run of the corridors. You'll be interested—" In their comfortable big way, the men went out the door.

Eileen sank down on the top stair as if frozen. I stood above her. "I wish Dick were here with you," I said.

"He isn't here." Eileen spoke to herself. "He's way, way away." She sat staring into the darkened well of the hall. Babs would have been crying hysterically in my arms but Eileen merely put out a thin hand in front of her. "I'll sit here and wait, where I can hear Barbie if she cries again. Why don't you run along? Why don't you run along and get a little sleep?"

I hesitated, aching to try to comfort her. But suddenly I realized that Eileen, whose father and mother had both been killed in an accident, had at that time learned a terrible lesson; something it is not good to learn, so young. She had learned to lean on no one. So I went to my room.

For a time I stood looking out into the inky street down which no one came. I walked about, straightening things that were already straight. And I listened. There was no sound of crying now. Had the onset of the disease put a stop to it? I mustn't assume that; this could be anything; it could be nothing. I stood by the bed. I saw long, long years ahead for Barbara Elizabeth, early years that should be full of play, school years and years in which she should fall in love, marry, and have children. And I saw years of a totally different kind.

I threw myself down on the bed, trying to rest, but my mind ran to and fro like a rat along the base of a sheer wall. There was no comfort, no peace, nowhere for my thoughts to turn. And then I found myself repeating something; comforting myself with words out of my childhood.

> Jesus, tender shepherd, hear me.
> Bless thy little lamb tonight.

No, that wasn't what I wanted to say. That was the little prayer we used to recite every night of our lives when we were small. But this was what I wanted to do. I slipped to my knees, my head against the cover.

"Oh, God," I began, "she's just a dear little girl. She enriches the world. We've done everything we can. Now we have to leave it to You. Please don't let anything happen to her; please, please, please—"

For a long time I lay there. I think I fell asleep.

It was Eileen's steps in the hall that woke me. I went out with a question in my eyes. She shook her head.

"She's still sleeping."

"Then let's go downstairs. I want to fix you something hot to drink."

We sat at the table together with our teacups before us. I looked down into mine.

"Do you believe in prayer?"

"You mean saying prayers, at night?" Eileen brought her mind by an obvious effort to this, to her, quite unrelated subject. "No, I don't think anything about it, one way or another. I haven't the slightest objection to a person's being religious," she added. "I just wasn't brought up that way." Then she looked at me, as an idea came to her. "Why, is Dick religious?"

"No. Yes, maybe. I really don't know—now," I said. "But I don't think I did enough for my children along that line. I believe every child should learn to trust in God, and to pray."

"Maybe." But Eileen was not even considering the subject.

"Hey, what are you two swing-shifters doing?" Babs stood in the doorway huddled in a white toweling bathrobe. "What's up? Anything good to eat?"

I told her about the baby. Before I could even finish she started to speak but broke off as Ed, Dr. Beard, and Charles came in. She said hello to them, then sat down beside me. "Why didn't you tell me?"

"Why get you up?" Ed said gently. "There wasn't anything you could do."

"What's the story?" Babs asked. I described the symptoms. "Listen," Babs said, "down at the store today I dumped Barbie on the counter while I shopped. She tried to pat the store cat and fell off. She hit her neck on the base of that big iron stove they have there. Do you think that could have anything to do with it?"

"Well, now I guess we can exclude polio." Dr. Beard slumped into a chair, his arms slack. "Say, Elizabeth, is there any more

81

of that, whatever it is you're drinking? If there is, I want it."
His face wore a tired look of affectionate exasperation.

So, under instructions from him, I put Eileen to bed with
something to make her sleep. Everyone else turned in. I went
once more to Barbara Elizabeth's room. The unaccustomed
bustle outside had wakened her a little and she lay small and
watchful beneath the blankets. I tucked them in securely. It was
time for me to turn in, too, but for a moment I stood looking
down at her. She was all right now. I was thinking of the years,
later, when she would be out in front, where Eileen and the
rest of us had been tonight. I thought of their possible terrible-
ness. And then I knew. Eileen had had no recourse but I had
had one. I had had the channel for my feelings made by childhood training. Someone had taught me to pray and I could teach
Barbara Elizabeth.

My voice is not too good and prayer out loud isn't really my
line, so to speak, but I took hold of the crib rail. "Jesus, tender
shepherd, hear me," I began.

Barbara Elizabeth twisted her small shoulders and with a
small sigh went contentedly to sleep.

"ONE CLUB." Ed sat back. His fingers tapped the table top and his eyes searched our faces, Margery Smith's, mine, and Ben Smith's, in turn.

Margery arranged her cards. "I'm simply woozy tonight," she announced. "I've been shopping all afternoon with Mary Lee trying to get her something to wear to the school party Friday night." Margery regarded her cards as if they somehow surprised her by being there.

"It's your bid, dear," Ben said patiently. Like Ed, Ben is a very good bridge player; he gets completely wrapped up in the game.

Margery looked at her hand. "May I review the bidding?"

"Ed dealt and bid a club," Ben said.

"I found a dream of a dress, but it was kind of expensive." Margery moved two cards next to three she had been holding slightly apart. "Still, I think I may get it. You know how hard it is to find anything just right for that age. All of a sudden, they look like Orphan Annies in anything childish and they haven't the figure for anything else. At the moment, Mary Lee has practically no waist."

"It's the way they eat all the time," I told her. "Food is the principal passion of Freddie's life and he shows it. But they lengthen out. Look at Charles." Charles is only a year older than Freddie and Mary Lee, but beside them he seems grown-up.

"Ed bid a club, dear," Ben said. There was no hint of exasperation in his voice.

"Even at that, she wouldn't be at all bad looking if it weren't for those braces," Margery complained. "We thought we'd get 'em off her teeth by now, but the dentist says no, she must keep them on another six months. And she has this gruesome way of snapping the rubber bands."

"Mary Lee is a grand kid," I came back warmly. "You just wait; in a couple of years she'll be a knockout. She's got lovely eyes and hair."

"Well, Margery?" Ben's voice was kind but it sounded discouraged.

"Oh, is it my bid?" Margery studied her cards. "I pass."

"I bid a diamond."

"I bid one spade," Ben came in promptly.

Ed bid two diamonds.

"It's Mary Lee's first high-school party." Margery's voice dropped to a hushed monotone. "I do want her to *look* like something."

"It's your bid, dear," Ben said.

"It is?" Margery considered. "I bid two spades. The whole thing is dreadfully difficult anyway. You know the minute they get in high school they'd die rather than walk in anywhere alone. Mary Lee says flatly she won't go unless somebody asks her and nobody has. Her father would go around with her, but no, that won't do."

"Of course it won't! Suppose somebody were to see her!" I laughed, remembering my early difficulties with Babs.

The bidding continued and at last Ed got the contract at three no trump. The first card was led. I put down my hand with some relief and settled back to watch the playing and the players. I thought of the games we'd had together over the years; one, the night before Freddie was born; another when Freddie lay tossing after a tonsil operation and we all sat quietly just outside his door until four in the morning when he dropped off into a deep sleep. I felt a surge of affection for the Smiths. Suddenly I said, "Listen, Margery, Freddie's going to that party. He'll take Mary Lee."

"Oh, Elizabeth, do you think he would?" Margery's face brightened. "Mary Lee would kill me if she knew I'd told you."

"She won't," I answered promptly. "I'll have Freddie call her up himself and invite her."

I chose the next day after school to break the news to Freddie.

84

I went to the pantry and mixing a lot of honey and peanut butter I made a plateful of juicy sandwiches. Freddie took my offering without suspicion. I said, "You're going around to the school party Friday night, aren't you?"

"Yeah." His honest round face told me nothing.

"Taking anybody?" I asked brightly.

"Who, me?" Freddie's tone was startled.

"Why don't you ask a girl?" I went on. "The boys take girls to parties when they get in high school, don't they?"

"Not the fellows I go around with," Freddie came back cheerfully. "The whole bunch of us is going together."

"Mary Lee hasn't anybody to take her," I began. "And I told Mrs. Smith you'd be glad to go around and pick her up. Don't talk with your mouth full!" I added.

Freddie's jaw hung open and now, all movement arrested, exposed a hunk of white bread. On all counts Freddie was too frustrated to speak so I went on, "The Smiths live near school and anyway Mary Lee is an awfully nice girl."

"Well, I can't, that's all," Freddie said. "I'm going with Bingo and Harold and Charlie and Pinhead Harris and Popeye Green and Ears Summers and a whole bunch of fellows."

"Listen," I said, "you play with Bingo and Harold every day of your life. I guess you can tear yourself away for once and go with Mary Lee. I told Mrs. Smith you would. And," I added for good measure, "I don't want to hear any more discussion about it, either."

Freddie put down his glass of milk and glared at me, his round brown face settling sullenly, his hazel-green eyes baffled and miserable; so miserable and so baffled that I was thoroughly exasperated. "It's perfectly ridiculous to make such a fuss, just because you have to walk three or four blocks out of your way," I told him. "I want you to call up Mary Lee tonight. Now, go do your homework!"

Freddie did not answer, but he went upstairs. I heard him banging his way defiantly along, a kick at every step. Why are kids so *difficult?* I wondered. I didn't know. Well, this one could just snap right out of it!

At seven-thirty that night I set off my time bomb in the quiet living room. Ed was busy with the paper. Eileen had put the baby to bed and was now sitting on the couch with Charles helping him with a math problem. Freddie was at my desk, having got there first.

"Have you called Mary Lee, Freddie?" I asked. "If not, I want you to do it right away."

"Gee, Mom, I can't. I told you 'safternoon." Freddie's tone implied that the whole business was settled and over with.

"And I said we'd have no discussion about it." I heard my own voice growing louder, like when you give a sudden twist to the radio knob.

"What's all the argument?" Ed's gray eyes were kind, but somehow his look made Freddie and me seem the same age.

"All of a sudden for no reason at all Moms wants me to take Mary Lee to the school party," Freddie said. "What's the matter with the girl—hasn't she got legs? Why should I have to lug her there?"

Ed glanced tolerantly from one to the other of us. "I don't see why you should, unless you want to. What's the idea, Moms?"

I turned on him indignantly. "You know perfectly well what the idea is," I said, "or you would, if you didn't sit at the bridge table and think all the time about who plays what card and why. Margery told us last night Mary Lee had nobody to go with and I said Freddie would take her. Margery Smith is my best friend and I guess if there's anything I can do for her I will."

"Freddie will, you mean." Ed corrected me.

"But Ed, I promised Margery." There were tears of anger in my eyes.

"Well, it's just too bad, Mom, but I can't." Freddie began to write busily.

Ed studied his son for a moment. Plainly he was puzzled. Freddie grumbles a lot but he is seldom downright un-co-operative.

"Have you any good reason for not taking Mary Lee?" Ed asked presently. "She doesn't look like a drip to me."

"Oh, Mary Lee's an all-right kid." Freddie said honestly. "She's a good outfielder. I just can't take her to any old party, that's all. I'm going with a bunch of fellas. I'm going with—"

I saw an opening. "Listen," I began. "Your friends are

around the house all the time and I'm just as nice to them as I can be. Now it's your turn to be nice to Daddy's and mine."

"Your mother's got a point there," Ed admitted.

"Lots of times you've put me out on a limb by bringing Bingo or Harold home to supper without asking me." I was heartened by a hint of support in Ed's manner and determined to press the advantage. "Maybe I shouldn't have promised Mrs. Smith without telling you first, but it's done, and you can't let me down."

"But gee, Mom," Freddie said, "the Missing Links are all going together; me and Bingo and Harold and Charlie and Pinhead and Popeye and Ears Sum—"

"If I hear those names again I shall scream." I meant it.

"What *are* the Missing Links?" Ed wanted to know. He gets behind on data like that.

"They're a club; me and Bingo and Harold and Charlie and Pinhead and Popeye and Ears—"

I stiffened.

"Wait a minute." Ed's face lit up with a brand new idea. "Why don't all the Missing Links go and call for Mary Lee?"

Charles sat up straight so suddenly that all his bits of paper careened to the floor. "We don't go 'round with girls. We train, and things like that."

"And *I'm* not going to ask her." Freddie's head went down and forward and his eyes asked, What do you think of that? He faced me with the courage of despair. "I won't," he said.

"You can't speak to your mother like that." At last Ed came to bat for me. He looked firmly, almost angrily at the defiant little boy before him. "Your mother has asked you to do something," he said. "I want you to do it, right away."

Every square inch of his stocky little body protesting, Freddie went slowly into the hall and back to the phone. We heard the door beside it thump with the impact of his foot. We listened shamelessly. In the fewest of words and with guarded inquiry, Freddie tried to get the word that Mary Lee had been asked by someone else. But she hadn't. At last he wound up his conversation by saying, "If you want, I'll come by for you."

I sighed with relief, smiling across at Ed. But Ed did not smile back. Half an hour later, up in our room, he said slowly, "You know, at that age girls are just a darn nuisance."

My stored-up indignation broke loose.

"It's too ridiculous," I said. "Perfectly nice little girls have to stay home and wait around while a bunch of Missing Links decide whether or not to take them somewhere. It used to infuriate me when Babs was that age and it does now."

"Those kids are too young for parties," Ed said, "especially the boys. But women promote that sort of thing."

"There's nothing you can do about it," I told him. "It's the system. They meet it as soon as they enter high school. Personally I don't think it hurts the boys; it teaches them manners."

Ed picked up his bathrobe. "Personally, I'm for the Missing Links."

"How about keeping it to yourself if you are?" I asked. "How about a united front toward the children?"

"True." Ed took a turn around the room. Then he stopped beside me. "But you've got to have a little imagination. You put poor old Freddie in a spot. I was asking Charles about the club. The coach started it. It seems nearly all the boys are Charles's age; Freddie is the littlest one. He's trying to be a big tough guy and here you go, making him look like a sissy. His whole future as a Missing Link is at stake."

I saw it now—the coach's plan—nothing definite, nothing you could fight, just a persistent influence against everything the girls would want—

Ed opened the window. "Well," he said, "it's done now."

"It's not serious." I tried to laugh it off. But doubt began to gnaw at my heart. Freddie's face, miserable and hot-eyed, came back to bother me. What would the Missing Links do? Tease him? Perhaps haze him? No, that went out with initiations. Put him out of the club? I crawled into bed unable to find comfort no matter how I turned.

At last it was Friday, the night of the party. Freddie had long since subsided into sullen silence. Efforts on the part of Eileen and Ed to kid him into better humor were notable failures. I stood in the hall as he came downstairs, hoping I wouldn't feel I had to comment on his appearance, but he was scrubbed and neat; evidently the antisocial tenets of the Missing Links did not extend to personal untidiness. Charles slid down the banister and joined us.

"Chop, chop," he admonished amiably. They went out to the street to go their separate ways. I knew the party, held in the school building, would be over early. Short as it was, however, I never saw an evening go so slowly.

Ed felt it too. "I wonder how poor old Freddie is making out?" he said. At ten-thirty he dialed to the news. Above the radio voice I heard the sound of the front door opening.

"Who's that?" I called. "Freddie?"

"Hiya!" Freddie came in on a breeze.

I looked up expectantly. "You're home nice and early."

"Uh-huh." He stood in the doorway.

"How was the party?" Eileen asked. "Did they have music for dancing?" Eileen and Babs have taught the boys what little they know about that art.

"Uh-huh." Freddie edged toward the hall.

"Come in and tell us all about it," I urged. "Does Mary Lee dance well?"

"I dunno." Freddie's face was a blank.

I smiled. "Didn't you dance with her, dear?"

"Dance with her?" Freddie spoke tonelessly.

"Do you mean to say you took a girl to a party and didn't dance with her?" I asked. "Well, at least you saw she had plenty of partners."

"*Partners?*" Freddie asked.

Ed had been watching Freddie; now I saw his gray eyes darken. Ed is old-fashioned about responsibility toward women. He opened his mouth to speak.

Suddenly my heart went out to Freddie. He looked so—so inadequate. "Well, never mind, dear," I said comfortingly, "you called for her and took her home. That's the main thing."

"Took her *home?*" Freddie stared at me with growing horror in his eyes.

"Do you mean to say," Ed stood up, "that you left a little girl alone in that big school building late at night? Where is she now?"

"I dunno." Freddie stood as if paralyzed.

Ed got up. "The first thing to do is to phone the Smiths," he said. "Call Mrs. Smith, Freddie, and explain," he ordered. "Then, if Mary Lee—"

89

"Wait a minute." I tried to think fast. I didn't want to alarm Margery unnecessarily. Especially, I couldn't bear to have Freddie put in such an extremely bad light. "You left early. Mary Lee must still be there. Get the car, Ed. You'll be over there in three minutes." I shoved the two of them out the door. "Mary Lee has sense enough not to try to go home alone through the dark streets," I called. "I hope," I added to myself.

They were back in a few minutes. "Everybody'd left," Ed said, as he hung up his hat. "The janitor was sweeping out. But he knows Mary Lee and he's sure she went off with a whole crowd of kids. Well—I guess I'd better call Ben Smith, myself, and make sure she's home," he said.

Out at the phone, he spoke in a tone too low for me to hear what he said. "She's there all right," he said briefly as he came back. He started to say something more, but evidently decided against it.

"Wonder what's holding up Charlie?" Freddie was making conversation.

Ed did not answer and some time passed. Then Charles came in with color high and eyes shining.

"Mr. Smith says you wanted me to come home; was that right?" he asked Ed. Without waiting for an answer he turned to Freddie. "You missed some party!"

"What do you mean? I was there. I just left," Freddie said.

"Not at school," Charles said. "At Mary Lee's."

"At Mary Lee's!" Freddie repeated.

"Yeah. She was looking all round for you after the party. There was a whole bunch of us outside the coatroom and she came over and asked had we seen you. Then she said anybody that wanted to could come to her house for cocoa and cake. Mrs. Smith kept passing it out. You'd ought to have seen it. It was twice as big as the one Norah makes."

"What kind?" Freddie asked darkly.

"Cocoanut layer. There was extra helps for the whole crowd."

"What do you mean, 'the whole crowd'?" Freddie spoke as if against his will.

"Oh, me and Pinhead and Popeye Harris and Ears Summers —and the whole bunch." Charles's voice was matter-of-course.

For a moment Freddie was too outraged to speak. His mouth

90

opened and shut. Then he said in a frozen tone, "You mean to tell me the Missing Links went home with Mary Lee? And me, sneaking out early because we don't go round with girls!"

"Being invited to people's houses for eats isn't going around with girls," Charles said.

"But gee, Charlie, *I* thought—" We heard Freddie arguing as they went upstairs. "Gee, nobody told *me* there was going to be cake."

I smiled at Ed. "So the littlest Link was the strongest."

"I don't know about that," Ed answered slowly. "It didn't have to stand the same amount of strain."

He went out. Presently I heard him moving about in the kitchen. At the foot of the stairs I met him. He was carrying a piled-up plate. He glanced at me sideways.

"Well, Freddie didn't *get* his cake," he said defensively. He went on up the stairs.

"THE LITCHFIELDS are coming, hooray, hooray!" Babs rocked me in a hug that fairly squeezed the letter from my hand. "George's father is the grandest guy," she released me, "and you'll simply adore his mother."

"I'm sure I shall, dear." I retrieved the small sheet of blue paper with the silver edges that told me the news. At this moment George was, presumably, somewhere on the North Atlantic. Urged, indeed nagged, by Babs, I had at last invited his family to visit us so that we might get acquainted.

My husband and I have talked your letter over, [Madelaine Litchfield wrote] and we find it will be possible for us to be with you the first of the week. Frank has to go down to New York to a directors' meeting and I shall go along and get some shopping done. We'll stop off to see you on the way back. We have taken rooms at the hotel near you (you know, men don't visit well), and we'll come to the house late in the afternoon. We want to see not only you and your husband and Babs, but also your son's wife and the baby.

Appreciatively—

"Mind if I read it myself, again?" Babs shook her dark bob back from a flushed face and perused its few impersonal lines. "Isn't it a darling letter? She's fixed everything. She always does. You ought to see her make the men in the family get in line. And do they eat it up!"

"What's she like?" I sat down and took up my sewing.

"Very smooth," Babs said. "Sort of carelessly elegant; everything matching but not too much. And she's so *gay*. The night I was there, before George sailed, the cook was out and left a

92

buffet supper. It seems their waitress has gone to work in a war plant. George's mother said we weren't to spoil our hands doing any old dishes. We just piled 'em up and left 'em for Bridget, next morning." Babs's eyes rested on me with some dissatisfaction. "Well, that's the way I like to live."

"Who doesn't?" I sighed. I did not say that in our house doing this to Norah would be considered a mean trick on a good friend.

Ed, coming in from the office, cut short our talk. We told him the news. "That's fine, glad to hear it." I saw he was tired. "Still time to hear the end of the ball game." He turned on the radio.

The voice of the commentator seemed to assume a monotone in its continuous excitement. Ed's eyes closed. Babs rose and, leaning down beside him, snapped the program off.

Instantly his eyes opened. "What's the idea?" he asked.

"Oh, good, you've waked up." Babs perched on the arm of his chair. "Because I have something to say to you my pet. I don't think George's father goes for the Dodgers."

"Bets on the Giants, does he?" Ed asked.

"No; he's just not the baseball type. The afternoon I was there he came in from the office, the maid brought tea, and he sat down and asked each one of us what we'd done all day. He was sort of gracious and formal. Not tired, like some people." She gave him a friendly dig.

Ed's expression did not change. His leveled gaze met mine. "And how long will he be with us?" he asked.

"Just for dinner," I put in hastily.

Ed got up. I knew he was going to another room and radio, away from interruption.

"Don't worry," I told Babs. "You know how darling Daddy will be when the time comes." Babs sat up and rammed an extra pillow beneath her arm.

"I'm not worrying," she said. "I might have once, when I was young," she went on without a trace of a smile, "but I know now it's the way you always say it is, real people are real people everywhere. It's just—well, it's *me*."

"What's the matter with you?" I asked.

"I don't know exactly. Ordinarily, I pass in a crowd."

93

"Perhaps it's motherly jealousy," I ventured. Patty had told Babs once to remember that George was "Mother's only boy." "It's hard to let a son go, even to a very nice girl." It had been hard for me, at first, to let Dick go, even to Eileen, whom I loved.

"No. Matter of fact, she and George's father are crazy about each other. They're sort of a closed corporation. That's one reason Patty and George have always been so close; they've been *another* little team. The thing is, that somehow"—She put her head on one side trying to frame her thoughts—"even if I *have* my ring they don't act as if they expected us to get married. It's little things they say, like, 'Of course, if this goes through we'll be very happy.' It sort of sends a chill down your spine."

I studied my daughter. She's broad-shouldered with a head of dark hair falling back from an eager face. Her brown eyes change constantly as her ideas are funny, romantic, or indignant. To us, she is a heart-warming girl. What were the reservations about the engagement in the back of the Litchfields' minds? I did not know.

On the afternoon of the eventful day a taxi stopped before our house. Both Ed and I hurried to the door. The couple who came forward were unusually attractive. Madelaine Litchfield wore a soft summer suit of grape color and the bow at her neck was a rare true blue. Her loose blond curls, the flawless curve of her face made her appear very young. Only her eyes, keen, aware, bespoke long experience of the world. The man beside her was ruddy, firmly built, not lean, but hard of muscle, which gave him a boyish look. The impression was not false; just a quick one you received and had to amend.

Madelaine Litchfield was the first to speak. She put out both hands. Her manner was friendly yet detached. "It was so nice of you to ask us. We came as soon as we could. These taxis—" Now she was greeting Ed and I was shaking hands with George's father and meeting the gaze of shrewd hazel eyes. Easy to meet, these people, and nobody's fools.

"Madelaine!" Babs came flying down the stairs. I recalled with a bit of a jolt that Mrs. Litchfield liked the young people to use her first name.

94

"Let me look at you, lambie!" Mrs. Litchfield leaned back. "You've got thin."

"She's all right; you leave her alone." Mr. Litchfield had his arm around Babs now. "Well, how are you, sport, huh?"

"Don't you want to sit down and be comfortable?" Babs led the way and we found ourselves following our guests in their unhurried possession of the living room. The nervousness I felt did not seem to communicate itself to anyone else. We spoke of crowded trains, of the general confusion of travel in wartime. Babs sat watchfully waiting as if expecting some miracle would happen and we would all hug and kiss each other. When none did, she fell to eying her future mother-in-law, all admiration.

"Are we too late to see the baby?" Mrs. Litchfield asked presently. I hesitated. Eileen was helping Norah.

"Maybe *you* could get her," I told Babs. Babs ran upstairs.

"She's a great girl," Mr. Litchfield said. "Lots of zip."

"We're all devoted to George," I responded warmly.

"Kind of young," Mr. Litchfield said. "Crazy. But they all are."

"George has the stuff, all right." Ed stared into space, his blue-gray eyes full of gentle thoughts.

Mrs. Litchfield shifted a long, graceful leg and then said, "We were glad to find you felt as we did; that you were opposed to early, hasty marriages."

"George talked it over with me," Ed said. "We were pretty well agreed."

Mr. Litchfield took out a cigar. "We've been through this sort of thing before," he said.

"What sort of thing do you mean?" My voice was quite steady.

"Not formal engagements, of course. George never plunged on a ring till he met Babs. But he's been a pretty popular fellow, you know. And he always picked the lookers. Remember that spring at Sea Island, in his sophomore year, the widow he was in love with?" He turned his face toward his wife with a reminiscent grin.

Mrs. Litchfield smiled back into his face. You saw how necessary it was for them to share a joke. "That was nothing," she said. "Remember that dreadful girl at Sun Valley? She

95

wasn't unlike Babs, in a way; glamour to the nth degree. She never got out of ski pants all the time we were there; went off from the hotel in them, when she left, and stepped aboard the plane still wearing them. I hear she's been married and unmarried a couple of times since."

Ed spoke, a little too heartily. I knew he wanted to boost Babs. "Know how that is. We've had plenty of trouble around here, too. Boys underfoot, all over the place."

Mrs. Litchfield was quick to see her husband had overdone it. "Now, Frank, you make your son sound like a southern belle," she told him. "And of course," she was not ungracious, "if this engagement lasts, I mean if the thing goes through at some future time, we'll be quite happy."

"Oh, quite." Mr. Litchfield followed her lead.

"If the thing goes through . . ." The phrase that had sent a chill down Babs's spine sent a chill down mine too. Before I could rally to reply, however, Babs came in leading Barbara Elizabeth. Barbie wore a blue pinafore and her chubby arms came out from perky white ruffles. Her damp hair wound into an upward spiral of curls topped by a small bow.

Eileen came hurrying in behind the two. I made the grown-up introductions.

Mrs. Litchfield leaned forward and held a slim hand to the baby. "Would you like to shake hands with me, dear?" she asked.

"No!" Barbara Elizabeth's voice, sweet as a bell, ended on an upward turn. It made her answer sound thoughtful, considered.

"She always says no to a direct question," Eileen explained in distress. "It's the age." She reframed the wording of the suggestion. "See if you have a hug for Mother's friend."

"Yes." Barbara Elizabeth's tone again swung upward, lovely and without emotion. She put out both her arms.

Mrs. Litchfield embraced her, a little awkwardly. "I haven't been around much with people this age," she confessed. "Not lately. What is it you want, you little mite? Oh, it's my purse."

In order to reach it, she shifted her position. In doing so she managed, somehow, to bring her heel down with some weight on the baby's almost bare toes.

96

Barbara Elizabeth drew back and began to cry in utter indignation. "The lady 'tep on me," she said.

Mrs. Litchfield was all remorse, almost bumping heads with Ed as they leaned to examine the little foot.

"I don't think the skin is broken." Eileen studied the foot anxiously. "I'll just take her up and disinfect it, to be on the safe side."

"But you've just come in. I'll go." I carried Barbara Elizabeth upstairs. The little toes were red but whole. I sat in the bathroom holding her. After a minute I brushed my eyes.

Barbara Elizabeth regarded me gravely. "Is you got soap in your eyes?" she asked. I shook my head. She thought a minute. "Is the lady 'tep on you?"

"No," I said, "not really. Oh, well—in a kind of a way, I guess she did." I put her down.

Dinner went off well, even gaily. Babs could not say and do enough for the guests. I watched her eager face and listened to her affectionate voice with a queer sadness all my own. Who said girls and mothers-in-law don't get on? They were having a gorgeous time discussing the subject nearest to them both; the one thing on which they would never disagree: the wonderful traits of George. I was the one who was really hard hit. The other woman, my own age, lovely, assured, with every right in the world to it, had taken a place with Babs seemingly equal to my own. Equal? I smiled ruefully; for the moment her place was superior.

With the coffee in the living room, Babs went up to help Eileen get Barbie to bed. I took the talk in hand. "I understand you're a serious golfer, like your husband."

"She plays a damn good game." Mr. Litchfield spoke for her.

"Get much time for it these days?" Ed asked him.

"Not much," Mr. Litchfield admitted. "But the fifth hole at our club is right at the end of our garden so Madelaine and I get out and knock 'em around a bit. Oh, tell them about your new clubs." He grinned at his wife.

"Oh, yes." His wife sat back, relaxed. "I don't know whether you've tried to buy any new clubs since the war but if you have, you'll appreciate this. Somehow, Frank managed to wangle a set of matched clubs for me from the pro at our club. They really were something. Well, George and I are about the same height, you know, and he liked them. When he joined the Navy, he asked me to give them to him."

Mr. Litchfield put in, "So, of course, Mother, here, parts with them. Nothing's too good for our boy in the service. I guess he figures the old man can afford another set. (He can't!) And she hadn't even tried them."

"Oh, yes, I had, once." His wife corrected him. "But the thing Frank and I can't understand is what in the world he'll do with them on a destroyer. I suppose they might put in somewhere, and he could go ashore and play. But I wouldn't think they would even have room for them aboard, not in wartime."

Ed did not answer. Instead he got up and went out. I heard him in the closet under the stairs. When he came back he was holding up a brand new golf bag full of shiny clubs. "From George to Babs on her nineteenth birthday, with love," he said.

"Well, I'll be damned." Mr. Litchfield sank back, clutching the arms of his chair, tears of laughter running out of his eyes. "That's one on you, Madelaine."

"Let me see them." Mrs. Litchfield leaned forward. "They're the ones, all right. They're mine. I mean, they were."

"Babs must give them back," I began. Then I saw Babs coming down the stairs.

Mr. Litchfield took over and with authority. "Your father's showing us the clubs George got for you," he said. "I say the boy has taste."

"Aren't they sump'n?" Babs took out a putter and swung lightly at a curled leaf that had blown from a bouquet to the rug. "Want to try it?" she asked Mrs. Litchfield.

"Thanks." The other's tone was kind but dry. "I won't bother. George let me hold them once."

"When we're married we want to live next to a golf course." Babs budged the leaf.

"Really? I always thought George wanted a smart little walk-up in town when he was married."

Babs kept her head down. "Nope. We both agree we're going to the country to live."

Mrs. Litchfield smiled remotely. "People change," she said.

Babs turned and looked at her. The gaze she met was noncommital, appraising. Something in Babs's seemed stricken. She dug viciously at the little leaf.

A bit later they left. They would run in, they told us, sometime in the morning, on their way to the train.

"Aren't they simply darling?" Babs asked, ignoring the chill.

I kissed her warmly so as not to answer. As we undressed, I said to Ed, "They could be; but somehow they weren't."

"You imagine things," my husband said. "Nice people, love their kids, everything."

But long after he had gone to sleep I lay staring into the darkness.

And then it was morning and time for them to come again. They walked up from the hotel, the two of them, and they and Ed and I sauntered across the garden to the place where Barbara Elizabeth was digging in her sandbox.

"Have to cook shebbels," Barbara Elizabeth said, pouring water from a large tin pail into a cup that would not hold it.

"What in the world are shebbels?" Mrs. Litchfield wanted to know.

"Vegetables," I said. "It sounds like that if you say it fast."

"It's so nice, why don't we stay out here?" Ed suggested.

"I think it would be lovely." Mrs. Litchfield sat down on the bench. Ed drew up two chairs.

"We can't stop too long, Madelaine." Mr. Litchfield's low tone was a warning.

I sat listening to the small talk. They would go soon, I was telling myself. I had failed to find the reason for their basic coolness to Babs, failed to dispel it, failed to warm them up in any real sense to our daughter.

"Hey!" Babs's voice reached us even before she came dashing out through the back door. "What do you know! A letter from the great man!"

"Where's it from?" Mrs. Litchfield looked up eagerly. "He can't be back—" She made room for Babs beside her.

"No. Somebody must have picked up their mail at sea and brought it in. It's the same old line, he's fine, glad to be at sea, he sends his love to you all. And—" Suddenly Babs closed both hands tightly about the letter.

"I wrote him about something and he says to do what ever I

99

think is the right thing, so I may as well tell you while you're all together. I'm not going back to college this fall. I'm going to business school."

"But, dear!" Mrs. Litchfield was distressed. "You can't do that. Rooming with Patty and all. In a way, this year's the nicest."

"I know. Don't think I haven't thought of all that. We've got that darling tower room and everything; but Patty thinks I'm right about it. I was only waiting to get the go-ahead signal from George."

Mr. Litchfield studied her with interest. "Why do you want to leave?" he asked.

Babs faced him earnestly. "Suppose the war ends tomorrow," she said. "All right, the men who had jobs before may get them back. George never had one; he was just out of college. We couldn't get married with no salary. We'd have to wait and wait till he found something. Well, if I had some money we could get married right away."

Mr. Litchfield smiled. "But George doesn't need—" He stopped at a signal from his wife.

"And I've had to think of this—" Babs looked across the garden as if we weren't there. "He might be wounded, so he couldn't support me at first; maybe not at all. Of course he *won't*, but we have to face that possibility. Well, I love that guy more than any old college or parties or—or even Patty. And I'm fixing it so I can marry him, no matter what, so there!"

She sprang up and as suddenly as she had come she ran into the house. "Eileen!" we heard her calling. "Eileen! I heard from George!"

Mrs. Litchfield leaned forward. A star sapphire on her finger winked brilliantly. For a moment she studied it, then her direct but unsimple blue eyes met mine.

"You see," she said slowly, "my husband and I have been exceptionally happily married. Let me talk, Frank." She brushed him aside with a tilted hand. "And when you are, you're concerned over your children's choices. You want them to have the best, too."

"I know," I said.

"And what we were afraid of was that Babs was just another in a series of glamour girls. Patty always harped on her roommate's popularity. And the first of George's friends to mention their engagement said how lucky George was—the reason he gave was that Babs had been the best dancer at their Junior Prom. What we wondered was, did she have the stuff and did she really love him, enough for a lifetime?"

We had risen now, in the stress of talk, and stood opposite each other under the motionless arms of the maple tree.

"But anybody that will leave college senior year to try to support that great big hulking son of ours—you won't let her, of course—" (and I knew at once we would not) "well, she must be dreadfully in love is all I can say."

She put both hands on my shoulders; strong, honest, deft hands they were. They all but shook me. She looked across to the house.

"Where is that girl of ours?" she asked.

CHAPTER

11

THE HAND THAT HELD the letter sank down beside my husband's coffee cup. He looked at me over the length of the breakfast table from which the children had already gone, leaving a marginal line of cereal dishes and bits of toast like the wrack along a seabeach.

"It's from Charles's father," he said. "He's come over with some sort of British mission to the United States."

"Captain Heather?" A pang of foreboding went through me. In the years since Charles came to us from England we've learned to think of him as one of our own. My voice sounded sharp as I asked, "What does *he* want?"

Ed's words came slowly. "He'd like to come out here tomorrow. He wants to see his own son, of course. And probably he intends to give us the once-over and find out what sort of job we're doing. Natural, I suppose." Ed tried to keep his tone casual and overshot the green.

"You're holding out on me." I was studying his face. "What else did he say?"

"That was about all, but somehow he made his coming sound sort of—sort of significant. Well, here," he picked up the letter, "it says, 'You can perhaps imagine my eagerness.' Wait; this is the part: 'My plans for Charles must necessarily be altered. I find it hard to put what I must say in a letter and will therefore leave it until we meet. Sincerely, Guy Heather.'"

Plans for Charles—altered plans! The words came to me like a little cold current striking a swimmer ahead of a changing tide. Both Ed and I looked out instinctively to the lawn where Charles and Freddie were busy at their Saturday-morning assignment

102

of leaf-rakings. Freddie is short like me, and stocky. In tweed knickers and a plaid lumberman's jacket he looks practically square. Charles, lithe and tall in the same sort of clothes, seemed older than he was. They were having trouble now with Blimp, who was racing through the yellowed maple leaves barking excitedly. At last Freddie thought to touch a match to the heap and Blimp backed away as the blue smoke rose skyward out of the flames like an Indian signal.

"It's going to be tough on Freddie," Ed said—he put it into words—"if Charles leaves us."

"I know," I answered. "I just can't give him back. Not even to his own mother."

"You get in the habit of thinking of the two of them together," Ed went on. "I've been putting away a little something each month in war bonds toward their education. I've entered them both at Blake." He got up and stood for a moment by the window, then walking past my chair he leaned down and kissed me. "Well," he said, "there are some things that are out of our control. I guess this is one of them. There's nothing we can do until Charles's father comes." He went out, trudging down the hall like a little boy.

I wandered upstairs. I wanted to talk. I knew there would be no more discussion of the subject with Ed so I was looking for Eileen. With my daughter-in-law I can nearly always be sure of understanding. As Ed once put it, she pays you the rare compliment of complete attention. I found her pushing the baby's arms and legs into a zippered playsuit. She set Barbara Elizabeth on the floor in a lump and listened with distress in her great gray-blue eyes.

"But Charles's father can't do that to us." Then "Oh, dear, I'd feel better if Babs were home."

"I think I'll call her up." I stood Barbara Elizabeth on uncertain feet. "If Charles's father did take him anywhere and Babs were away at college, she'd never forgive us."

I went down to the phone. It was something to do and inaction was telling on me. Then, too, the other Missing Links were coming around to our house Sunday afternoon and I would have to order extra milk, peanut butter, and honey. Like a dog trotting happily down a well-worn path, my mind found comfort in these simple and familiar thoughts.

Babs caught an early bus and appeared Sunday morning before we were even up.

"I practically came down on the milk train." Her voice woke me. She was standing in the doorway, the bold green and white plaid of her coat contrasting with her high color and brown eyes. In the morning sunlight she looked fresh and sharp at the edges, as is the way of youth. "Hello, my pet." She sat down next to her sleeping daddy. He did not move. "O. K., if you want to be like that," she told the back of his head. She turned toward me; then, "Does Charlie know?"

"Only that his father is coming." I sat up. "Shut the windows, will you?"

"Patty and I were up practically half the night discussing it," Babs said. She banged the windows down and walked back to the foot of the bed. "It's rugged. The way we figure is this: A, we could hide Charles somewhere. B, we could simply give in and let him go back to his mother; but gosh, that might ruin his whole future. C, we could all make a terrific play for his father so he'd adore us and want Charles to stay." Babs sat down again at the foot of the bed, her face alive with her ideas.

"You've got something." Ed opened the eye that was not in the pillow and winked.

"Well, well! Fancy meeting *you* here." Babs clutched his foot through the bedclothes and wiggled it to and fro. "Or we could be ourselves and let nature take its course."

"I'm afraid that's just what's going to happen." I pulled my bathrobe about me. "I have a very strong hunch that all this has to do with his mother. Think how wonderful it would be for the three of them to be together again. Think of that man going home, Charles with him, and walking in the door to his wife."

"Good old Mom," Babs said. "Drip, drip, drip!"

Ed looked up at his daughter for a moment with a curious expression. He knows the hardness of youth is due not to lack of heart but to lack of experience, yet somehow Ed never gets used to it.

All he said, however, was, "And now if you don't mind—"

"I guess I know when I'm not wanted." Babs walked to the

104

door with her nose in the air. A moment later her face reappeared in the crack. It wore an expression of real concern. "Say, Mom," she wanted to know, "is there any orange marmalade or honey or something?" Her tone was as anxious as it had been over Charles.

I sighed. "Go ask Norah and tell her we'll all be right down. And Babs!" I called after her. "Jog up the boys, will you? If they don't get going now, they'll never be on time for Sunday school."

The family awaited the arrival of Charles's father that afternoon with suppressed excitement. Ed busied himself putting long thin cigars in a glass container. "My best ones, and I don't even want the man to come," he said. Eileen brought Barbara Elizabeth down in a tiny red shirt and dark blue overalls.

"I thought of dressing her all up," she told me, "but she likes to play, and Captain Heather probably doesn't care about little kids, anyway."

In front of the hall mirror Babs applied more lipstick, critically pressing her lips. "I don't know why I'm prettying up so," she said. "I never wanted to see anybody less in my life."

"Where on earth are Freddie and Charles? Boys!" I put my head back and called.

They came pounding in. "Go slick your hair down," I told Freddie. "You look like a little toughie with that spike on the top of your head."

Now I turned my attention to Charles. It came to me that only Charles, who was most concerned, had said very little about his father's impending visit. That he was immensely proud of him I knew—I remembered how he had burst into our room with his mother's letter telling about the captaincy. But to the news that his dad was coming his reaction had been an almost startled silence.

"Let me see you." I studied him from top to toe, recalling as I did so the little boy of ten who came in out of the dark that winter night, so expectant, so small, so shy, yet bred to make his blue eyes meet yours, as they still do, unafraid. That was the year of the great London blitz. His mother and father had wanted to get him far away from the violence coming out of the skies.

Charles turned restless under my scrutiny. "O. K.?" he asked at last.

"Come here, chop, chop!" Babs beckoned and paced slowly around him. "You'll do. I can see you a few years from now, breaking all the hearts on campus."

"Dry up." Charles lunged at her. Together they went over the arm of a chair in a semiserious tussle.

That's it, I told myself. He can hold his own now; which he couldn't once. He's sturdy. I suppose it's the rough-and-tumble of life in a family—or it could be a quart of milk a day, I added practically.

What happened after that came so fast that, in Freddie's phrase, I rocked with the blows.

First the front door opened and the Missing Links came in. Bingo Brown was still on roller skates. Racing down the hall, he caught the draperies at the far end and came to a swinging stop. I pelted after him.

"We've already got your fingerprints, Bingo!" I showed him the grimy marks on the rumpled fold. "Sit right down and take off your skates." To my surprise Bingo seemed quelled. In fact, silence fell on all six boys. Not used to such a response, I glanced up surprised. It was then I saw him.

The man standing in the doorway was fairly tall but compact, with the compactness that seemed the result of hardy living and the pressure of responsibility. A fine tan raincoat was buttoned over some sort of uniform; British, of course, but I could not be sure exactly what, and he held a pipe in his hand as if it were a part of him. His skin was the ruddy brown that comes from exposure to all kinds of weather. But it was his eyes you noticed most. They were sea-colored and profoundly grave with just a little light on top. He was watching the group of boys now, searching among them for his own.

"Charles!" I called over my shoulder in what was almost a note of alarm. "Charles, it's your father!" Charles appeared in the back hall, brushing Bingo aside. For just a second, as he passed, he looked at me. Then he hurried to his father.

"Well, well, let's have a look at you, son. It's been a long time, hasn't it?" There was no masking the glow of tenderness in his face, yet he did not hold out his arms as Ed might have done. Instead, he gave his boy a hard masculine handclasp.

"Father!" Charles jumped like a small child. "How's Mommy, Father?"

"I have something here for you. It's a present from your mother." Captain Heather felt in his pocket, then held out a wrist watch. It was bulky, square, and handsome in a manly style.

"Oh, Charles, how beautiful!" I welcomed our guest, adding, "I hope your wife is well?"

He did not reply and now the whole family crowded forward. I led them into the living room. Captain Heather chose a comfortable but uncushioned chair. He sat relaxed yet alert as I had often seen a man rest in the saddle after pulling a high-spirited mare to a walk.

He refused Ed's cigars with a nod. "Have my pipe, if you don't mind." With no effort whatever he had taken command of the room. It had been our intention to set him at ease, then to prod him gently with questions. No chance for that, I saw now. He was interrogating us.

He had a word for each one in the family. "Is she only a bit under three, really?" he asked Eileen, his voice running down and up the scale as he held out a hand to Barbara Elizabeth. "I'd have said she was four at least." "Do they make you study very hard?" he wanted to know from Babs. "No time for boys and parties and that sort of thing?" Babs launched at once into an explanation about George and a description of a coed campus in wartime with all the boys in military training. "It's the men who have to be in early with lights out now," she said. Captain Heather laughed. "That must be a change." He questioned Ed about business conditions a bit and then he turned to Charles.

Now it comes, I thought. He's going to tell us he's taking Charles away. Instead, he began to put questions about the other boys. The Missing Links had been introduced and gone to the cellar, which that winter was serving as their hideout. "You've quite a group of friends, haven't you?" he asked. "And who was the lad on roller skates who fell down as I came in?"

"That's Bingo." Charles found it hard, I could see, to put into words the driving spirit that inhabits Bingo's nervous little body.

"He's sort of a fixture in our house. He arrives every night —about desserttime," I explained.

"I see. And what are they doing down below?" he asked.

"We're making an airplane model." Freddie stood up in front of him.

"Are you, indeed?" Charles's father puffed interestedly. "Some sort of paper, I suppose?"

"Oh, no, sir. It's plywood. We've got a small engine, too," Charles explained. "It'll be a bomber." The gaze fixed on Charles was darkened now and became suddenly deadly serious. These English people, I thought, they've been through things we know nothing about; and I was suddenly moved to say, "You know, Captain Heather, terrible as the blitz was for you, it *did* serve to bring the English and Americans together as nothing else could have done. No one can fail to see the stuff in the British, after that."

"After all, there isn't much we English can do but go right on living, is there?" It was a statement, not a question. He was staring ahead of him.

"It's about over, isn't it?" Ed asked. "Just a stray robot now and then?"

"I suppose so." He tires easily, this man, I thought. Suddenly he looked haggard. Perhaps a hot cup of something—

"Babs, how about some tea?" Norah, I knew, was out for the afternoon. Babs followed me into the kitchen.

"Gosh, Mom, I wish he'd give," she said over the soft clatter of cups and spoons. "Why doesn't he put us out of our misery?"

"I don't know. Don't put any cloves in the lemon," I told her. I remembered an English friend who calls our American tea bewitched water. "And he may want hot milk as well as cream."

Charles was standing near the door as we came back into the room. Freddie had already left. "May I go now?" Charles asked more of me than of his father. "Those kids might rook that cylinder—"

"Yes, dear. You boys can take a couple of bottles of milk downstairs and there's a platter of sandwiches in the pantry."

108

Suddenly I glanced anxiously at Captain Heather. Perhaps he would be hurt at Charles's nonchalance.

"Run along." Captain Heather took his tea. "I'll be down myself later to have a look. He's very fond of you," he told me after Charles had gone.

"We love *him*," I said simply. "We're a very casual family in some ways, I'm afraid, but we do love each other to death and Charles—well, he's just one of us."

"I can see that." He sipped his tea for a moment in silence. Then setting down his cup, he lifted his head and gazed resolutely about the room as if aware of danger, and facing it. From below came the confused noise of boys' shouts and an occasional thud.

"I don't want to seem rude," he said at last, "but there may not be as good an opportunity again. Mrs. Breton, I wonder if I might speak to you and your husband alone?" He glanced at the two girls with the utmost kindness in eyes that nevertheless remained unsmiling.

"It's time for Barbara's bath anyway," Babs said. "Come on, *amigo*." She went out of the room swinging the baby over her shoulder. Barbara Elizabeth laughed delightedly. Eileen followed.

"Mr. Breton, and you, Mrs. Breton—" Guy Heather leaned forward as if the importance of what he had to say urged him into physical action. "It would be absurd for me to try in any way to repay you or even to thank you for what you've done. Charles came from a country in great peril. He was a frightened little boy. You've made him into a sturdy lad, almost a man."

"It was all there," Ed said gently. "We just stood by and let him grow."

"Oh, no." Captain Heather withdrew his pipe decisively. "You've given him the rarest thing in the world today—security. Before deciding to send him here," he went on, "we had considered putting him in a boarding school somewhere at home. But—" He paused so long it seemed he had forgotten that he had been talking. "Charles's cousin was in school in southern France when war broke out. He was just seven at the time. He got home to England, finally. We never knew just how, and he was too young to tell us. He spoke of loud noises and of men fighting and of the cold sea water. He was unbelievably dirty. One never knows—" He paused, then finished. "One doesn't want a child away at school; one likes to feel he's with a family."

"I know." Things were safer now in England; quite safe. He'd want to take Charles home. I must let him go gracefully— generously.

"My wife and I found a little place up north from London." The Captain was staring now at an intricate design in the rug. "It was not too hard to get to, when I had leave. My wife had a rose garden, and we bought some good hens. It was up the lane from one of the inland waterways and we'd planned on buying Charles a small sailboat. We thought there he would be well and safe." He got up and took a nervous turn about the room. He's a very considerate person, I thought. He knows how we're going to feel at losing Charles and he hates to come right out and say he's taking him back. Now he was talking again, his arm crooked on the ledge above the fireplace.

"My son is very happy with you," he said at last. "The life he lives is right and—and good. I know it's a great deal to ask." His eyes went from one to the other of us as if searching us. "I'd like Charles to stay on with you. I'd like you to keep him if you can."

He's going to stay! He's going to stay! My heart was chanting it.

Captain Heather swung about now. He stood back to us. Both of his lean hands grasped the mantel.

"It was only a chance bomb." He spoke as though alone. "One of those meaningless robots aimed at nothing in particular. My wife was killed."

For a time we sat in unbelieving silence. Then Ed cleared his throat, twice. He rose and put a hand on the man's shoulder.

But Captain Heather was still in command. He turned abruptly. "I have to get back to my port tonight," he said. "But I would like to see what the boys are making. Shall we?" He bowed and stood back for me to lead the way.

12

IN SPITE OF HER PLANS, we persuaded Babs to go back to college. I was on my way, now, to revisit the old school and to see her, too.

The train ran over the trestle across the river and pulled up at the little station that served the college town. The brakeman helped me down onto the wooden platform. I looked around. I had hoped Babs would meet me.

Suddenly she came pelting the length of the platform. Her brown hair was blowing, her dark eyes were eager, and her arms were flying out of her red topcoat.

"Oh, Mom! I didn't see you, at first! I was so afraid something had happened and you hadn't come. Gosh, I'm glad you're here!" She released me and stared at a tall, ponderous man who got off the train behind me. "Oh, good morning, President Moon," she said. "This is my mother."

"Ah!" The president bowed slightly. "Let's see, Miss Breton, didn't your parents graduate from here?"

We were walking away now from the freight shed toward the road. "It was Daddy who graduated," Babs said.

"But I did go to college here, too," I put in. "I left, my junior year—" I stopped. It seemed nobody's business but my own that I had cut short my education to marry Ed during the First World War.

"Let me take your bag." Babs seized my suitcase, which was evidently beneath the president's dignity or perhaps beneath his line of vision, and we all climbed into a waiting bus.

"He knows you," I said after we had climbed out and separated from him at the college gate.

"Oh, I'm a celebrity around here. I don't think he actually knew about me." Babs lapsed into honesty. "But it's quite a lot for him even to know my name. I hope you're properly impressed."

"I am!" I squeezed her arm. We walked along the paths running between lovely magnolias and under enormous arching elms to the dormitory. The hall was a very old one; beside the new colonial brick residence houses it seemed gloomy and unattractive. It was, however, in the very heart of the campus and therefore the first choice with those in the know. Inside the shabby doorway, a group of girls was clustered around the mailboxes. Babs pushed her way through and peered into one of many small glass panes lining the wall.

"Nothing for me," she announced gloomily. We went upstairs. The room that Babs and Patty shared was high and narrow with an adjoining cubbyhole which held two cots. To offset the darkness, the transom was embellished with a big round sun cut out of orange paper. One of the two narrow beds ran beneath the windows and there was a dresser on either side of the door. While Barbara deposited my suitcase in the inner room, I sat down and looked about me. It was easy to see which dresser was which. Patty's man is a flier, and pictures of a boy in khaki wearing flying insignia dominated her corner of the room. On Babs's side were photographs of George; George in a football suit complete with helmet, George and Babs side by side on the beach, George on the steps of the fraternity house, and a new portrait of George in the uniform of the Navy. It was a good-looking, friendly face with steady eyes. Only the lower lip, protruding slightly, betrayed an impulsiveness that together with a real generosity of spirit made George an immensely attractive boy.

"Doesn't he look adorable in his sailor suit?" Babs asked. "I had to practically beat him to get him to have it taken. Patty helped."

"You're close as a clam about George lately." I settled back.

"Well, that's what I wanted to tell you. Here, get comfortable." Babs pushed a couple of pillows behind me. I knew better than to prod her into confidences; instead I let my eyes wander across the court and rest on a girl on the floor of a room below.

She was lying face down, taking notes from a book. A portable radio on the floor beside her gave off a flow of tune; her jaws moved rhythmically, and her rope-clad soles sawed in air.

"Term paper," Babs explained, her eyes following mine. "Everybody's doing them. About George—I thought I wrote you. All the while he was training, you know, he was attached to this new ship. Well, when they left for the North Atlantic they went in that same ship. He wrote me he had been pretty glad to shove off and it was good to be at sea, and apparently he still feels that way. All he thinks about is that old ship. He doesn't—he doesn't even need me."

"The service comes first with them," I agreed. "And besides, he hasn't been gone very long. He'll come home someday and want you terribly; you'll see."

"Do you really think so?" Babs asked, wistfully. "I don't know; now I've got my ring I'm apparently supposed to keep quiet till the war's over. He's so busy with his old Navy, he doesn't even think about me, rotting here in this hellhole." She fished about in a pile of tiny candies on sticks that were acting collectively as a paperweight. "Want a lollypop?"

"Thanks; if I do I'll take one."

"Then I decided since there was nothing else to do I might as well work. See that?" She indicated the pile of reference books and papers. "My lifework—my term paper. "'Beowulf and the Rise of the English Spirit.'"

"Dear me!" I sat up and respectfully patted the somewhat disordered papers into a neat pile.

"It's an old Anglo-Saxon epic," Babs explained. "It's sort of fascinating, at that. Marauding monsters and underwater fighting; boy, you couldn't faze 'em! You see where the British got their stuff. That little lifework of mine—well, it just *might* have a future." She unwrapped a pink lollypop and sucked it tentatively. "Wouldn't it knock 'em for a loop at home," she asked, "If I turned out to be a Brain, after all?"

I sat looking at my big half-grown-up daughter. It seemed to me perfectly wonderful that at this moment in her life she could be part of a happy, orderly, academic society. It seemed wonderful, too, that forces, working however obliquely, had carried her into a scholarly channel. Ed would be so pleased when I told him.

"Listen," Babs broke in on my thoughts, "speaking of that, I have to go around to the English office and pick up the outline of the last half of the paper. Miss Geeber asked to see it for some reason. She's the head of the department. We might meet Patty on the way."

At that hour of the day the campus was filled with students. It was all familiar; when a middle-aged figure passed sedately pedaling a bicycle, brown tweed skirt bulging over the rear wheel, I smiled inwardly, feeling no older than Babs.

"That reminds me. Patty and I sold our bicycles," Babs told me as we stepped back onto the tar walk. "Could you find my roller skates and send them up? I'd save a lot of time on them."

I promised to look for them. And now we saw Patty. She dashed forward. I kissed her delightedly. Patty is small, blond, appealing, and wholly lovable. Together we went into the building that housed the English Department. A woman was just closing the wide oak door to the English office.

"Miss Geeber!" Babs caught up with her. "I came for my outline." The professor turned and faced us. She was short with graying red hair and pale but keen eyes. Her manner, not cordial, was genuine. She stood a moment as if trying to recall something. Then she said, "It's on my desk. You can go right into my office and get it."

"This is my mother." Babs turned to me. "Patty and I are showing her around."

Miss Geeber smiled and suddenly her whole face sparkled with feeling and intelligence. But all she said was, "Come and have a cup of tea with me, all of you, if you have time." With a nod that terminated the talk, she left us.

"She's the faculty resident at our house," Patty explained.

I was studying a wooden plaque on the wall. It bore a list of names in black lettering under the title, "Mehitabel B. Moogins Award."

I remarked, "I don't remember this."

"It's given each year to a member of the junior class," Patty explained. "It's one of the biggest things in college."

114

"Really? In my day the basketball team was about the biggest thing. That and hockey."

It was Patty's turn to be surprised. "People go in for brains now," she said. "Basketball is—well, it's kid stuff."

Babs opened the door and joined us. There was a peculiar glitter in her big eyes. "Listen," her voice was practically a hoarse whisper, "come on down to the lunchroom. I've got to tell you something."

We found a small table and sat down. Babs brought us straws and bottles.

"I went to pick up my paper," Babs looked cautiously around, "And then—gosh! I didn't mean to, but I saw this letter. It had my name, Barbara Breton, 'forty-six, in the first line. You could have knocked me down with a canary feather. I didn't mean to read it; honest. It just leaped right out at me."

"What was in it, for goodness sake?" Patty demanded.

"It was a recommendation to the committee for the junior English prize," Babs informed us. "Geeber was recommending *me*."

"For the Mehitabel B. Moogins Award?" I asked unbelievingly.

Patty gazed awe-struck at her roommate. "You will walk out on the platform at Commencement." Her eyes were dreamy. "You'll get a medal. People'll clap. Your name will be engraved on the program. Fame comes to Room Two-o-two without my lifting a finger."

"We'll have to lure Daddy up here somehow or other," I said. "He'll just burst with pride."

"Listen, that doesn't mean it's settled. I'll have to get this paper finished and in on time. Geeber doesn't take any alibis. It has to be in Friday morning, but if I sit up nights, I can do it. But the thing is," she finished confidentially, "Geeber is head of the department and what she says usually goes."

Suddenly I saw that winning this prize meant something to Babs; that it meant in fact a very great deal; that it was not only her surprise bid for campus fame, but also, winning it, I saw, would give her her first tremendous satisfying sense of achievement. I saw what I had to do.

"I'm going home tonight," I told her, "and leave you free to work."

But Babs dissented. "Stay over till tomorrow morning," she urged. "There's a show at the students' building tonight; I want to take you. Then tomorrow I'll go into the silences with Beowulf. I've still got hours and hours of work to do on it." And so I agreed.

Miss Geeber was having tea when I knocked at her sitting room. The girls had gone upstairs to brush up so I entered alone. One hardly noticed the woman at first for the room, which was crowded with the spoils of travel: an old ivory chess set, priceless bits of porcelain, fine photographs, too numerous to be hung. As I sat down, Miss Geeber opened the conversation on what she probably thought was our only mental meeting ground.

"Your daughter," she said, "is doing some very excellent work for me. Some students come to college with C minds and remain C minds to the end. Barbara will be a B or a B-plus student when she leaves. Sugar?"

"Thank you," I said, "one lump. I mean spoonful."

"The average girl," Miss Geeber handed me a teacup, "comes here with smooth hair, smooth manners, and just as smooth a mind. If there's anything individual under the surface, we don't find it. Barbara is not a smooth girl." (Ooh, how she'd hate that, I thought.) "Her first reaction to scholarly material is one of surprise. Her attack is fresh. Cookies?"

"Thank you, just tea," I told her.

"If she keeps up her good work through next year, I'd really like to see Barbara come back and work for a graduate degree." Miss Geeber lowered her voice. "I think I could find a niche for her in my department. I'm going to talk to her; after certain things have taken place."

I studied the face opposite my own with a feeling compounded of respect and compassion. There was something selfless in her devotion to her students; she was singlehearted in her scholarship.

"Are we too late?" Neat and shining, Babs and Patty stood in the doorway. The intimate conversation was over.

I was able during supper, at which I sat between Babs and

116

Patty, to ask news of the latter's man. George, I learned, liked him immensely, but Patty's father did not approve. Realizing how much of a pet she was at home, I wondered if her father would ever warm up to a man she really loved; it seemed unlikely. With both her parents and the Army to contend with, Patty's plight had not, however, turned her toward her work. Instead, she was drifting. I felt equally sorry for them; their men wholly committed to a life which seemed to leave no room for girls and with an insecurity ahead that shook the heart.

"And you ought to see his letters," Patty said. "Full of juicy bits like the floor plan of their new quarters." She stopped indignantly.

"At least you *get* letters. Does anybody mind if we wait for the late mail?" Babs added. "They bring it over Saturday night. George's ship just might be in, and could be he'd write me."

We put off going to the students' building till after the mail arrived. It brought no letter, however, and in a somewhat subdued mood we slipped into the back of the darkened auditorium. The program was a series of separate sketches and the curtain was just going down on the fourth.

Number Five, we were informed from the platform, would be a lecture on human anatomy, "Sex to You." The part of the lecturer was taken by a young instructor, outrageously costumed in a red satin evening dress heavily weighted on one shoulder by a bunch of violets pinned to a trailing boa of ostrich feathers. She came down stage carrying a large knitting bag and pushing before her a dressmaker's mannequin; one of those wire affairs covered with gray cambric and mounted on wheels. Smiling with what was not so much a smile as a leer, she reached into the knitting bag, pulled out a paper sunflower and a big plush bee both of which she hastily put back. "The advanced course," she said in a stage aside. Next came a big pink satin heart which she skewered onto the cambric chest of the mannequin, using two hatpins. From time to time she supplemented this with objects pulled from the interior of the dress form—a pair of gasping bellows, a whirring eggbeater, a bouncing bedspring. It was all so silly; such an innocent kind of fun. I laughed till my ribs ached.

It was eleven o'clock when we came back to our own hall out

of the starry, breezy darkness. Everybody had late permission and now they were gathering in the dining room where the housemother had set out milk and graham crackers. Even the faculty residents joined the crowd in front of the long table.

Babs and Miss Geeber stood together reminding each other of the good gags; Babs giggling reminiscently.

Suddenly a face appeared in a dark low window at my left which opened onto the back hall and a voice said anxiously, "Hey, Breton! Phone call for you. Long-distance is burning up waiting to locate you. Make it snappy."

Patty looked at me and I looked at her. Miss Geeber's mind, exquisitely sensitive to impressions, told her that this was important. "I hope nothing's wrong at home?" she offered.

"It's probably the man Babs is engaged to. The Navy doesn't stop to write or telegraph; it phones." I smiled.

After what seemed an interminable time Babs's head and shoulders came poking through the window. She swung a long leg over the low sill and stood beside us. Her eyes were glowing.

"It was George. They just got in and he wants me. He says he simply has to see me right away." Babs heaved a sigh of utter contentment.

"So he's coming up." My words were not even a question.

"No, I'm meeting him. They'll only be in four or five days and he has to go home to see his father and mother, too. So he wants me to come there, right away. I said I'd leave first thing in the morning. That was all right, wasn't it?" Her eyes went from me to Patty.

"If he wants you, you'll have to go. I don't suppose he inquired about his sister but I'm going home with you," Patty went on with that quick tact of hers which was so endearing. "It'll be easier for you both, all around, if I'm along."

"But Babs! What about—" I hesitated. "What about your lifework—the *Beowulf* paper?"

"Oh, gosh, I forgot all about it. I— I don't suppose I could get an extension of time?" She eyed Miss Geeber. Suddenly the full import of the decision she was making struck her. All her achievement, her fame on the campus, her admission to a charmed circle—she was throwing it all way with a single impulsive gesture.

118

The professor looked fully and sadly back. "It's part of your education, Barbara, to learn to do a thing not only well but also within certain limits of time. I can give you an extension," she went on, slowly, "and I will. But I shall also give you a merely passing mark for the paper."

For a moment longer the two faced each other. Barbara stood, swept by a strong emotion. Yet I realized her choice was made. However much she might seem to hesitate, the tide of her life was setting away, now, from formal learning. And in the steady renunciatory gaze of the little woman opposite her I read the fact that at some time Miss Geeber, for what reasons we shall never know, had made an opposite choice.

"The young man is asking a good deal of you," she said slowly. "One can only hope he's worth the sacrifice." She turned away.

Babs stared at the receding back. "You'd think the Navy was just nothing. And me coming right back! It's only I can't finish the paper in time. Oh, well, the Mehitabel B. Moogins crowd will have to struggle along without me. This is War."

She slipped her arm through mine and squeezed it in pure ecstasy.

"IT'S LIKE WHEN I was small and went out in the snow to slide," I told Ed. "My little brother used to sit down on my sled and expect me to drag him uphill."

I waited for my husband to act as if he heard me. He had been poking a furry rod into the stem of a pipe. Now he blew busily into the shank, looking not at me but at the opposite wall.

"Sometimes it seems as if nobody in this family could pull his own weight. The boys need their sneakers for gym at school, so *I* have to grub around in the closet under the stairs and find them. Babs comes home from college to buy a winter coat (that's what she's here for, in case you didn't know it) and she gets all wrought up if I give her *any* advice but she won't look for one without me. Even Eileen—" I hesitated; my daughter-in-law is my special pet. With Dick overseas she and her little girl are alone in the world except for us. But I went on, relentlessly, "Even Eileen can't take Barbara Elizabeth out without asking me what she should put on her. I get awfully tired," I finished.

Ed did not comment. Instead, he set the pipe on the table and began to walk around the room. He was plainly absorbed in thoughts of his own and his thoughts were far away. I could tell this by his eyes. Ed's eyes are a warm gray. They have a depth that is clear but they are by no means easy to read. But I've seen that look when Ed is thinking back to before 1940 when he manufactured toys and sometimes even designed them. He used to like that. Occasionally he would bring one home—I remembered a silly yellow beetle that ran very fast, lifting its wings as it went, and how we all laughed over it. Now his business was the grim one of munitions.

Suddenly he stopped pacing. His eyes changed. *"You're tired!"* It wasn't sarcasm; it was just an exclamation. "Listen, I'm so dead I could sleep for a week."

He sat down. The shade from the reading lamp put his eyes in shadow but let the light fall strongly on the lower part of his face. He looked bad. You don't notice things in a person you're with every day but now I saw that the area under his cheekbones, the one that tells the story, was sunken and that the flesh sagged. The line of his mouth was harsh and I didn't like his color.

For a moment neither of us spoke.

"How would you like to have a real vacation?" he said at last. "This is something I've been thinking about for a long time," he went on slowly. "I thought we'd go away somewhere, just you and me, without telling anybody where we were, not even the kids."

"It would be wonderful! But I hear it's awfully uncomfortable traveling and that we're asked not to." I was trying to marshal my thoughts. A dozen reasons why I couldn't leave home stood before my mind.

"We needn't go far." Ed's mouth wasn't harsh now; it was curved into a smile. "We'll just find a good hotel somewhere, and hole in. There'll be no phone calls, no mail, no secretary reminding me what I've got to do, and *you* won't have the kids on your neck. We'll have breakfast in bed and sleep all day if we want to. Would you like that, hm?"

I walked across the room to the arm of Ed's chair. His upturned face was eager and strained like a child's, as if he was afraid I might say no, it was impossible.

I put the difficulties resolutely on the back shelf of my mind.

"What do you think?" I leaned down and pulled his head toward me. "I'd simply adore it."

The family received the news of our plans with astonished indignation. We did not tell them until late the next afternoon when we were actually starting to pack our bags. They gathered in our room, even Eileen appearing in the doorway with Barbara Elizabeth, a sleepy bundle held tight in her arms.

"My goodness," Babs said, popping down on the slipper chair

and folding her hands. "Walking out like this. You can't do that to us."

"Gonna take your golf clubs?" Freddie wanted to know. "'Cause if you are, Charlie and I could go along and caddy for you." Ed did not answer this. He wandered around the room, alternately saying, "Let's see" to his open bag and whistling a tune from *Show Boat:*

> We can make believe I love you—
> Only make believe that you love me.

"I think it's the most wonderful idea I ever heard of," Eileen said. She watched me as I folded a nightgown and a negligee. Her gray eyes above the baby's head had streaks of sadness in them as they so often had, but there was no envy; there isn't an atom of selfishness in Eileen's whole make-up. When she said simply, "We won't know what to do without you," I knew she was thinking of the responsibility of Barbara Elizabeth.

Babs continued to watch us, fascinated. Babs is all eyes anyway. Presently she said, "Well, you've got to tell somebody where you *are* going. You can't just *disappear,* like a couple of bodies."

"I'm leaving our address with Dr. Beard." Ed was enjoying hugely the family's reaction to the news. "And now," he pulled out his watch, "who wants to phone for a taxi for Daddy?"

"That gag," Freddie said. "Who wants to get the paper for Daddy, who—"

"I'll phone for one." Babs gave Freddie a superior look. "Personally, I think it is the most romantic thing that's ever happened in this family."

Safe in a cab we sped across the half-darkened city. "Ed, we've passed the turn to the railroad station." I peered out anxiously. "This driver doesn't know where he's going."

"He knows." Ed sat back and lit a cigar. At last we drew up before a red brick building with lights across a wide white door, the town's one really good hotel. It stood beyond the station, up a few blocks.

"Well, this is it." Ed did not get out at first; instead he sat watching me. "This is where we're going to spend our vacation."

"Right here? Right here in town?" I couldn't believe it.

"Why not? Do you know of a better place or easier to get to? No catching a train, no standing up for hours to get into the diner. This place has the best food you ever tasted. Here you are, driver." He shoved a bag toward the door.

Standing by Ed as he wrote our names in the hotel register I had a queer sensation of being someone else. It persisted as we stood in our room looking around at the decorator's green on the walls and the peach-colored bedspreads and hangings.

"Not bad!" Ed gave the place an appreciative glance.

"I feel like the new girl in a dormitory," I told him.

"Well, you're not in any girls' dormitory." Suddenly Ed put his arms around the whole of me, as if I were a bundle. "All I want is for you to have a good time. This is our vacation," he said. "We'll stay at least a week; maybe two."

Ed had inquired to good purpose. The food was excellent. Dinner was a matter of prolonged consultation with a solicitous maître d'hôtel. "If you *like* that, why don't you have it?" Ed would ask me. The conference over the meal ended, conversation flagged. For myself, I could sit contentedly beside Ed forever in silence. It crossed my mind, however, that he might like a more amusing dinner-table companion. It had been years and years since Ed and I ate a meal without children on either side of the table demanding an ear. The effect had been numbing. I decided to make an effort—

Ed looked up from his plate. "I think the thing that tires me most," he said, "is always having to pay attention. At home it's the kids, in the office it's the help. And even if you go out with your friends, you've got to keep your mind on what they're saying. Thank God, you don't *have* to be entertained." He devoted himself to a bit of beef in a clear brown gravy.

Over the coffee Ed informed me that he was opening our vacation by taking us to the theater. "It's a new show. It's kind of rough, I hear; but they tell me it's awfully funny."

Our seats were down front, two on the aisle. With a whirl of music the curtain went up on a bevy of dazzling girls in an exotic setting. It was gay, startling, unreal; and it was very funny. Ed wiped the tears of laughter from his eyes. Now and then he glanced at me to be sure I wasn't missing anything. It ran through my mind that Ed and I hadn't gone to a show like this for years, and that in our younger days he would rather have hoped that I wouldn't get some of the jokes. A circling comedian appearing to dwindle into a pair of baggy trousers before our very eyes failed to enlist my entire attention and my mind went back to a line from a French essayist, "Naïveté, charming in the young, is a sign of stupidity in the old." Just then, a roar of masculine laughter greeted one crack that was meaningless to me. I would ask Ed about it later.

Safely back in our room, I did. He explained it. He told me a story he'd heard.

"Do you know any more as good as that?" I asked, when I could speak again.

"Trouble is, I forget jokes," Ed said. "Bad memory, I suppose. I did hear one the other day—" When Ed turned out the lamp we were still giggling like children.

I woke the next morning from a profound sleep to see the sunlight coming in rather bleakly under dark shades. I gazed about me, confused by the unfamiliar green walls with the meaningless landscapes. I leaned on my elbow and looked for Ed. Oh, yes, there he was in another bed, sleeping, like one drugged. I stretched luxuriously. No children, no noise—and no coffee. No coffee! I sat up. What to do? If I phoned Room Service the waiter might wake Ed. He was certainly good for another hour. I dressed and went down to the coffee shop. Sitting on a soft high stool at a chromium-covered counter, I ate through No. 3: prunes, hot cereal, coffee, and cinnamon buns. I began to feel simply wonderful.

When I came back to the room Ed was sitting up in the arm-chair in his bathrobe. He looked rather forlorn. The black shades were still drawn. "I *wondered* where you were!" His voice was plaintive.

"I tried not to wake you." I ran up the shades and let the warm sunlight flow in around him. "Shall I order you some breakfast? Orange juice? Coffee? Ham and eggs?" I bent down and kissed him, solidly and hard. "Where are your slippers? Here." I put them in front of him. "Oh, and I'd better tell them to send you up the morning paper."

Ed watched me pick up the phone. Then he said, "I hope you don't die first."

124

"Goodness, what a thing to say." I looked at him in utter astonishment. "I've no intention of dying for at least fifty years."

"I'll bet you won't, either." Then, "Why don't you leave the beds until the chambermaid comes?" he asked. "Lord knows we're paying plenty for service."

"Because I don't want you to eat your breakfast in a messy old room. Can't I just smooth 'em up?"

"Well, O. K." Ed was magnanimous.

There was a knock at the door and a narrow table on wheels came in propelled by a white-coated and smiling waiter. Each glistening metal cover had to be lifted while Ed passed on the food beneath it. The morning paper lay folded beside the coffee pot. Properly tipped, the waiter vanished. Ed looked at the repast with anticipation.

"Have some coffee." He pushed a cup toward me. The forlorn look was gone and now even the lines of weariness were less deep. "This is the life," he said. "No rushing to the office, nothing to tend to." He looked up belligerently as a chambermaid tried her key in the door.

I took a "Do not disturb" sign from the closet and put it on the outside doorknob. "There," I said.

"Good. That's the girl." He settled back with his paper.

A small armchair stood within the sunlight by the other window. I sat down and looked out at the unfamiliar outlines of the factories, at the clouds above, at the traffic below with the cars resembling Ed's yellow beetle jerking along the street. A faint honk from a horn reached me now and then; but it was all very far away. It was as if we were flying. I'd been up, once, and seen the town far below in an angry little cloud of its own making. I was as remote from it all here as there. The leisure was solid, satisfying, like a big chunk of candy when you were a child.

Ed felt it too. As he filled this pipe he said, "Pretty nice, isn't it? We've got this coming to us, you and I. I say let's stay two whole weeks if we want to."

And so the morning passed. Just before noon, Ed dressed. "How's about lunch?" He selected a tie from at least a dozen in his bag, taking a bold plaid that Babs had given him but he had never worn. "They say there's a little sun-porch café here that's open at noon."

I suppose I shall never forget the peculiar enchantment of the sheltered terrace where we ate our lunch. The place must have been an orchard once, for old fruit trees still stood on either side. A curving hill not fifty yards away cut off the breeze. The sheltered, sunny slope was thick with withered grasses.

The foreign-looking maître d'hôtel again concerned himself with our slightest whim.

"I know," I told Ed, as the man moved away with the order. "He reminds me of that waiter we liked so much in Florence." Ed and I once made a brief trip there together, after the first war ended.

"We'll go there again," Ed said. But he did not look at me. He knew it was not so.

"I don't understand the military significance of northern Italy," I said. "Is it important or isn't it?"

"Most people don't understand it." Ed began to draw on the tablecloth with a fork. "The thing is, there are two passes through the Alps, here, and here. They fan outward from Italy. Armies coming into Italy meet on a plain but going north they come out into widely separated territory. There's never been an invasion into Europe *from* Italy for that reason. They won't crack the European fortress through the Alps, I'm afraid. But by air it isn't far to the Balkans and the oil fields." He put a salt and pepper shaker at the upper right to represent them.

"How do you know so much?" I asked, admiringly.

"Well," he said, "what do you think I read the papers so carefully for every morning? Just for the tax news and comics? Besides, I have a rather fine collection of books on military strategy down at the office. I've been buying them ever since the last war."

"You have? I never realized that."

For half an hour or more, he talked on while history went by me like a landscape slipping past a train window. This was a side of Ed I had not known; our hours of mental companionship are so few.

Over our second cup of coffee I said, "Dick must be about here." I touched a spot within the border.

Instantly Ed's face changed. The shadow of something bleak and grim fell across it.

"Could be." He paused. "Well, are you all through? Because if you are, I'm going to find a barbershop and get myself the works, sun lamp and all."

"I'm through." I put down my napkin. The enchantment was broken. I wished that I had Ed's ability to put everything aside, to go all out for business one day and all out for fun the next. I followed him thoughtfully into the lobby. Once there, he turned. He was almost gay again. He pulled out a handful of bills. "Here," he said, "go buy yourself a silly hat or blouse— anything you want and wouldn't ordinarily blow yourself to. There's a cocktail lounge somewhere around here in the hotel— I'll meet you there," he pulled out his watch, "at half past four."

The hat was like something dreamed up by an ultramodern artist. It consisted of a bit of ribbon, a bicycle clip, and two tail feathers dyed red. But the girl was right, it did something for my sage-green dress; and for me. At her suggestion I bought a lipstick to match. Back in the room I spent a full fifteen minutes, a lot of time for me, getting an effect. Fred Beard once said he could tell the age of a woman patient most quickly by the way she put on her lipstick. I did mine as Babs would have done, with a firm clear outline. I wanted the woman who met Ed in the lounge to seem both young and very, very attractive.

I found him in a comfortable armchair near the bar. He got up to greet me with a low whistle. "Some lid," he said. "Turn around. Let's see."

"There isn't any back!" But I pivoted.

"It's all right; it's O. K." His eyes were frankly admiring. "I won't know who I'm out with." He pushed a little cushioned chair forward for me. He called an order to the waiter and began to nibble on some durable-looking potato chips set out before us.

"Oh, you mustn't eat them," I warned him. "I'm sure they're part of the permanent fixtures."

Ed laughed. At home, they would have taken that for a dumb mistake and corrected me patiently. Or they'd have thought it accidental and pointed out laboriously to me the joke I had happened to make.

"Have some peanuts." Ed pushed them toward me. "I ate a few; but they're so old I'd hate to pick on 'em."

I sat back contentedly. There was no doubt about it. The red feather was doing its stuff. Some people across the room studied it. "Pretty good-looking girl I've got." Ed reached for my hand.

"Do you really think I'm good-looking?" I wanted to know.

"I think you're lovely. I always have and I always will." His hand gripped mine.

I was unbelievably touched. It was his voice, too. But what I said was "This'll baffle the bartender. I'm sure he thought you were waiting to pick up some dizzy blonde."

"You don't know bartenders," he told me. "Nothing baffles 'em."

Time went by, warmly, quietly. At last Ed said, "Let's have the menu and decide what we want for dinner. I'd like to eat early and then tonight just go up and sit peacefully in our room."

In spite of myself as the dinner hour drew near I began to wonder what was happening at home. I thought of suggesting that we call up the children. But with a little effort I decided against it. Ed wanted to shut out everybody and I wanted him to have his way.

Ed was ahead of me in the room, turning on the softly shaded lights. The room, strange this morning, now seemed familiar, even dear.

Ed looked appreciatively about him. "As far as I'm concerned, I'd like to live here forever," he said.

"I love it for a holiday but not for keeps," I told him. "Hotel life is too idle for me. And there are times when work at home is a comfort. I remember when my mother was dying out in California; I house-cleaned my rooms, dumbly, all day. I even did up the ruffled curtains."

"Don't let's think about that." Ed drew me down beside him. "Let's think about us, right now."

And then suddenly, with nightcap in hand, Ed began to talk. He began to tell me about himself when he was a kid; things he had never said to me, perhaps not to anyone. He told me how he used to fight his way to school, as if it were something he wanted to remember very clearly and then to forget forever.

"And I mean fight," he said. "There was one block where the toughest kids in town hung out. I had to go through there every day. It was no use going around; they found you and beat you up worse. I remember one of the gang especially. He was a great big hulk with black eyes and a knife scar on his face. He was my nightmare. I used to dream about him and when I started to school in the morning, I'd stand on the corner before I went into that block and get a good grip on my book strap with my fists clenched. And lots of times I used to cry. I was so scared. Going around that corner was the toughest thing I ever had to do in my life."

"How awful," I said. "Wasn't there anyone to help you?"

"Nope. But maybe at that it taught me something." He sighed deeply. It was as if the telling had eased him somehow; had taken a weight from him. "Well, it's all over now," he said. "Let's not think about anything but you and me."

Perhaps I am slower than Ed to free my mind of the threads that tangle me with a household of everyday living. Perhaps it was rather that he had been consciously freeing himself for a couple of days and had a head start. But I was with him now. No need to ask me to think only of this moment. His warm hard figure was the ultimate reality.

It was perhaps ten o'clock when the phone whirred startlingly into the deep silence. Ed answered it and Babs's voice rippled across the wires. After a moment he said, "O. K., we'll be right there."

"We've got to get home in a hurry—the baby—got a hold of something, a little key." He was already up and pulling on his clothes. "Something always happens to us." Anxiety brought a note of exasperation into his voice.

I wanted to phone but Ed stopped me. "No, no, we'll be there in a little while. If she's swallowed it, a few minutes isn't going to matter."

"It won't kill her, will it? I mean, they can get those things out, can't they?" I asked as we drove hurriedly back again into semidarkness over the route we had taken so gaily the night before.

"Don't ask me. I suppose so. We'll see what Fred Beard has

to say when we get there." Suddenly Ed laid his hand upon mine. It was meant to be a reassuring touch but his fingers were cold and they shook a little. "Why couldn't those kids be careful —and I wanted you not to have to worry about anything."

"Here they are." As we opened the door Babs called out and Eileen came down the stairs with the boys shoving behind her.

"Where's Barbie? What's Fred doing?"

"We couldn't get the doctor," Eileen began.

"He was on a confident case," Charles broke in, "helping somebody have a baby. We made his girl give us your phone number."

"But I fixed Barbara Elizabeth up all right," Babs said. "I remembered the time Freddie swallowed a prune pit."

"*You* remembered?" Freddie's tone was bitter.

"So I held her upside down and shook it out."

Freddie grinned. "If there'd been any nickels we'd have got 'em."

"It was all my fault," Eileen said. "I was sitting on the bed with the tin safety box I keep Dick's letters in. I opened it so as to read some of them over again. Barbara Elizabeth was on the bed beside me. I must have put down the key without thinking. All of a sudden, I heard a sort of gurgle and she had the key in her mouth. I put my finger in and tried to get it. It seems that was the worst thing to do. It pushed it down her throat. She was choking on it. Look!" She held up a tiny flat object. "I spoiled your lovely vacation." Eileen's eyes were wide and remorseful. "But I was so frightened. I just *had* to reach you."

"That's all right, dear." Ed spoke slowly, his hand on her shoulder. "That's what families are for."

In our room that night I stood with my arms about him. "Our lovely vacation—"

"I know," he said, "everything was just right; the timing— everything."

Something small and hard pressed into both of us. Ed drew away and took out the hotel key with its wooden tag.

"I forgot to turn it in. Room Forty-eight. Well, we had a wonderful day; a perfectly wonderful day. They can't take that away from us, not if we live to be a hundred."

He stood turning the key softly in his hand.

14

NINETEEN, ENGAGED, and her father's darling, Babs had privileges and used them. She was using them now. She drew up a stool in front of his big chair, sat down, and took the evening paper out of his hands. "I need your undivided attention, my pet," she told him.

Ed gave one regretful glance at the sports page, now on the floor, then fixed his eyes on his long-legged, dark-haired daughter. A corn-yellow suit with a scarf of Sicilian red warmed the round face and eager brown eyes.

"What's the matter?" Ed asked. "You've got a ring with a diamond big as a rock. Don't tell me you're agitating now in favor of getting married!"

Babs rocked back on the stool, her legs stretching out on either side like oars at rest. "You'll never believe it, Daddy," she went on, "but I *think* George wants to. You know how I practically died getting him definitely engaged? I guess he's been planning to age me a little first, because he's never said 'boo' about a date for our wedding." She turned the ring on her finger slowly. "And, well as I know the guy," she went on, "I never liked to bring it up."

"And so?" Ed asked.

"Well, then he got involved with the Navy and turned serious on me. At first I thought it was the life that was getting him down. But it wasn't that. I could tell by his letters—for the first time George really needs *me*." She paused. "I don't know if you'll understand it," she said.

"I think I do." Ed's face was in shadow, but the light from the reading lamp fell sharply on his wide mouth. For a time his lips moved, making words he did not say aloud. Then, "and so George wants to get married soon. Is that it?"

"It's just my hunch," Babs told him. "But it's a great big one. I'm the intuitive type, I guess." She leaned forward, her lifted eyebrows pointing up and in. "This is the situation. George's ship is in again, and he has this seven-day leave, beginning yesterday. He stopped off to see his family. He's coming here tomorrow for the rest of the time. What I want to know is, if he wants to get married pronto, will you let me?" She studied Ed's face. "Moms is O. K. about it. But I'm so afraid you'll try to stop us, and Daddy, George is the most wonderful man in the whole world and I'd marry him tomorrow and follow him around the ocean in a rowboat. That's how I am about that guy," she finished.

"I see." Ed didn't go on for a moment. Then, "I guess you can count on your daddy for almost anything," he told her.

"Thanks, Toots." Babs got up. "Now you can read your old paper." She went out. I heard her on the stairs.

Ed did not go on reading, however. Instead he said, "You know, Elizabeth, there's something about that boy that worries me."

I was surprised, and said so.

"Yes, but we've never seen him up against anything—anything real, I mean," Ed went on. "He's had everything handed to him on a silver platter. It's all been too easy."

"It won't be easy for him now," I put in. "It isn't easy in the Navy."

"That's another thing," Ed said, almost irritably. "Why did he go in that way? He'd been deferred to be a doctor. He was starting out for a commission in the Medical Corps, and then, next thing we hear, he's enlisted as a common sailor. What I'm afraid of is that the boy is restless, doesn't know *what* he wants, can't stick to anything. What kind of husband will a man like that make for our Babs?"

I considered. "Men *are* restless—real ones," I told him. "Remember you, last war?"

Ed dismissed this. "It's the shifting about I don't like," he explained. "I'm afraid he is unstable. And this wanting to marry Babs, on the spur of the moment—"

132

"I'd hardly call it that." I couldn't stop a smile. "After all, they've known each other for almost two years. And they *are* engaged."

"I know that," Ed said. "But what's the rush?"

And he picked up his paper, through talking. . . .

Of all the young people who come in and out of our house, George makes you the most aware of himself. We had no idea within several hours when he was coming; yet as the whole family wandered into the living room directly after lunch that Saturday, we suddenly knew he was at the door.

He stood at the entrance to the room like a child at a surprise party. Indeed, in his navy-blue suit he looked not unlike a very large child. Only his eyes, although they were dancing now, were too troubled underneath to be boyish.

"Hello," he said. "Can the Navy come in?"

Babs got there first, but everybody pounced on him. Ed was gripping his hand and saying, "Sit down. Sit down." Babs had slipped into the curve of his other arm. George grinned at me.

"I'd *like* to shake hands with your mother and Eileen," he explained to the top of Babs's head.

He sat down on the couch, Babs beside him. Ed, Eileen, and I drew up our chairs to form a half-circle, while the two boys pushed in like terriers, close to their hero. They began at once to question him. They wanted to discuss with him the structure of a PT boat, about which they'd been having a dispute. They are avid if rather indiscriminate readers. They had just finished several comic books and now were deep in *They Were Expendable*.

"But George is on a destroyer," Babs said. "Can't you see him dashing along an iron deck—with waves coming over big as mountains—dropping ashcans on submarines way down below? You *do* hold on tight, don't you?" She stared anxiously up at him.

George smiled down with an odd look in his blue eyes. Before he could speak Eileen broke in. "Won't the war be over pretty soon, don't you think?" She studied George's face as if, being in the service, he must know.

"I think they're bound to send your husband home for a while before long, whatever happens," he said in his friendly way, his eyes full of kindness for Eileen. "Dick's been over ever since Casablanca, hasn't he? It's about time he saw his baby. Where is she, anyway?"

"Want to see her?" Eileen went out and returned, presently, leading Barbara Elizabeth. Barbie was dressed in corduroy overalls, and in her hand was a carefully clutched piece of white tissue paper. The two girls and George dropped on the rug beside her, with Charles behind them. Freddie hung over the chair back in a discouraged way. I knew he was thinking, well, what about PT boats? On the rug, Barbara Elizabeth threw her right foot stoutly out before her and sat suddenly down.

George held his arm out stiff as a rail for her to clutch. "Careful, sport," he said.

"There's an awful good picture downtown," Freddie put in. "All about convoys. Pretty interesting, huh? Like to see it?" he urged.

"I was thinking you might care to take a run down to the plant," Ed said to George. "We made a lot of changes since you saw it. We've got a new machine that's a honey."

"That so?" George put an arm across Babs's shoulders and drew her nearer as he listened.

"Of course, we could go next week just as well," Ed said, "but I thought you might like to see it."

"I'd like to, sometime, sir." George set Barbie, who was hanging onto his knee, on the floor and got up. "But just today, I thought Babs and I would go places."

"Of course," I interrupted, before any further plans could be put to him. "Run right along."

George followed Babs into the hall, and stood watching her as she ducked toward the mirror. "Come on. You look fine. You know sump'n? We're going to buy you some flowers. What do you like? Camellias? Orchids?"

"Orchids," Babs said promptly. "Only I wouldn't know it was me, wearing 'em."

George let his eyes travel over the soft hair, the vivid face of the girl before him. "O. K., let's shove off." He waved to us and they went out, their clasped hands swinging. Their going drained the room of all excitement and fun. The family fell apart. Eileen, a sad look in her big gray eyes, picked up the baby and went to her room. After a brief conference, the boys left for Bingo's house. Ed thought of something he had to see to in the garage.

Only Ed had come back when George and Babs returned. They were still tightly holding hands, and a spray of tiny yellow orchids on Babs's shoulder showed what their errand had been. "Now we're going somewhere and dance," George announced, "and then we'll have dinner downtown and go to a show. We intend to find all the fun the town offers. But this girl insists on changing her clothes," he told me.

"I *won't* wear a sweater with orchids," Babs explained. "Honestly—just look at them! Did you ever see anything so perfectly gorgeous?"

George cut off any comment. He looked at his wrist watch. "I'll give you ten minutes."

Babs went upstairs. George stood looking gravely down at Ed. "I'd like to talk to you, sir, if you have a little time."

"I'll go up and help Babs." I put my knitting down on the couch.

"Don't go." George did not look at me but he sat down on the couch with me.

Ed filled his pipe. "I've got all the time in the world."

"Well," George began, "it's like this. I've never wanted anything in my life the way I wanted to marry Babs on this leave. I guess I was counting on it all the time I was out there in the Atlantic. I didn't think about much of anything else. I guess Babs caught on from my letters, although I never said anything definite, because I was trying to make up my mind." He picked up a cigarette and stood turning it in his well-kept, even graceful fingers. Then he put it back. "I was up against the first thing in my life I couldn't fix."

Something in me tightened. What did a boy do when for the first time in all his young, careless years he couldn't fix things?

George felt the strain. "Maybe I'd better fill in the background first," he went on, "about why I shifted to being a sailor."

"Why did you?" Ed's face was a mask, as I've seen it sometimes when he's talking business.

"When I got put in the reserve the war didn't look so big,"

George said. "At least not to us fellows still in college. It was just another fight with those Germans. We'd been taught all about propaganda. The Japs were sort of yellow-peril stuff, too. Even after Pearl Harbor, a few of us had to be shown." He looked across questioningly to Ed.

"None of us thought it would be so bad," Ed said. "We all hated the idea of being sucked in."

"So I wasn't in any hurry," George went on, relaxing a bit. "When Dad suggested I get deferred and try for a medical commission in the Navy, it was O. K. with me; he's always wanted me to be a doctor. And I thought that way Babs and I could get married and have quite a lot of time together. Marrying Babs came first with me." He stiffened again. "It was what I cared most about." I felt the arm next to mine tremble.

"I suppose seeing your friends getting in made the difference," Ed suggested.

"I don't know—" George hesitated. "I think it was reading about the chap who was shot up on the bridge of that submarine and just lay there and said, 'Take her down!' I—I wanted to carry on from where he left off. I wanted to have a crack at 'em for myself. I couldn't get a Navy commission, of course, when I was turning down the chance they'd given me; so I had to wait for the draft or go in as a sailor. Well, being a sailor was very O. K. with me."

"I see." Ed's face was set. "And so you want to get married before you ship out again and maybe run into real fighting— is that it?"

"No, sir." George got up and walked restlessly around the room. "I've been thinking a lot during the months I've been in." He faced Ed and eyed him almost sternly. "You and I both love Babs, sir. She's very young. We want to protect her. I thought I might get shore duty this time, but even then, if I married her and let her trail along after me wherever she could, I'd be taking on something I couldn't handle. I'd be on duty; and Babs would be anywhere. I think the best place for her is right here." He looked almost lovingly around the living room. "I'd like you to take care of her for me until I come back."

"That's if you go to sea again." I was fighting for what Babs

136

would want. "There are lots of necessary and worth-while jobs ashore."

George gave me a long, direct look. "I'll be at sea."

There was a moment of silence.

"But it would have been awfully nice the other way," George said.

Ed lifted his hand and let it fall palm down on the arm of his chair. "Have you got your orders?" he asked, at last.

"I'm due to report back tomorrow; I'm still attached to the same ship." George's tone was even. "The rest of my leave's been canceled. So I'll have to get the midnight train."

"Have you told Babs?" Ed asked.

"Not yet." George hesitated. "That's the hard part. If you don't mind, I'm going to take her out somewhere and do it my own way."

"She's coming now." Ed gave me a warning glance.

"Here I am!" Babs had put on a cool gray dress on which the yellow flowers rested like butterflies. I could not face the look of utter happiness in her eyes. She came over to me and gave me a hug of sheer exuberance. "You don't have to sit up and worry tonight," she said, releasing my head from her arms. "I'm all taken care of."

George held out his hand. "Come on." At the door he turned as if there was something he ought to say to me. He must have thought better of it. "Good night, sir." He shook hands with Ed.

They went off, their talk and their laughter coming back clearly.

Time passed—much time, and very slowly. The family got to bed; the household settled into a deep quiet.

At a few minutes after twelve Ed came down in his bathrobe.

"Oh, *this* is where you are," he said.

"I'm waiting for Babs."

"So am I. She must have gone with him to the station."

He opened the front door and we stared into the darkened street. A light but steady rain was falling. Presently the hooded lights of a cab crawled around the corner. It stopped at our house and Babs got out.

She came in, but now she was very still. The little orchids were damp and crushed. Her hair was flattened by the rain.

She must have followed him out in the storm, I thought. She must have run down the platform, trying to keep up with the train.

She flung her purse on the hall table. "You knew," she said. "George told you. You knew all the time."

"Only just before he left, while you were dressing."

I put my arm through hers. It was not a caress. She would not want one—not from me, not now.

"We waited up for you, Mom and I." Ed's hands had been rammed into his bathrobe pockets. Now he drew them out, indecisively. Then he said, "I guess an old family isn't much use right now."

"Let's sit down a few minutes before we go to bed." I took Babs into the living room. Ed drifted off.

I pulled Babs down beside me on the couch. Suddenly, Ed appeared from the direction of the pantry. Three stemmed glasses sprouted from his left hand. In his right was a green bottle.

"Champagne," he announced. "I was going to save it for the wedding, but now—I thought we'd have a little drink together, just the three of us."

He set the glasses in the lamplight and filled them carefully. He handed us each one. For the first time Babs raised her eyes.

I thought, He's going to propose a toast. But he didn't. Instead he lifted his glass and bent his head just a little.

"They don't come any better than your guy," he said.

CHAPTER

15

"THAT'S SOME TOY Daddy bought for Barbara Elizabeth," Babs said. "But nothing's too good for a first grandchild, eh, Grandma?" She gave me a friendly grin.

Out on the grass before us, Barbara Elizabeth was running about busy with a new possession. A light wind blew the last leaves across the lawn. I had been trying to get the best of them with a big bamboo rake. But under a cross fire of comment I had given it up and gone to sit on the steps with Eileen. The wind drove the leaves around Barbie's feet. She did not notice them. She was busy getting the hang of her big toy.

It was more than a toy. It was a wooden slide made of varnished oak. You ascended a stout red ladder, debouched onto a platform, then slid wildly down and out into space. A person had to be quick, to land with legs well apart, to come off standing instead of sprawling on the grass. Barbara Elizabeth was still a little uncertain about it all. We saw her now, her green corduroy-covered legs, her red-clad shoulders, her topknot of curls, wavering a moment at the platform's edge, against the sky. I felt Eileen stiffen. But Barbie rocked to safety and sat down.

"Ca'ful." She warned herself. "Watch it!" She slid to the grass.

"I'd like to do that myself," Babs said. "Wouldn't you know it would be Daddy who'd think of a thing like that?" Babs is always in Ed's corner even when she's in there quarreling with him.

"It's so good because it uses the long muscles," Eileen explained. She has a book that tells her these things.

"And," I added, "she can play on it all by herself."

These unprophetic words had hardly left my lips when we heard a protracted scream. It was, in fact, a series of whoops, and it came from beyond our garage. Just beyond the garage door a path leads out of a growth of small trees and underbrush known as the Woods. From it, a boy and girl came racing out onto the lawn.

They wore identical brown sweaters and their shorts and skirt were cut from the same faded wool. They might have been four or six (actually they were five). The girl's flying pigtails and the boy's flailing arms were all the color of hickory nuts.

"Oh, dear, it's those twins." Eileen leaned forward, alert. "They've moved into the house back of the Woods. They come through here a dozen times a day." The path, plus our drive, is an unofficial right of way between our block and the one behind it for all the small fry in the neighborhood.

"Lookit, Bill!" Belle, the sister, had seen it first. Her yell checked her twin. They wheeled and hurled themselves toward the slide.

Barbara Elizabeth's small rear was just going over the top as the twins hit the ladder. The boy shoved her aside and shot down. His sister followed. Her eyes were straight ahead. "Look out for me," she shouted.

Eileen jumped up and ran to protect her child. But Barbara Elizabeth needed no help. She knew when the company she was traveling in was too rough for her. Lying on her stomach, she backed onto the ladder and slid to the ground. She ran to her mother.

Palms in, Eileen's long hands pressed the baby against her knees. Barbara Elizabeth began to cry. Eileen looked darkly at the twins. "The slide is Barbara Elizabeth's," she told them, "and you mustn't shove her like that."

The twins came up standing in front of her and watched her with interest. Insulating themselves against criticism was an old art with them. Their sandy faces, their bright beady eyes were utterly uncommunicative. They told you nothing.

Babs, coming up to the scene, struck where a blow might tell. "Does your mother know where you are?" she asked.

"Our mother don't never know *where* we are," the little girl

140

paid. Her voice held overtones; the desperation of a harried mother and the smugness of her own satisfaction. The boy chimed in. "She don't never know *where* we are."

And now, as if conjured out of the air, three other children stood before us. The largest was a skinny little boy of perhaps seven with a solemn face and big ears. Goaded by some memory of training he said to Eileen, "These are my friends." He started toward the ladder.

The twins went into action. They moved in formation, arms flying, with shrill yells. "Sissy pants, sissy pants!" The boy with the big ears fell back from the ladder, stumbling against his friends. The three children gathered themselves up from the grass, the twins pursuing, and ran shrieking into the Woods.

The noise brought Ed out of the garage. With gas rationing he couldn't use his car much but he tinkered happily with the engine. He walked toward us, wiping his hands with a bit of waste. He looked pleased at the slide.

"Well," he said, "I'm glad I got that thing. Pretty nice toy for the whole neighborhood." He patted the back of Barbara Elizabeth's head. Babs eyed him with affectionate exasperation. "It is," she admitted. "But it's a heck of a time to mention it."

What catnip is to kittens, our slide was, for a while, to the children for blocks around. Squatters' rights made it, in their own eyes at least, the twins' property. With it they appropriated Barbara Elizabeth, or perhaps it would be more accurate to say that they appropriated Barbara Elizabeth and therefore what was hers was theirs. "It ain't your slide!" said a child who was being pushed away. To which they promptly answered, "It's ours! It's Barbara Elizabeth's. It's ours!"

Forced off her own property by the others, Barbara Elizabeth looked on unhappily from the side lines. Her eyes sagged. She watched attentively while the twins pushed and poked. She took to retreating toward the house. Occasionally the girl twin would come for Barbara Elizabeth. Some first impulse of motherliness would make her turn wildly and lovingly toward the smaller child. She would wrap her arms around her, lift her off the ground. "Want to play with me?" she would ask. Rare moments, but they gave Barbara Elizabeth a taste of companionship.

But more and more Barbara Elizabeth spent her time under the porch where a low door in the latticed woodwork opened into an earthy, cavelike aperture. No one joined her there. Once a long-legged cat came and rubbed herself against the outside wood. She was a thin, yellow creature with a shrewish face and desolate eyes. Barbara Elizabeth's head appeared in the doorway. Here at least was companionship of a sort. "Want to come in my house, cat?" she asked softly. But the cat, alarmed, made off across the lawn.

"I wouldn't mind the other children playing here if they weren't so rough," Eileen said one morning.

We were sitting at breakfast, Babs by her father, Barbara Elizabeth in a high chair between her mother and me. We could see Belle and Bill already playing on our grass. Barbara Elizabeth saw them, too. "Want to get down." She slid terrifyingly under the tray of the high chair. I saw her feet thrust out. It seemed as if her whole weight hung by her chin against the tray's edge. Eileen hoisted the small figure in the pink bathrobe to a sitting position again. "First we eat," she said.

"The way I see it," Ed was answering Eileen's remark, "kids have to learn to get on with other children sometime. They must learn to be good sports themselves and to stick up for themselves if other people aren't."

"Daddy! Have a heart." Babs pushed a pot of honey away from her plate. "This masculine stuff is all right in its place, but listen, my pet, Barbara Elizabeth is only just *three*."

"But I don't want her to fight!" Eileen's face was serious. "I don't want her to have to stick up for herself. I want to bring her up with nice manners."

"Nothing like 'em," Babs agreed. "I ought to know. My ankles were always sore from Mother's meaning nudges." She adopted a syrupy tone. "'Babs will be glad to let Marie have her tricycle, won't you, dear?' That's the kind of thing Mother dished out."

"Well, it didn't hurt you," Ed said. "But I still think Barbara Elizabeth has to learn to stand up for herself." There was just a glint of tears in Eileen's eyes and Babs saw it. "And if Mother could reach that far," Babs told Ed, "your ankle would be black and blue now."

142

And then, as suddenly as it had come, the tide of children swept away from our lawn. It passed us by. Looking out, we saw the twins, followed by other tots, go down our driveway to the street.

"I guess they've found a new attraction." Ed spoke almost regretfully.

"They're making a beeline for someplace," I said.

"They've found another dive," Babs wisecracked over my shoulder.

"And during the lull," Eileen put in, "I'll just run down to the drugstore. Barbara Elizabeth will be all right, alone in the back yard." She went out.

I went out once to make certain. "Where are you, dear?" I called.

A small soft voice answered from under the porch. "I'm here."

"I just wanted to be sure you were there," I called back.

Barbara Elizabeth's curly head came out from below. "I don't want to be there. I want to be here." She began to cry.

"Well, I just wanted to be sure you were all right." I was a little confused by her reply. I went back into the house, uncomfortably aware that she had been contentedly at play and I had disrupted it. But she would settle down to something else. . . .

Perhaps half an hour later Eileen came back. She set her small parcels on the table. "Where's Barbara Elizabeth?" she asked.

"Playing by the back porch," I told her, comfortably.

"No, she isn't. She isn't anywhere in the yard." Eileen's voice had a tinge of anxiety.

"Probably she went into the cellar." I preceded Eileen to the stairs, turning on the light as I went down. Unlike many cellars, ours is one great room. It has the usual complement of old trunks, discarded rockers, and boxes at one end; but it is whitewashed throughout, not uncheerful and rather a favorite place with children. Its nooks are known to all of us. Barbara Elizabeth was not in any one of them.

"Babs," I called, as we came out into the front hall again, "are you upstairs, dear? See if the baby is anywhere around."

We heard her going in and out of the various bedrooms. "Where are you, Midget?" In a moment she joined us, coming down the back stairs into the kitchen. "Norah says she didn't come into the house," she told us. "She hasn't been in at all, all morning."

And now we began to hunt in earnest. We started from the back porch where she had last been seen. For Eileen's sake I tried to conceal my rising sense of alarm. Perhaps the baby had gone around the block, I suggested. The journey to the end of the block around the corner and back along a fence at the foot of the yards was an adventurous journey, forbidden to her. But every now and then, in spite of us, she made it.

Eileen started off with Babs beside her. I followed more slowly, looking carefully in every front yard. "Barbara Elizabeth, Barbara Elizabeth!" Eileen's voice carried thin and high along the wide sunny street, empty except for a single child on a tricycle. There was no answer. Something inside of me turned to a round lump of lead. It was I who was responsible. It was I who had let her run off.

I cut through a lawn and met the girls coming back along the white fence. Eileen was crying now. Her wide mouth trembled. She said quietly, as if to herself, "What'll I do, what'll I do?" We walked toward our yard, side by side, not looking at each other.

"Let's *think*." Babs stopped by the slide. "Maybe she went up the path—"

We hurried toward the Woods. At first they offered no invitation to straying. A tangle of blackberry bushes was inaccessible to all but an elderly rabbit whose homeward way led under them. He hopped off as we came near. "He's just like Barbara Elizabeth," I thought. "We don't scare him, but we bother him terribly."

"I used to love to sit out on the bare rock, farther up." Babs was making conversation. "Maybe we'll find her there." She broke into a run, Eileen behind her. I went more slowly, looking from side to side. "Barbara Elizabeth," I called softly into the Woods. She was so small we could pass her by and not see her. She might not answer; she might not be able to. . . .

The Woods cover one side of a very small hill. Almost at

144

the top a round shoulder of rock appears between the trees. It is imbedded in checkerberry leaves and strewn with pine needles.

Eileen stumbled out into the open. "Baby! Are you there?" But there was no one. Only a small snake, sunning himself on a sun-warmed stone, slid like liquid into the ground.

The Woods came to an end, just beyond the rock, against a stone wall. Something was moving there. I looked up. The twins stood staring over at us.

We ran up to the wall. Beyond a strip of unkempt grass on the other side we could see their yard and porch.

"Hey, kids, is Barbara Elizabeth at your house?" Babs asked.

The twins shook their heads. There was almost no expression on their faces.

"Have you seen her?" Eileen's voice was shaking.

The twins nodded, moving their heads solemnly up and down. "She wented that way." The little girl pointed north.

"She wented that way," her brother agreed, but he pointed in exactly the opposite direction.

The little girl proffered something further. "Prob'ly she got runned over."

Bill agreed. "She got flatted by a truck. Prob'ly she did."

I heard Eileen suck in her breath, but Babs spoke. Her voice was short. "Of course she didn't get run over. We'd have heard —" She paused. These two knew something. Rattling around in their little minds was a kernel of information, like a penny in a pig.

If we could only shake it out of them. Babs studied them angrily. Then following the only clue they had offered, she went on, "Why should she get run over?"

"If you cross the road, you get runned over, prob'ly." The little girl was plainly repeating a warning she had often heard.

"Did Barbara Elizabeth cross the road?" Eileen's great staring eyes were fixed on the child's face.

"Mhm, she crossted the road with us." Belle was pleased with the effect she was creating.

"Where did you go?" Now Babs's tone was very sharp.

The twins were aggrieved. "We only just wented to the swing," they said. They climbed up and sat down on the wall.

"I know! I know what they mean." Babs whirled toward us;

the twins were forgotten now. "There's a new family in the street beyond the McDonalds' garden—they have a swing."

We were hurrying along the path now, Indian file. The Mc-Donalds live directly across the street from us. So that was where the beeline had been going; the swing was the magnet that had drawn all the children so suddenly away from us. And now we were standing on the sidewalk in front of our house. A bus drew up at the corner and another thundered past on the far side going in the other direction. Eileen looked fearfully up and down the street.

"Come on! We can cross now." Babs shepherded us to the far sidewalk.

"Playing with other kids is a good thing," she went on breathlessly, as we hurried past the McDonalds' yard. "Learn to share the equipment—" Babs, trying to be casual and comforting, sounded so like Ed that I almost smiled.

The lot behind the huge building swarmed with children, running, shouting. I could not see the beloved little red-and-green clad figure, the little brown head.

"There she is, there she is!" Babs pointed excitedly.

"Baby! Barbara Elizabeth!" Eileen started to run.

She was facing us. At the sound of her mother's voice she looked in our direction. But only for a moment. She had other things to attend to. Her whole being was centered on the swing.

The swing hung from a bar held by two stout steel poles. It had a low, inviting seat and already the ground beneath it was worn bald. Barbara Elizabeth had been headed straight for the seat. In the split second when she faltered at the sound of her name, however, someone had got ahead of her. It was a little boy in a sailor suit. His black hair fell in a cowlick over a determined face. Now his hands were on the ropes.

Barbara Elizabeth stepped up and shoved. She was not rough. But she was utterly determined. The boy slipped suddenly to the earth.

Barbara Elizabeth composed herself on the low seat. She grasped the ropes firmly. Her heels dug into the dirt. The swing moved slowly up and back. As it came down she thrust both feet out into the air.

"Watch out!" She warned the world. "Watch out for me!"

146

IT BEGAN WITH Ed's deciding that the boys should earn their spending money. He was working on the theory that a person with a regular income will learn not to run into debt, and not to spend foolishly. It's a nice theory but I cannot agree that it's wholly sound. From the time he was a small boy, Dick had budgeted his expenses and always had enough for football games, baseball equipment, and so on; while to Babs a box of bubble bath powders may seem a wise expenditure. Spending, then, is a matter of temperament. But we both agreed that the boys could get some business experience and learn the value of money by trying to earn it.

Freddie has had a small allowance ever since he was eight years old and when Charles came to us from England, Ed put him right on the payroll, too. But this year things were different.

"Remember there's a war going on," Ed began, "and anyway, you're old enough to make what you spend. Why, when I was your age I had money in the bank."

Freddie, who was practicing a card trick, allowed Charles to draw a card, study it, and return it to the pack. "Yeah?" he asked, without enthusiasm.

"I saw you," Charles said triumphantly. "I saw you put another one on the bottom."

"I had a paper route," Ed went on. "Delivered fifty papers every day after school."

Freddie put the pack down in a discouraged way. "Bingo's got that for his racket and we can't cut in on it," he told his father.

"There you are," Ed said. "Bingo has initiative. Why, I bet he even makes enough to give his mother something."

"He gives it all to her," Charles explained. He looked up at Ed, his wide blue eyes serious. "He has to. They don't have milk but twice a week at their house."

Ed tamped his pipe in silence. There's nothing we can do about Bingo except fill him up when he comes into the kitchen after school with the boys.

"And anyway," Freddie went on, "Bingo was lucky. His uncle had the paper route and was killed and that's how Bingo got it. Ya gotta have the breaks."

"Yes," Charles chimed in, "you must have luck. Norah says that's the important thing."

"Don't be silly." Ed's voice was sharp. "You don't make money by luck. Money is made by honest work and I want you boys to find something regular to do."

"Errands?" Babs asked hopefully from the couch, which she had pre-empted by the simple expedient of putting her feet up on it.

Freddy's voice was studiedly bitter. "We do those anyway. Unless," he brightened and looked sideways at me, "we could get paid, huh?"

"Nothing doing," I said. "Everybody puts something into a family. Your 'put' is errands."

"Well, it doesn't matter what you do," Ed said, "so long as the profit you make is a just and fair one. It's a pretty nice feeling," he added, "to have money in your pocket that you earned by real hard work."

Babs got up from the sofa. "No swapping one nice, big nickel for two itsy-bitsy dimes?" She put her arms along the back of his chair. "We know," she said. "*You* made your own way. Nobody gave *you* a start. O.K., we get it." She rumpled his hair for him.

Egged on by Ed, Freddie and Charles gave a good deal of thought to their changed financial future. I heard them after supper pointing out to each other profitable pursuits and openings as offered in the advertisements.

"There's a couple here," I heard Charles say. "Here's one.

148

'Raise poultry for profit.' Gosh; we could keep about a hundred hens in the back yard. . . . ''

"I don't guess Moms would stand for that," Freddie said practically.

"Well, then," Charles ran his finger down the page, "how's this? 'Learn to write verses for popular songs.' It says all you need is to buy this book on rhyming."

"With what?" Freddie's tone dripped sarcasm. "Wait, I saw sump'n good, somewhere here." He flipped over the pages. " 'Do schoolmates avoid you on account of pimples?' " He grunted. "Naw, that isn't the one. Mine was about a lucky stone. Here. It's something about Indians," he said.

"Yeah?" Charles bent fascinated over the item. " 'Possessing this stone assures you fortune,' " he read. "But you have to send money for this, too," he announced, "so it's no good either."

"Yeah; well—hey, how's this one? 'Stupendous offer—beautiful colors and suitable sentiments.' And it says, 'Send no money.' "

I settled back comfortably. Anything that said 'Send no money' couldn't possibly do any harm.

"Listen, Moms." Freddie stood by the desk at which, a few days later, I was writing a letter. "How much do Christmas cards cost?"

"Oh, you can get very inexpensive ones," I said without looking up.

A short silence told me this was the wrong answer.

"Yeah, but how much do *you* pay?" he persisted. "Would you give ten cents apiece for a really gorgeous card, one with a suitable sentiment in beautiful colors?"

I looked up at his anxious face. Freddie's whole countenance has a certain validity about it; when he asks a serious question, he is honestly trying to get not only the material facts but information as to how a person would behave under given circumstances. Freddie is a warm, aware, and interested human being, and he merits your undivided attention. I pushed my writing aside.

"I usually have them printed with Daddy's and my name on them," I explained, "but this year I didn't. I'll probably pay ten or fifteen cents apiece, and on a few I'll spend a quarter."

A look of satisfaction glowed in Freddie's round face. "Well, don't buy any," he said. "I think I can help you out." He went to the bookcase and, obviously trying not to look too important, took a brown paper parcel from the lower shelf. "Five hundred gorgeous Christmas cards. Five hundred," he announced.

Charles stood by. Together they forced back the twine.

"We took advantage of this stupendous offer," Charles said.

"Yeah, we got 'em for a cent apiece." Freddie undid the top.

"How in the world did you pay for them?" I asked.

"That part's all right. We didn't have to send any money. We can pay for them all as soon as we've sold a few. The way I figure, the very least we can make is fifty dollars." He took one out and handed it to me. It was made of cheap, dirty white paper with muddy red and green printing. What had been a silver star had already lost its shiny dust. "Like it, huh?" Freddie watched me anxiously.

"I'll take a dozen," I told him promptly. "I think I can use that many." Babs, coming by, studied the card without comment. She followed me to my room.

"Moms," she began, "you can't send out cheesy cards like that and you just can't let the boys sell them to people we know."

I laughed. "People we know can take care of themselves."

"But charging ten cents or even five is just—just an imposition." She waited for me to say I thought so, too. "Honestly, Moms," she concluded disappointedly, "sometimes I just don't understand you."

At first the Christmas greeting business was fairly brisk. Norah was a customer at five cents a card and so were two or three of the neighbors. The boys disposed of some to the boys and girls at school. Then came a lull. Things, I gathered, were not going so well. In fact, two days before Christmas found them in a worried huddle. I tried to encourage them.

"You ought to be able to make a lot of last-minute sales today," I said.

"Yeah." Freddie sat biting a pencil. "We gotta have a different plan, though. Tell you what." He turned to Charles. "Let's see what Bingo thinks. He's had lots of experience. We can whack up some with him," he added, expansively. "If we sell the rest we can afford to."

That was at three o'clock. At half past, Norah came in indignantly from the kitchen and stood in the doorway of the living room. "They'd a right to ask you, Mrs. Breton," she began, her eyes snapping. "The boys is just gone out with our mahogany tea tray tied onto that Bingo Brown. They put a couple of Mr. Breton's neckties through the handles and off they went."

I looked up, puzzled. "What on earth are they up to?"

"It's a kind of peddler's tray," Norah explained. " They spread those Christmas cards out on it. They're down the street."

I went to the door and looked out. Sure enough, stationed on the corner was Bingo, his wares hung from his neck. Fanned out on the street were Freddie and Charles, accosting passers-by. I watched. Occasionally someone stopped to examine their stock. Evidently they were making sales. I would let them alone.

I told Ed about it as we went to bed. "I'm sure Bingo had the idea," I said. "And he must have stood them up plenty or he wouldn't have hung around the street corner like a shoestring peddler for hours on end."

"Well, anyway, they've got pep. They might make a good thing out of those cards." Ed put out the light. "My bet is, they'll clean up."

Christmas day came and went. Among other things it brought Charles and Freddie some magic apparatus. They were working on it in the middle of the living room when Ed walked in from the office. He stood watching for a while. Presently he sat down in his big chair. Instead of retiring behind the evening papers as he usually does, he looked on at the family. His mood was expansive. Suddenly he asked, "By the way, boys, how'd you make out with your Christmas cards?"

"O.K." Freddie went on studying a chart. "And we got a lot left we can sell next year, too."

"How much did you take in?" Ed was curious. "Well, let's count it and see."

Both boys got up. Freddie brought in an old cigar box from the bookcase and put it on the table next to Ed. The lifted cover exposed a miser's heap. Shielding the coins with his hand, Freddie turned them out.

"You pile the dimes," Charles ordered, "and I'll do the nickels." It took them a minute or two to separate and stack the coins. "Three dollars and forty cents." Charles's voice was jubilant. "That's not so bad."

But Freddie was staring at the stacks. He raised his eyes gloomily to meet Ed's. Realization was written on his round face.

"Fifty cents for Bingo. That's his cut for helping." He set a pile of nickels aside. "And we have to send five dollars to the company we bought them from—we didn't make money," he said slowly, "we lost it. We're in the hole."

"What do you mean?" Charles's blue eyes were incredulous.

"We gotta pay the company, haven't we, you dope?" Freddie said. "Well."

Ed cleared his throat. The shade from the lamp veiled his eyes but the light fell on his mouth. I saw it move before he spoke as if he was undecided what to say. Then, "Well, about paying the company," he said, "don't worry too much about that. Matter of fact, the cards came collect. I just happened to meet the postman at the door. I took care of that. We can fix that all up later sometime," he said, talking rather fast and avoiding my eyes.

"It's awfully nice of you, sir," Charles said in his well-mannered English way.

"Yeah, well—" Freddie's gaze was still stricken. "Whoever paid it out, we did all that hard work for nothing. And we got to pay you, sometime. It's just like I told you, you have to be lucky, like Bingo with his uncle dying."

"But Bingo works hard, taking all those papers around," Ed said.

"Yeah, but that's no good without the breaks." Freddie's voice was doleful with disillusionment.

What with this and what with that, the boys' financial problems entirely left my mind, for a time. Certainly nothing was further from my thoughts, or indeed from theirs, when I turned toward home late one afternoon to see a straggling crowd gathered on our corner. A driving rain had come and gone and now a lemon light from the sky touched the faces of some score of men, women, and children pressing forward over what must be something at the edge of the curb. An accident? Ed? Freddie —Charles? I ran to the fringe of the crowd. "It's a poor little cat that was washed down the sewer by the rain," an elderly woman told me. I pushed forward, worming my way in.

On his knees, beside the sewer opening from which the grate had been removed, was Freddie. He was peering down and holding a length of clothesline that twisted slowly in his hand. Opposite him, Charles leaned dizzily over the cavity, shouting directions. Now the tipped corners of a cardboard box appeared above the level of the sidewalk. Clinging to it was a miserable scrap of kittenhood, its flattened fur dripping with muck. Its meowing was weak but fierce. I saw Charles press the little animal down within the high walls of the box as bystanders swung it securely onto the pavement. The crowd began to drift away.

"You can't leave that little half-drowned creature here, in this cold," a brisk female voice said. "It will die of exposure."

"We know a woman who will be glad to have it." Charles's voice was superior.

"My mother will let it live in our cellar," Freddie said.

I heaved a deep sigh. I had left Norah ranting a quarter of an hour earlier because the boys had taken her clothesline without so much as by-your-leave. How was she going to feel when it came back wet with sewer water and attached to a dirty half-drowned kitten? I brought up the homeward-bound procession well in the rear.

Thoroughly washed with brown soap and a hand spray, the kitten emerged no worse for her grueling experience. The boys were in constant attendance on her. She was persuaded to drink a little warm milk, and a small heap of old dusting cloths reluctantly given up by Norah was made into a little home in a warm corner. On account of Blimp, the newcomer had to remain in the cellar and it would be quite impossible to keep her permanently. But for the time being she was the little Pussycat Princess in person, rewarding a delighted retinue with tiny shakings of her paw, whisks of a fluffy blue-gray tail, and a purr loud out of all proportion to her size, a purr which even through her heavy hair made the tips of one's fingers tingle.

153

Word of the rescue spread and children trooped in all the next day to have a look at the heroine of the adventure.

And then just before supper the doorbell rang again.

"Run see who it is, Freddie," I said.

He came back into the living room followed by a pretty woman in a mink coat. I got a quick impression of luxury; smooth hair piled high by expert fingers, great jeweled buttons at the ears, a face that was a mask of expensive make-up. Through the window I saw a driver standing by the door of a waiting taxi. Rather astonishingly, the woman before me had a bath towel folded under one arm.

"I'm Angela Part," she said. "You've seen me, of course, in pictures. I'm appearing in person across the country for the bond drive. A Mrs. Morcisson tells me that your little boys saved a kitten from drowning in the sewer. I think she must be my Angelina. She ran out of the hotel in the storm and the bellhop couldn't reach her."

"Come and see." I led her to the cellar. Freddie and Charles followed, hostile-eyed and silent as Indians. Moving gracefully toward the small nest of rags, the woman swooped to the floor and picked up the bit of fluff and pressed it to her face.

"Angelina, darling," she said. "How could you run away and frighten your mommy so? If these children hadn't saved you I'd never have seen you again." She rolled the cat deftly in the Turkish towel and preceded us up the stairs, talking all the while to the bundle in her arms, from which a little heart-shaped face peered uncomplainingly out. We could even hear a rattling purr. Angelina knew on which side her bread was buttered.

We stood in the hall. I didn't dare to look at Freddie and Charles, cut to the heart, I knew, by the disappointment of losing their new pet so suddenly. I would comfort them when she was gone by telling them we would have had to get rid of the cat anyway. We couldn't have kept her in the same house with Blimp for long.

Just inside the door the lady in the mink coat reached into her pocket and, carelessly drawing out a bunch of bills, handed them to Charles.

"You little boys can divide this between you."

"No, no." I touched Charles's arm gently. "You mustn't give

154

them all that money. They don't need to be paid for saving a cat's life."

"But a Persian like Angelina is worth that five times over." The woman ignored the gestures with which Charles, obedient to my look, held the money toward her. "Why, her mother won any number of blue ribbons. Besides, Mother wouldn't know what to do if she really lost her little angel-face." She lifted the kitten and kissed the unresisting nose. The door closed behind her.

"Lemme see." Freddie tugged Charles's hand. They hurried in to the light of Ed's reading lamp. "Fifteen smackers! Holy gee!"

"What's all this?" Ed leaned forward.

"It's fifteen iron men," Freddie told him. "There's gold in them-thar sewers. I told you so. Getting the breaks is what counts."

"It's just like Norah said. It's luck that brings the money. Hey, Norah!" They ran pell-mell to the kitchen.

The evening paper sagged unread in Ed's hands. Slowly he shook his head.

"I give up," he said. "You train 'em. Because if fishing kittens out of sewers is a business, I'm nuts."

UP TO THIS YEAR, there had never been anything in Babs's life that a father couldn't fix. When as a little girl she got splinters in her feet, Ed pulled them out. At the time her tonsils were removed, he bought her her first ring, a tiny gold one with a turquoise heart. Once when she swam to a little island in the lake and was afraid to come back, he went after her, pacing his long stroke to her short one all the way home to the beach. When, in college, she got into an occasional jam financially, it was he who, over my protests, pulled her out with an extra check. "I guess Daddy can fix that," he would say comfortably.

Now the forces working against her happiness were too vast for Ed or any father to handle. When the Navy took George to sea and to war, we knew that Ed couldn't make things all right for her any longer. But being Ed, he could try!

The morning in question was a Saturday, and we sat at the breakfast table. Ed, who takes the serious part of the paper to read in the bus, as befits a man of affairs, was catching up, over his eggs, with the desperate doings of the characters in the comics. Freddie and Charles had already gone out. Eileen was parceling out bits of toast with jelly on top to Barbara Elizabeth. Barbara Elizabeth looked gravely at her mother and carefully turned each piece upside down. When she took a bite the ruby lumps slid down her bib. Eileen, who is patient, retrieved them with a teaspoon. Now Babs came in.

"Good morning, dear, you're late, aren't you?" I asked.

Babs slid into her chair, settling down like some big bright bird. She wore a brilliant green dress and over it a semimilitary jacket buckled tight at the waist. Her long, carelessly curled hair and the absence of any make-up, except a little lipstick casually applied, made her seem like a junior high school girl instead of an upperclassman at college.

"Keep your teeth in, Mother." Babs's voice was amicable. "Morning, everybody. Anything good to eat, Norah? I'm practically gnawing my fingers."

"Yes, and you have a letter." Norah set down a plate of fried eggs in front of Babs and then felt in her apron pocket, her face serious. She knows that Babs watches the mail slot like a cat at a mousehole.

"Let's have it." Babs's lips, an imperfectly colored geranium, blew a kiss toward the envelope. "O-o-o-oh." Her voice slid desolately down the scale. "It's just an old ad."

"Dick's letters come in bunches," Eileen explained, turning from Barbara Elizabeth but still holding a teaspoon high in the air.

"Bunches are fine. Bunches would be wonderful," Babs said, "but all I get is silence." She sprinkled brown sugar over her corn flakes.

Ed lowered his paper, scarcely suppressing a sigh. Ed has never accustomed himself to Babs's continuous patter of words. He would like to change her habit of talking so much, but doesn't quite know how. "If she'd only pipe down a little!" he had said one night after a party at our house and, chuckling unwillingly, he had repeated a remark he'd overheard. "That girl's got looks; personality—why, if she were only dumb, she'd have everything."

The telephone rang, out in the hall. It was a single long, insistent ring. Babs jumped up, taking the corner like a skater. In a moment her head reappeared, the instrument held to one ear. "Long-distance," she said in a low, thrilled whisper. "New York—Yes, this is Barbara Breton. *Yes.*" Her hand went over the transmitter. "It's a buddy of George's, a Mr. Syfax. He wants to come out from New York this morning to see me. O.K. if I ask him to lunch?"

"Of course," I told her. "We'd be delighted."

She put the telephone back on the table. "He'll be here about twelve. Isn't it too exciting?" For a moment the brightness in her face went out as if someone had turned off the light. "I wish it was George. Well, I've got to dash! I lost my best lipstick. I have to zoom down and get one right away."

"Awfully nice of this boy, whoever he is." Ed gathered up his papers. Now he, too, had to leave. "It's quite a gesture, spending two hours on the train just to see a friend's girl." He got up and walked around the table.

"It is; it's unusually nice." My mind was turning it over. "Come home for lunch, dear," I went on, abstractedly. "I'd feel a lot better if I had you here."

"I can't promise. I might, but I very much doubt it." Ed turned toward the door.

I called after him. "Hey, how about my good-by kiss?"

"But I just did kiss you!" He turned and smiled at Eileen. "Sometimes I wonder about Mommer," he said.

As Norah was hard at work on lunch I set the table, using the favorite yellow crockery which Ed and I bought in Italy years ago. As I did so, my mind gripped the hard fact that a friend of George's was making an extraordinary effort to see a girl who could mean little or nothing to him. Or did a few hours on a train seem trivial to a man used to steaming thousands of miles over the ocean? I wondered.

At a little after twelve Babs came in. It did not surprise me to find that Ed was with her. She poked her head into the dining room. "Your table looks simply beautiful." Babs exacts a good deal of effort from you but she always rewards you by appreciating the results.

The boys came in. Eileen gave Barbie her lunch and took her away for a nap. A bus thundered past, gathering momentum after its stop at our corner. Almost immediately the bell rang. Ed hurried to the door and threw it open.

I don't know what I expected to see; I suppose, subconsciously, I thought I'd see a fresh-faced, clear-eyed lad in a sailor suit, like the boys in the Navy posters. But the man who stood before us was definitely older. He was small, wiry, and yellow-skinned, either from malaria or China duty, or both. A pair of protruding ears gave him a cautious, inquiring look. He nevertheless produced an impression of warmth. Not genial, radiating warmth, like Ed's, but a glow shut up within him. I was very much drawn to him right away.

He stepped carefully over the threshold like one accustomed to lifting his feet over the high coamings on shipboard, and put out his hand. Ed took it. "Come in, come in. We're so glad to have you here."

"Glad to make your acquaintance." Mr. Syfax shook hands with us all. By now others in the family had joined us. He moved on to Babs. "You're just like your pictures."

Babs spoke to him almost shyly. "I suppose you're on the same ship, aren't you? Why couldn't he come home—I mean, couldn't he get any time off, too?" she amended hastily.

"I'll have to tell you about that." He withdrew his hand.

Catching Norah's signal I led the way toward the luncheon table. Somewhat diffidently he pulled out the chair indicated at my right and sat down.

But he did not tell her. Instead he went on, "George is quite a boy. He worked for me. I showed him the ropes. I really did."

And then, crouching over his plate, he began to talk about his experiences in Jap-occupied China before Pearl Harbor. He greatly entertained Ed, who is an ardent baseball fan, by describing how the Japanese played the game; their fondness for it and the way in which the man at bat, when a strike was called, took off his hat and bowed very low to the umpire. Next had come a long siege of malaria, after which he'd wound up on Atlantic duty. As he talked, he used his eyes, which were reddish-brown, as another might use his hands, for emphasis; peering sideways, rolling them upward, or suddenly hooding them with his yellowed lids as the mood of his narrative changed. They seemed to have an entity of their own; to be always watching, always reporting to the brain inside. That brain was careful. If he had come to say anything important, he would do so at his own time.

It was after a second helping of gingerbread and applesauce that he leaned forward and clasped his hands on the table. They were thin, work-worn, and strong. The ability to help was in them, like a potential caress.

"Mr. Breton," he asked, "I wonder if you and I—"

"Certainly." Ed rose at once. They went out into the hall.

"I could shake that guy," Babs said. "My gosh, you'd think he'd give a little. I certainly didn't invite him to lunch to hear how the Japs differ from the Dodgers. He doesn't even act as though he thought George was important." She reached for a cigarette and lighted it with an irritated gesture. "I guess George is just another sailor to him."

Eileen's steady eyes met mine for just a moment. Listening carefully, she had noticed, as had I, that the two men had stopped in the small room across the front hall which for want of a better word we call the office. Like me, Eileen was alarmed. I looked thoughtfully at Babs. Nothing has ever happened to frighten her, I thought; nothing in her life. Of course she isn't nervous. Why should she be?

"I guess you boys ought to be starting back to school." I spoke abruptly. An invisible hand squeezed my heart and the cords back of my knees ached with tension. What were they talking about? If only Ed would come back—

But he did not come back at once. Instead, he called Freddie and Charles. (Had he thought of school, it would not have mattered. Ed believes that sometimes education is where you find it!) "Come on in here, boys. Mr. Syfax has some Jap souvenirs to show you."

Had they gone to that room, he and this man, only to discuss souvenirs? Or—

Suddenly, however, I looked up and saw Ed in the doorway. He came in quietly and stood behind Babs's chair. He put out his hand and moved it over the curve of her head, over her soft hair. Then he said, "George has been hurt, dear."

"*Daddy!*" Babs jumped and stiffened electrically.

"The convoy was attacked," he went on slowly. "He got one of his legs pretty badly smashed up."

"Oh, *no*." I saw George dancing with Babs, cheek to cheek. My mind chanted the words, the song they had loved to dance to; "Brazil, Brazil, Brazil!"

"Daddy, where is George? Did Mr. Syfax tell you? Can I go see him?" Babs started up.

"Sit down," Ed said almost harshly. He turned away, pacing up and down the room. "Syfax doesn't know. George was moved to a bigger ship along with the rest of the wounded. That's *all* he knows." He picked up a fork and balanced it on his finger. He did not look at any of us.

160

Babs sank back. "But Daddy, he'll—George'll be all *right*, won't he?" she asked.

Ed moved his shoulders restlessly, as if shifting a weight. His mouth was working, framing words now, without a sound. His clear, gray-blue eyes seemed farther back in his head; they gleamed under the lids that fell over them in sharp folds. He put the fork down. Eileen broke the silence. "I'd better see if Barbara Elizabeth is covered up."

"Yes, do, dear." I lifted my glass nervously. The brilliant sunlight thrown back from the shaking surface of the water danced in a rainbow under the ceiling.

"This isn't going to be anything," Ed said. "Nowadays, they fix 'em up in no time. Sulfa drugs, modern surgery—it's not like the last war. Why, I'll bet a leg wound doesn't amount to a hill of beans any more."

Babs was sitting with her shoulders hunched forward, as if a cold wind were blowing on her back. Her great eyes were fixed on her father.

Abruptly he said, "I'd better put through a call to George's father. They may not know."

The Litchfields, he found, had received word. They had been waiting, hoping to get something definite before calling us. Mr. Litchfield had taken steps to learn more. "Let us know what you hear."

Ed swung away from the phone. "Better take care of your little girl," he told me. Without even saying good-by, he strode across the room and down the hall. We heard the front door bang behind him.

I pushed my chair back and opened my arms. What else was there to do? "Come here, dear." As if released by a spring, Babs was in them.

Her sobs shook both of us. How terrible it is to be young, I thought, as my hand traveled up and down the bright wool sleeve; when grief strikes the heart, the body, and the mind all in one, running through them like lightning, tearing you apart. I did not speak. I only gazed across her shaking form to the squares of empty sunlight on the shining floor.

And Babs had been told so gently. This little man had come so far that she might be gently told. I considered his kindness;

the kindness of a man at home in the deep waters of human feeling. Then I thought of Ed.

I knew what Ed was doing. He was ramming along the street somewhere with his hat pulled down over his eyes so he wouldn't have to speak to anyone, trying to get above that feeling of frustration, trying to accept the fact that when she most needed him he could not help his daughter. Why do men go *out* to fight their troubles? If Ed would just sit quietly in his room or throw himself down on the bed—at least I would know where he was. . . .

As if she had heard his name Babs suddenly stopped sobbing and lifted her head. She said, "I guess I'm not being a very good sport, acting like this. I guess that's what Daddy thinks."

"This has nothing to do with sportsmanship," I said.

Babs looked up at me. Her lashes and eyebrows were askew with tears. "I guess a lot of other girls are going through the same thing," she said, "and some of them a whole lot worse."

"The fact that other people are suffering doesn't make what's happened to you any easier to bear," I told her. "Maybe it does keep you from feeling you've been picked out by fate. But it doesn't make your suffering any less."

"But I'm not thinking of myself," Babs said. "It's George. I wanted everything in his life to be perfect, absolutely perfect. and now—" She stood up and ran her hands backward over her disordered hair, pushing it back from her wet face.

Suddenly I heard Ed, making an awkward business of coming in the front door. He opened it almost fumblingly. I held my breath. He came into the dining room holding a box, which had made handling the door difficult. His gray eyes were a little too dark, a little too bright, but the taut muscles of his face around his mouth had relaxed. Ed wore an air of peace.

He walked toward Babs, taking the cover off the box. "I brought you something."

He took out a bouquet of roses—red Jacqueminot roses—and stood holding them in his hand, like a little boy. Like a little boy he pushed the flowers toward her.

"Here!" he said.

"Oh, *Daddy!*" Babs's streaked face went down into the mass of petals as into a bowl of clear, cold water.

162

BABS WAS HOME for her spring vacation. When Ed put his head into the living room and called to Babs, "Someplace I never heard of is on the phone for you," I reached the door second only to my daughter. My aim, however, was not to go with her but to close the door. Five members of the family were sitting about within earshot. Anyone who suffers from the need expressed by the poet to "be alone with Heaven" is out of luck in our house. I meant to give Babs a break.

Ed dropped into his big chair and as he did so gave me the name of the place that had called. I stared down at him. "But that's the big new naval hospital," I told him. "Do you suppose —could George possibly be back in the country?"

"Might be." Ed too was frankly waiting. A silence fell that said we were all listening for news. My mind went over the little we knew about George's injury; a leg wound, suffered in action at sea, after which he had been hospitalized. That was all.

After what seemed an hour and was actually much longer than the "others are waiting" five-minute period desired by the telephone company, Babs came dreamily into the room. "He's landed," she said. "He's here. That was him. George! He sounded as if he was right in the next room."

"Babs!" Eileen jumped up. "When can you go to see him?"

"He says it's no use beating it down there; he's going to be moved any minute. They're sending him nearer home. Once he's there, he will be let out on a pass and can come to see *me*."

We gazed raptly at Babs; Eileen and I practically wet-eyed, Freddie and Charles evincing that intense interest devoid of any emotion characteristic of boys of their age, Ed with affection written on his face.

"Did he sound the same?" I asked.

"Did he?" Babs spun on a dime. "Oh, boy, oh, boy, oh, boy!"

The next morning, Babs, wearing a pair of slanting glasses with red rims which she removed in order to read better, consulted a letter in her hand.

"It's from my mother-in-law," she announced. "She wants me to spend next week end with them. Here's what she says. 'You and I have a lot to talk about, with our "hero" coming home.' I don't know why she puts quotation marks around hero; he certainly is one! Well, anyway, 'We'll be looking for you sometime Saturday. Affectionately, Madelaine.'" Babs bent her head belligerently. *"And I'm going."*

"Of course, you ought to." My mind went at once to details. "I'd wear your gray suit and take your green crepe. You can make the same accessories do for both."

Babs, who had turned to go, stopped in her tracks. She looked me up and down as if I were something she'd never seen before. "Mother, honestly. I just don't understand you. Here George is wounded and I'm going to his family and all you can think of is what I'll wear."

I defended my position. "You represent the family."

"George loves me the way I am," Babs said. "I hope his family does, too."

I couldn't resist the opening. "Has he ever seen you the way you are?" I asked pointedly.

But instead of continuing to argue Babs gathered me into a breath-taking squeeze. "I don't know," she said. "And I don't care. All I'm going to do from now till George comes home is just think and think and think about him."

As I freed myself I put my hands on her shoulders and her brown eyes met mine. I saw the brilliance in them. Partly with my mind but mostly with my heart I remembered. I remembered the glow that comes with being really in love for the first time; how one wakes in the morning unable to think at first what makes life so wonderful, the sense of apartness as one walks around the house and of kindness toward the people one sees inside it and out; the glory that rests on the street as warm air fills a tunnel; the whole careless enchantment over a world that has the other person in it. I decided to skip the maroon accessories.

Friday afternoon Ed and I drove Babs to the station. Through the car window I looked into the grimy waiting room. It was filled with men in uniform, girls with babies, solemn, anxious-looking old people. Suddenly I had a disturbing awareness of a country on the move. How lucky we were, I thought, that Babs was at home. Then I heard the hoarse, alarming hoot of the train that was carrying her away. I was glad when Ed climbed back into the car.

As if he, too, felt an undercurrent of alarm he put his hand over mine and said, "You're coming out to dinner with me."

After we had settled down in the pink and silver striped lounge of a downtown restaurant Ed said, "I've been thinking about George getting home. And I've been remembering a leave I had in Paris in the last war."

"Without me." I still felt a pang of envy.

"You weren't around, so I took an English girl out to dinner; damn good-looking she was, too." Ed grinned reminiscently. "I wanted everything to be gay and clean after the mud and dirt up at the front. I had to settle for a restaurant with dark red paper on the walls and awful lace curtains. Now this," he lifted his hand, "would have suited me perfectly. I was thinking," he went on slowly, "I'd fix it up for Babs and George to have dinner here, the night he gets home. This seems like the right place."

"The younger crowd likes a spot where you can dance," I told him.

Ed glanced at me oddly, "Not on crutches they don't." As if to soften the reproach he added, "Those places usually have a bar, and if there's one thing you can't stand after you've been overseas it's the sight of fat civilians pawing for the rail." He prepared to attack a formidable helping of duck lying amid black cherries. "They may not want to go," he finished, "but if they do they can. And I'll pick up a couple of tickets for the new musical show."

I considered Ed's intelligent face. It was heavier than when he took that Paris leave; heavier and much more lined. Some of the lines were put there by responsibility but most of them were the residuary marks of sure, recurrent tides of human feeling.

"You know," I said, "for just an old businessman, you have a lot of imagination. I think it's a wonderful idea."

Babs came back from the visit late Sunday evening. Had we known the time of her arrival we would have met her train, for in our family it is considered sort of mean to let anyone land unwelcomed; this has been true ever since the time when Dick as a small boy arrived home from camp unmet and later remarked, "I wouldn't of minded only last night we caught a porcupine and when I got off the train there wasn't anyone to tell." Babs dropped her bag in the front hall with a thud, entered the living room, and said in a low tone, "Hello."

"Hello." Ed put a small black notebook he had been consulting back into his pocket and smiled. "Have a good time?"

"Of course." Babs did not smile in answer. "What a funny question!"

Ed's eyebrows went up just a fraction of an inch. I thought it wise to open the all-important subject. "How is George?"

"Oh, fine. He called up both nights." Babs snapped her purse shut and then snapped it open again.

"Is he coming soon, or what?" Ed wanted to know.

"He's coming. He's going to stop off first and see his father and mother."

"He is?" Ed was surprised. That wasn't the way he would have managed it.

"Listen," Babs said, "I doped it all out with him on the phone when Madelaine wasn't there. We figure he can get away with just staying overnight at home and have the rest of the time with me until he has to go back to the hospital. I'm not so dumb. At least, not that way I'm not." Suddenly she rose and went upstairs.

"Do you suppose anything's wrong?" I asked Ed.

"Of course not," Ed said. "You're always imagining things." Ed took up his paper and dismissed the subject.

"Mother," Babs came into my room next morning as I was setting it to rights, "are you busy?"

166

"No," I said. "I can crawl under the bureau after Daddy's slippers some other time." I did not say it was a recurring mystery how they got there.

"I'll get them for you. Here." Babs handed them to me and sat down in front of the dressing table. The latter she regarded with dissatisfaction. "Madelaine has a lucite set with initials in black," she told me. "You ought to get one. But then, Madelaine's terribly up-to-the-last-minutey about everything."

Mentally I saw Babs's future other mother; slim, better than smartly dressed in lovely colors molded to perfect lines. I remembered her quick-witted patter. I tucked Ed's slippers into the shoe rack. I made no comment.

"She's so—so brainy," Babs said. "For instance, about George coming home. All I was thinking, dumb old me, was how wonderful it was he got off without being injured for life and now he was coming home and I could get my hands on him. I honestly thought that's all there was to it."

"Well, isn't it?" I asked. I sat down companionably.

"Oh, no." Babs was scornful. "The Returning Serviceman is a psychological problem. Madelaine took a course."

"A course?" I asked. "What kind?"

Sometimes Babs is as literal-minded as her three-year-old niece. "Is that fun?" I asked Barbara Elizabeth the other day as she swung on the nursery gate. To which she replied gravely, "No. It's a gate." Now Babs said, "A lecture course."

"What about?" I settled back to listen.

"I told you. The Returning Serviceman. It was on how to act when he gets home."

"Can't you just act the way you feel?" I asked.

"Goodness no!" Babs's feet were covered with bands of leopard-colored fur. She rubbed one toe over the other. "To begin with, you mustn't act as if you were watching him. All the same you've got to keep an eye on him all the time. Now how're you going to do that?" Babs crossed her eyes.

"Babs! You look like the idiot child," I told her sharply. "But maybe crossing your eyes would be the best method. What else did the lecturer say?" In spite of myself, I was interested. A son of my own was coming home from Italy, eventually, I hoped. I might learn something.

"Wait a minute, I took notes." She pulled a slip of paper from her pocket. "Oh, yes—and B, you're not supposed to ask him a lot of questions. Golly, it's good I found that out. I was going to make him tell me what happened every single minute since he went away."

I digested this. "Well, what's C?" I inquired presently.

"C is, you must try to act perfectly natural. That's what the woman said. How the heck can you act natural if you've got to *try?*"

"I don't know but I wouldn't worry," I told her. "He'll be the same old George."

"No, he won't!" Babs sat up very straight. "That's just the point. The woman says he'll be different. That's what scares me so." She turned her head away so that I could not see her eyes. "He's seen things; he's had an experience that was a very great shock; he'll be sort of numb to people back home who don't know what he's been through; he'll be numb to me."

"George? Numb? It doesn't sound like him," I said.

"You don't understand. He used to like just ordinary people like me. But now he'll be different. He'll be looking for the ones that can understand. And I don't want him to be different." Suddenly she plunged forward, throwing herself lengthwise across the bed. She lay with her head on her arms, her fur-tipped feet thrashing wildly in the air. "I want him to be just the same," she said.

On the following Saturday afternoon a taxi stopped before the house. I looked out idly, then with intense excitement I saw a crutch thrust through the opening door.

"Babs!" I sprang to my feet. "Babs, darling, run! It's George! He's coming up our walk."

She had been awaiting him all day; twirling the radio dial, dressing and then changing her whole costume; pacing the house. Now she was meeting him, out there in the hall. . . .

Five minutes later, he entered the living room. He was wearing the ordinary blues of a sailor. He came with a vital push, bringing a sense of freshness, like a change of wind at sea. In prewar days George was good at sports, used to rackets, ski poles; now he handled his crutches as if they were some such equipment, swinging rhythmically on them. It was hard to be-

168

lieve anything had happened to him, except for the inevitable deliberation of his gait, a seriousness in his eyes, and a deep, deep red over his face. Before I had time to wonder about that he took a hand from his crutch and held it out.

"How *are* you? You all look just about the same!" His smile was for me, for the boys near by, for the room; for the very pictures on the wall.

I indicated the couch. "Do sit down." Freddie sat astride a low stool. Charles took a pose with an elbow on the fireplace mantel. Babs, instead of settling down beside him as she once would have done, drew away a little, finding a small stiff chair.

Somewhat awkwardly I began, "Is there anything I could do for you, George? Can't I get you something? Maybe a cup of coffee?"

"Now, Mother." Babs shifted restlessly.

George brought his crutches to rest side by side and said, "Don't start spoiling me, like *my* mother."

"How is your mother?" It was a routine question.

But George's answer was not perfunctory. He studied the opposite wall. "Mother seemed changed, somehow," he said slowly. "Not herself. She was, well, I can only say unnaturally meek; pussy-footing all the time. Mother's not that kind, you know. If she'd had any real contact, I'd say it was a case of war nerves. Something's broken her spirit. I wasn't there long enough to get the data and figure it out."

Babs, her face unglowing, started to speak, but Freddie cut in ahead of her. "I'd be very interested to hear how you got wounded, and about the battle and all."

Babs clenched her hands into little fists and beat on her own knees. "Don't ask him to talk about it," she said, almost desperately.

George gave her a puzzled look. I thought he seemed a bit disappointed. But in answer to Freddie he remarked, "It's a long story, kid. Guess it would bore the rest of the family. You and I'll go over the ground some other time."

"I'm planning to join up with the Marines," Charles announced. "Next year when school's over; well, anyway, year after next." He had met my eye.

George's glance traveled up the lanky figure to the almost

childish face. In his warm voice he said, "There's no hurry!" There was a pause as large as a house.

It was at this point that Ed came in. Before George could get in motion Ed's hand was on his shoulder. "Well, well, well, how are you?" Ed's tone implied there was only one possible answer. He drew up a chair. "All ready to get out and have some fun, I'll bet."

"Daddy, *please*. . . ." Babs's voice was sharp with worry.

Ed ignored her. "I figured you'd just about be fixed to step out, you and Babs. I took a host's privilege of deciding for you what to do. I reserved a table for two for dinner, in the Vienna Room; it's our one good place, you know. And here." He reached in his pocket and brought out two bits of gray pasteboard. "These are for a new musical that's trying out here before opening on Broadway. They say it's a lulu. Here you are; two on the aisle." He held them out.

George's face was unreadable as he said in an almost muffled tone, "Thank you, sir."

Babs could contain herself no longer. "Daddy, I *told* you. You aren't to push George like that. Maybe he doesn't feel—maybe he won't want to see a silly Broadway show. Maybe he doesn't want to go anywhere *at all*." She stopped, almost in tears. It had cost her something, too, to make this gesture.

"Who, me? Not want to take in a theater? For Pete's sake, why not?" George turned to her with surprise all over his face. "Babs, what's got into you, acting like that when your father is giving us the party of the ages? Where's the old gratitude?"

"But George, I thought, I mean your mother and I were sure —we heard a woman talking. She gave a lecture and your mother went—"

George stared. Then slowly, so that you could almost see him doing it, he put the pieces of his home-coming together. It made a picture he could read.

A born trouble-shooter, George could deal with any difficulty once he knew what it was. He had got to the bottom of this; he could handle it.

His eyes rested on Babs with amusement and something far, far deeper.

"Come on, you mental Four-F," he said. "Where's your hat?"

CHAPTER

19

THERE IS NO DOUBT about it; the loyalty of men to some of their own kind can be extremely trying. Take any foursome of dreadfully dressed old codgers coming in from the last green and among them is bound to be one whose presence causes sighs of resignation among the wives. Yet as far as such a little closed corporation is concerned, no member could ever be replaced. Out of such durable affection, too, the fiber of heroism is made. ("We're taking this ride together," said the pilot of the plunging plane as he found his injured crewmate could not bail out.) Women who are both experienced and kind accept their men on these terms, knowing that real friendship, wherever found, is on the plus side of life.

But little girls are not experienced; and the loyalty starts back in days when boys are the age of Freddie, Charles, and Bingo.

I was sitting in the drugstore after a bout of marketing. I had taken Barbara Elizabeth with me; she takes terrific pleasure in pushing a double-decked wire basket down the long counters. We had returned her unrequested acquisitions—a dog-bone package, a five-pound box of candy—and now we sat side by side eating ice cream and watching the world go by.

Looking out, I saw Mary Lee come to the counter and buy a stamp. Not yet fourteen, she is a perfect example of the fact that if you have a certain something, you cannot muffle it. Like all her kind, however, she does her best. You got a glimpse of brief navy shorts; otherwise her costume apparently consisted of one garment, a huge man's shirt of faded blue; it hung as shapeless as your grandfather's nightshirt used to. Her shining honey-colored hair was half hidden under a kerchief. Below

171

this drooping and witchlike headgear her face was all rose and tan and her steady eyes were the shade of high-bush blueberries.

I leaned out of the booth. "How about having something with us?"

"Oh, Mrs. Breton! I didn't see you. Gosh, that would be simply super." She slid into the seat opposite. "Hi, Barbie!"

Barbara Elizabeth ate two mouthfuls, then, aware of the amenities, said gravely, "Hi."

I ordered for Mary Lee. Something based on a banana and complete with chocolate and a cherry came. "Now," I said, "bring me up to date. What's going on?"

"Hasn't Mother told you?" Mary Lee's spoon paused in surprise. "I guess she hasn't had a chance yet. Well, Jane (she's my cousin) is coming out from New York Saturday and Daddy is giving me a party. We're going to the circus. I'm taking the boys and Sally (she's my oldest and dearest friend), and we're to have a box right down in the front row. The kids usually come by here, afternoons. I was going to tell 'em." She looked the length of the window, beyond the counter. There was no one in sight.

"How old is Jane, exactly?" I asked.

"Fifteen and a half. And she's very ultra." Mary Lee sighed. "All she talks about is plays she's seen and men she knows. You know how *we* kids are. We just gab. I've decided to ask Stewie Turnbull for her."

This should have given me the picture. I was occupied, however, with the appearance of my own Freddie and Charles coming along toward the entrance; and appearance is just what I mean. I thought I had seldom seen less attractive figures. Freddie, once fat, is now a solid slab under a dishrag shirt and shrunken dungarees. His socks curl like dead leaves over tennis shoes handed down by Ed, although Ed doesn't know it. Charles goes in for shorts at the top of his long thin legs. He now wore a sort of crew shirt with the name of a distant airfield printed on it. I never found out how he came by it.

"Hi!" "Hi!" they said right after each other just like that. They came up to our table. "How about moving over?" Freddie sat down and gave Mary Lee a friendly dig of the elbow.

Charlie went for a chair and not until then did I notice Bingo

Brown hanging around near the door. There is nothing about Bingo to attract attention. His clothes are grayish and carefully mended and without the extraordinary style, peculiar but undeniable, of the other boys' shorts and dungarees and queer shirts. But you glance a second time at his face. His eyes, once beady and fierce, are warm and have an intense concentration. His alert, unsmiling mouth is alive in every line. He is ill at ease with older people and even after years of eating cake at our house he never seems to see me if he can help it.

"Ask Bingo if he wants a chocolate malted," I told Charles. A decision in advance would do away with the agony of talk; and anyway I was quite familiar with his preferences as to flavor.

Given the word by Charles, Bingo pulled over a stool and sat perched on it. We did not come within his line of vision.

To start the ball rolling I began rather stupidly, "Mary Lee was telling us about the circus."

For just a second Mary Lee's eyes met mine and I saw something like panic in them. She glanced up sideways at Bingo. But then she went smoothly on.

"Daddy saw it in New York last year. He says there's a horse that dances; he's all black with a white harness and he doesn't *follow* the music. He leads the band with his front paw."

"Hoof, dimwit," Freddie told her.

Unexpectedly, Bingo spoke. He stared between us, at a spot on the wall. "The big cats are best. You can't tame 'em. They put women in the cage while the act is on. They'd eat 'em up if the men didn't prod 'em back; this guy was telling me." He continued to look into space, his mind captivated by the idea of the leopards who would eat the beautiful women alive.

There is something compelling about Bingo. Against your will, almost, his imagination carries you as in a current. I, too, saw the big cats— "Have you ever seen them?" I asked.

"I sorta helped take the cages off the train, one time. I just happened to be down at the freight yards." He shot a glance at me which I was careful not to meet. "You'd be surprised how they smell. I saw the elephants too; about a hundred, I guess, all tied in a field. They rocked all at once, like crazy. I might get a job there and see it this year. I dunno."

Mary Lee moved uneasily. "Gosh, I just remembered. I gotta be home. Gee, thanks just loads, Mrs. Breton! Hey, let me out of this firetrap, Freddie, will you?" She shoved.

Freddie saved himself with an exaggerated clutch of the end of the table. Mary Lee was on her way.

Too bad about Bingo, I thought. This will hurt him; he's a boy who wants things so intensely. I did not like to think about it.

The bridge table was set out in the Smiths' living room. Ben, the best of hosts, found me an especially comfortable chair while Margery fussed about bringing up a battery of smokes and ash trays. She sat down at my right, quite silently. This was unusual, but I did not notice her quietness. I had a tricky hand and all my mind was on the playing of it.

During the scoring she turned to me. "So Freddie and Charles have gone high hat on us," she said.

"They have? How come?" Gossip about our respective children is the idle table talk at every bridge session.

"Mary Lee called up Freddie before supper to ask him and Charles to a party for Jane," Margery said slowly.

"I'll say she did," Ed broke in. "I had the boys at the Club trying for half an hour to get in on our wire."

Ben grinned. " 'Others are waiting' doesn't mean anything to her."

But Margery did not smile. "I must have picked the wrong form of entertainment for your sons." Her voice had a bit of an edge to it.

"But they've been simply wild to see the circus." I put down the cards I was studying. "You can't mean they refused the invitation!"

"But they did." Margery lit a cigarette. Then, "That's just what they did."

Ben glanced quickly at us in turn. His face showed surprise and something else, too. But all he said was, "Somebody might have told me, before I bought that box this afternoon."

"But of course Mary Lee was so sure Freddie and Charles could go. It never occurred to me," Mary Lee's mother went on. "Stewie is away; he'll be back Saturday, though. I don't know how he'll feel about it when he finds he's the only man," she added wryly. "We'd have all girls if it weren't for Jane."

"Could the boys be scared of Jane, do you suppose?" I was still trying to figure it out. "Mary Lee's the only girl they ever see."

"I don't know. They argued a long time. Mary Lee wasn't at all communicative. She knew we were all playing bridge tonight and she is always so afraid we'll talk over her affairs and I'll tell something I shouldn't."

"I wonder why." Ben's voice was a little grim.

"All she did was ask me not to tell *you*," Margery finished.

I tried to get an appeal for help across to Ed. Why didn't he say something? But he continued to look restlessly from the ash tray to the cards and back again. If he wouldn't help, I would. I announced, "I'll fix it. I'll make them go; both of them."

"I'd a little rather you didn't, Elizabeth." Ben spoke. He kept his eyes on a burned place at the edge of the table. The four fingers of his right hand drummed nervously beside the spot. His mouth went on working as if he were making words but they did not come out.

Mary Lee is his darling and I realized, belatedly, that he could not tolerate the idea of any boy being *required* to go out with her. To him, an invitation from her was a wonderful break for any lad, whoever he might be. I saw, too, that this sort of thing could get worse. Tension over children may be too much even for friendship to stand.

Ed felt the strain, too. "My idea," he said comfortably, "is there's some joker attached we old folks don't know about. I agree with you, Ben. Let the kids work it out themselves. I'm sure of one thing: no son of mine would be fool enough not to jump at the chance to go out with Mary Lee. I wish I was young enough to be in the running myself." He smiled warmly at Ben. And he meant what he said. Next to his own children he likes Mary Lee best.

In spite of Ben and Ed, however, I decided to go to the mat for Mary Lee. At sixteen one may have a reserve list of masculine acquaintances. At fourteen minus, one has the gang one knows intimately, or no one. Jane, from New York, made the presence of boys all-important. Mary Lee's prestige was at stake.

Therefore when I heard the occasional sound of voices from the sleeping porch the next day, I marched determinedly out. Freddie was there, playing gin rummy. But it was not Charles opposite him; it was Mary Lee. They sat cross-legged on the rough blanket of Ed's and my bed, the cards between them. Both of them looked at me and then away again as if they had seen nobody.

With an odd sensation of being invisible, I went into my dressing room and closed the door halfway. I put on a dressing gown instead of my suit and lay down. Idly, I considered something Mary Lee was wearing: a gingham shirt of really devastating plaid in reds and greens; outsize, as usual. It rang a bell in my mind.

Through the open door their voices reached me. They had evidently stopped playing to argue. Mary Lee's tone was reasonable, even placating. "What's the matter with Stewie, I'd like to know? I gotta ask him for Jane. He goes to boarding school and Jane likes that sort of a man."

"He's a stinker," Freddie came back. "That's all. His family *had* to send him away. Nobody here'd go round with him. Sissy-pants Stew."

"He is not," Mary Lee said indignantly. "And there isn't just any comparison between Stewie and Bingo Brown as a person for a party. I don't see how you can even *think* of them in the same breath."

So this was it. Suddenly the whole thing stood out clearly before me. Freddie and Charles had decided Bingo was to be the third boy. As if putting my thoughts in words Freddie said, "But Bingo goes round with me and Charlie." There was no hint of argument; he stated a simple fact.

"Listen, dope," Mary Lee said, "my cousin Jane is used to men around sixteen and seventeen. I don't want her thinking *I* go with brats like Bingo. Take our class party." She warmed to the telling. "Every time the teacher shoved him on us girls at the class party he told us about the time he saw some men dissect a cow. Well! He doesn't even know how to *talk* to girls. He's never been around; Stew has."

"*Ask* Sissy-pants," Freddie said calmly. "Charlie and I won't be there; so he won't have any competition."

"But he isn't enough, all alone." Mary Lee was close to tears. "And you won't even *try* to be nice."

"It's just like I told you; Bingo goes 'round with me and Charlie; we all go 'round together. And Bingo'd ought to be asked."

"Freddie Breton, I guess I can invite who I want to to my own party." There was a scuffling sound followed by a thud as Mary Lee hit the deck. She came pounding through my room. Her unseeing gaze went over me and on. She tore off the plaid shirt, revealing a halter underneath, and flung it on a chair. She pulled both lips in, until the edges of her mouth formed a firm angry line. Now she ran from the room, down the stairs, and out of the house. I saw her racing across the lawn as she set out for home.

I rose and faced Freddie as he came in and tried to pass. "Now, listen to me, Freddie Breton," I began.

He resorted to an art of which he is master. He opened on a side issue. "I never said she could take Dad's shirt. We just happened to be looking in his drawer; she was crazy about the plaid one and she *made* me let her try it on." He edged toward the hall door.

Of course! It was the new shirt Ed had bought to wear out at the lake. If I'd only thought quickly enough—Mary Lee felt so badly and I knew Ed loved her and would, quite literally, give her the shirt off his back. I pulled my mind up with a jerk; Freddie's ruse had almost succeeded.

"Never mind about the shirt," I said sternly. "You have no right to tell Mary Lee who she can have at her party."

Freddie shoved a chair in front of him. "She'd ought to have her head examined."

"*I* think it's very selfish of Bingo to *let* you refuse on his account."

Freddie stared at me. "What do you think I am? He doesn't even know there's going to *be* a party. But she can't have us without Bingo."

"Of course she can!" But something inside me shriveled under the scorn of his onion-colored eyes.

He gave the chair a violent poke. He said, "You and Mary Lee both, you just haven't got any imagination!"

The next day was one of the most uneasy that ever passed me by. Almost invariably Margery calls me sometime before lunch for what she designates as the morning laugh. We regale each other with the funny things that happen daily in a household, or discuss the events ahead and what our two families are going to do about them. But I did not hear from her; and somehow I could not call her up. I was really sick about the whole affair.

Friday afternoon came. I finished the job of marketing again and once more went into the drugstore. In a few moments, and not all by accident, I felt sure, Mary Lee sauntered in again and up to the stamp counter.

I began to see a rhythm and order to her comings and goings. I felt sure the boys would arrive soon. "Hello, Mary Lee. How about having something with me?"

"Gee, Mrs. Breton, that would be simply super." Mary Lee, who never nurses a grudge, beamed as she came toward me.

"Here you are, Mrs. Breton." The clerk put a glass on the counter. "Freddie just went out of here." He did not even glance at Mary Lee; yet I knew the information was given for her benefit, not mine. "He and Charlie, they're out helping Bingo Brown deliver orders for us. Well, what'll it be?"

"Can I have a double strawberry cone?" Mary Lee did not climb up beside me. Instead, she stood freewheeling, as it were; ready—

And now Bingo Brown was coming in the door. As usual, his intense brown eyes were fixed on a spot beyond our shoulders. He appeared not even to see Mary Lee and me. Freddie and Charles stood out on the street, backs to us.

"'Scuse me, Mrs. Breton." Mary Lee went after Bingo in the direction of the back counter.

The clerk appeared from behind the high rear shelves. "Better step on it; there's a very sick child at this address." He held out a single package.

"Wait a minute, Bing!" Mary Lee was hurrying back with him through the store. "I want to ask you something—would you like to go to the circus tomorrow night? With Daddy and me and Freddie and Charles and Sally? Want to?" Her voice was soft, almost pleading.

Bingo gave her a brief glance. It was almost as if he noticed her for the first time. But all he said was, "Charlie and Freddie going? I didn't hear nothing about it."

"I don't guess they realize they're going. But they will!" Mary Lee held her cone like one lifting a torch. "You tell 'em; you kids all come by my house after supper, Saturday."

"O.K." Bingo's tone was level. Suddenly he studied Mary Lee. Then he headed for the boys, to whom he was to take the word. His voice hit an upper clef, dived a whole octave, plus a half note, then slid up again. "O.K.!"

He went out. The three boys moved away together without looking back, sauntering, ever so slowly, toward the house of the very sick child. I saw my son Freddie clasp his hands and shake them, high in the air, after a manner of one who wins a fight in the ring.

Mary Lee climbed to the stool next to mine.

"Well, I guess you heard," she said. "I had to have Bingo, after all." She paused. "The way I figure it, Stewie's never going to be anything in my life and Jane'll go back to New York. But I gotta *live* with Freddie!" She sighed deeply and fell to her ice-cream cone.

PERHAPS IF I hadn't been tired I wouldn't have gone so far off the beam about the committee meeting. But Norah's cousin had picked that time to have her baby and Norah was off taking care of the older children. For a week I had been cooking for a family of six; seven, including three-year-old Barbara Elizabeth. So when Margery asked me to entertain the War Activities Committee in her place, I took it hard. Ben's mother, it seemed, was coming unexpectedly on a visit. Margery was anxious about this meeting because now that the war news was so good everybody was sort of sitting back, just when they ought to be out raising money. It would make a lot of difference if the committee could be gathered together in the right spirit.

"I suppose they'll have to be fed," I offered. "What do they like?"

"Good food and plenty of it." Margery was glib. "Mrs. Morcisson's the chairman, you know, and when she had them before the drive last year, everything was done in silver and lavender. Even the little cakes had lavender icing and silver candies on top. But I don't think that's *essential*." She stopped to giggle. "I'd do whatever is easiest," she finished unrealistically. "If it's at your house, it's sure to be lovely." She hung up.

The meeting was scheduled for Saturday at three. Friday morning I lingered at the breakfast table with Ed and my daughter-in-law to discuss plans. The boys had gone off with the other Missing Links; Babs was not down yet. Ed was behind the paper. The sunlight fell in golden rectangles across the floor; breakfast had been good; I really felt pretty cheerful about the whole thing.

"I'm going to keep it simple," I told Eileen. "I'll have plenty of iced coffee. We'll order the ice cream from the drugstore. I'll make the cup cakes."

Ed lowered his paper. "Are we winning the war with cup cakes?" he asked with a grin.

"They help," I said contentedly. "And anyway, dear, we have this pretty house and the nice things and I like a chance to show them off once in a while."

"I know you do." Ed came by me and put his hand on my hair. "And why shouldn't you?" He went to the front door. Inside it, Barbara Elizabeth was riding a rocking horse. It had a black and white head, a blue plank body, and a pink plank seat. It was prettier than the ones our children used to have— prettier and far less substantial. She was singing loudly, inaccurately, and off key an old song she had heard at a birthday party. "The barmer in the dell," she shouted, "the barmer in the dell . . ." The rocker slatted on the hardwood floor. And now she saw something; something the postman was putting through the slot. Her voice floated up. "The door caughted a letter!"

Ed came back with it. It was marked "Free" but we knew at once it was not for Eileen; hers always bore air-mail marks. It was for Babs, from George in the naval hospital.

"Better put this away in asbestos until Babs comes down." He laid the letter on the table. For a minute he stood looking down at me. "And don't wear yourself all out getting ready for those people," he said. "You know Mother," he smiled at Eileen. "You'd think company was going to peek into every corner in the house!" He kissed me on the mouth and went out.

I was standing on top of the stepladder in the pantry taking out the best plates. Out in the kitchen Babs was plunging the breakfast dishes into a mound of foam.

Ed came into the pantry. "Oh, *here* you are! Don't forget about my bridge game," he said. "We're playing here this afternoon, you know."

"Oh, Ed, you *aren't?*" I pivoted on the top step.

"Hey, look out! You'll fall!" He steadied me. "I don't have to go down to the plant today," he went on as if that were good news. "I'll be around to give you a hand."

I began the nervous job of taking the tall glasses off the shelf and going backward down the stepladder with them. As I felt for the next step, my foot touched Ed. There he was again! He was holding up a bunch of letters and printed matter.

"What'll I do with these?" he asked.

I peered around. "Where did you get them?"

"Off your desk. Just tidying up for you." He stood looking up at me.

There was a ring at the back door. "It's the ice cream." Babs was there, now.

I opened the refrigerator and stacked it in, like giant dominoes. "I put all the cup cakes in here, too, on cookie sheets, so the maple frosting will harden," I told her.

"I'm sure you did, my pet," Babs said. "It sounds just like you." She glanced at the clock. "Gosh, I didn't know it was so late. Mind if I just go up and run a comb through my hair? George is coming sometime this morning; didn't I tell you?" She saw a look of concern cross my face. "Don't worry, he'll only be here for lunch. He's taking me out to dinner tonight." She bolted up the back stairs.

He'll only be here for lunch. I took Babs's place at the sink. In it, the handle of a frying pan stuck out like a spar from a sunken ship.

It's their offhandedness that's so hard to take, I thought as I polished the porcelain. And their pace is different. Today I wanted everyone to drive hard toward one end—the party at three. Instead, one by one, they were drifting away on their own affairs. I would have felt better if, as Barbara Elizabeth sometimes does, I could just scream with frustration. When, a few minutes later, I almost fell over Barbara Elizabeth waiting in the hall for her mother, and she came back to my "Darling, you're in my way" with an indignant "It's *not* your way, it's my way," it seemed to me she had put into words what was practically the slogan of every member of the family.

Now the doorbell sounded once more. I hurried along the hall, sure that I knew that tentative ring. It would be the twins.

But Babs was ahead of me and it wasn't the twins; it was George.

"No crutches!" Babs was looking out through the screen door.

"No, only this gadget." George waved a heavy, rubber-tipped cane. He looked very handsome, very fit. "Please, lady, can I come in?"

"You sound like the small fry."

Now he was in the hall and Babs was under his free arm. I welcomed him and then went back to the pantry. Well, Babs must definitely be counted out. I had the table to set. I mustn't forget to fix up the sewing room. The bridge game would have to go on up there.

At last everything was done. The table stood lovely to look at, with its lace cloth, decorative plates, and gleaming silver. I had sent the boys to the drugstore for sandwiches for all, and the crowd was fed. Next I moved mounds of unmended clothing from the sewing room and set out cards on the card table there, and glanced around, rather proud of my efficiency.

Ed poked his head in the door. He saw the cards. "Oh, it's too bad you bothered," he said. "We're not going to play, after all. Ben Smith thinks he ought to stay home and entertain his mother. Listen." He took the chair from my clutch. "You've been ramping around since dawn with a dustcloth in the hand and fire in the eye. Go upstairs and lie down a little while before you dress." And because any answer I could make would have choked me, I obeyed.

A relaxing bath, a short bout with hairbrush and lipstick, however, and I felt better. In fact, I felt wonderful. I consulted my watch. Twenty to three. Time now to take out all the little cakes and arrange them in the four tall compotes set out for them in the pantry. I ran down the back stairs and went at once to the refrigerator.

Before the open door I fell back aghast. The pasteboard boxes still stood in rows but from them a pinkish-brown liquid now dribbled slowly to the shelf below. Under it, the cakes lay in a sodden mass. I stood numbed, tied to the spot.

"Oh, *here* you are." It was Ed's cheerful voice. "I defrosted your refrigerator for you. I noticed last night it needed it, so when the bridge game was called off—" He stopped. He had seen the sticky ruins of the party food. "Oh, darling, gee—gosh, I'm sorry. I knew you had a basket of ice for the coffee down cellar—I never thought—I'm—I'm *so* sorry."

"Couldn't you have *asked* me?" My tone was frozen.

"Take the people to the hotel." He tried to sound nonchalant. "Send the bill to me."

"How can I? Don't be ridiculous." I stood like stone.

Ed moved uneasily. "I've said I'm sorry. I don't know what more I can do." His head went up. "Good Lord, what's that?"

The crashing sound came from the dining room. We ran there.

A cascade of spoons lay across the rug. Beyond them was a pile of shattered china. The lace cloth, caught in the pointed rocker of the horse, was pulled half off the table. Beside its folds, Barbara Elizabeth sat very still in the pink saddle.

Eileen was coming, on the run. "Mother *told* you," she began. "I *said* you weren't to go in there."

Barbara Elizabeth looked at no one, as if, that way, no one could look at her. She was too frightened at what she had done to cry. Her face puckered up.

"She didn't mean to." Ed leaned over and curved his hand over the back of Barbara Elizabeth's head. As if his touch had released her, she began to rock again, backing away from the table.

"Of course she didn't but couldn't *one* of you have kept an eye on her?" I asked despairingly.

"She won't do it again." Ed spoke as much to her as to me.

Both Babs and Eileen were on their knees, picking up the debris. George, from the living room, was calling to the baby, "Here, horsie, come here!"

We might have been alone, as Ed looked wistfully at me and said, "We won't do it again, either of us."

It was as if for me too Ed had loosened something that was under unbearable pressure. Utterly unexpectedly to myself, I burst into violent tears.

Now Ed did not hesitate. He took me in his arms. He patted my back. Because he would let me, which was rare, I cried unrestrainedly onto his tweed shoulder.

184

At last he lifted my head. "Better pull yourself together. I hear someone at the hall. It's probably the first of your guests." He poked a few hairs into what he thought were their places.

But it was Margery. "Anybody home? I came around to help. Hi, Babs." Her voice, with the lift in it, rose. "*George!* Nobody told me!" Her glance fell on Eileen and Babs, on their knees in the dining room. "Hello, girls, playing horsie?" she asked.

Now I would have to tell her everything. I walked slowly into the living room.

Not for nothing, however, have I had a best friend in Margery Smith for twenty-odd years. She had seen my eyes, red with what I honestly believed to be disaster. She saw Ed, looking, she told me later, as forlorn as a young husband pacing the hall of a maternity hospital. She did not know what was wrong, but she knew it was something and she acted.

She took a step toward George and turned her face up. Her own thirteen-year-old daughter could not have done it more adoringly. She said, slowly, "I've got the most stupendous idea." Her pretty, round face under its ruff of blond hair was very earnest. "These people who are coming—George," her voice could not have been more blatantly coaxing, "would you make a little speech?"

"Hey, Mrs. Smith, have a heart!" George fell back, alarmed.

"Just because something happens, and Mother's upset—" Babs was beside him now, and because she was angry she turned on me. "You're not going to exploit George. Honestly, Mother—"

But Margery, having known Babs from the bassinet, felt free to ignore her. "A hero would be very useful at this point," she offered.

"Listen, Mrs. Smith." George backed away some more. "I am not a hero. I am a guy who unintentionally put out his foot and stopped some ammunition." Then because George is always in command of the situation he shifted the talk. "Who are these people, the ones who are coming?"

To my surprise it was Ed who answered. "Just the female of the species 'civilian,' " he put in. "The salt-of-the-earth citizens who are trying in their dumb way to stand behind you."

185

A certain coldness slid off George's face. It slipped off as if he had removed a mask. I could have hugged Ed. George said, "They do, sir. Wherever you go anywhere in the world, if you're an American you feel the strength of your country behind you. When you come home, it meets you here."

He walked around in a circle, then paused. His eyes went from Ed's face to mine and then to Babs. "I could tell you about one little thing somebody raised the money for." He stood looking into space as if he saw something we did not.

"They evacuated us by plane," he said. "This boy with me— he was so young you'd never believe it, but he had three children. The oldest was a little curlyhead of four. He was—well, he was just the core of this sailor's life. The mother'd written he was very ill—a bad case of scarlet fever; since then he hadn't heard. It would jerk your heart to see him, lying there, just glaring at the bottom of the bunk above him—"

"We put in at the Azores. He hadn't expected that delay, and it sort of made him wild. . . . Well, the nurse and I talked about it. She knew the ropes all right. We were taken to a big base hospital after we reached the States. We'd hardly hit our bunks when up comes the nurse and says, 'How would you like to call your home out in Texas?' And with that, the corpsman plugs in a cord and hands him a white French phone."

George stopped and smiled down at Babs.

"Go on," she urged. "What happened?"

"He put in the call. He lay there—his bed was out in the aisle in the center of the ward—in his pajamas, sort of curled up around that phone as if it were something alive. He kept talking into it, kind of low. . . ." Abruptly George walked to the window and stared out.

"What about the little boy?" I said at last.

"Oh, he was fine. Somebody raised the money for that 'phone call," George finished. "I guess I could tell them about that."

Ed's eyes met mine. His were suddenly very, very dark. And now like sinking stones, the unimportant things of life fell out of sight, into their unimportant places.

"There's the bell!" Babs ran forward, as George, his young face oddly tender and oddly stern, turned and stood facing the door.

CHAPTER

21

BEING A WOMAN, I tell what I have to tell all in a rush, any time, anywhere. A man's thoughts come out late at night, like mice. If I hear Ed's, it is when I am relaxed yet attentive too. It's not that his thoughts are mouselike, but they keep the same hours.

One night at about eleven I brought a bowl of fruit and joined him in the living room. Ed was talking. He was saying, "I got it back today."

I quartered a pear. "Got what back, dear?" I asked.

"I just told you . . . a hundred dollars I loaned a man who used to work for me, years ago; quite a nice little sum to get out of the blue. I put it in our joint bank account."

"That's good." I sighed. "We'll have to outfit Babs to marry George before too long. We'll need it."

Ed's eyes narrowed. He looked almost appraisingly at me. "We're always shelling out for the kids," he said at last. "I thought this time we'd get something for ourselves; something for our wedding anniversary." He put his hand out, palm up.

I fitted mine into it. There is this about Ed's hand; it carries a strong current. Once that current was strange, unpredictable. It used to short-circuit my heart. Now it was familiar, powerful but steady, and in the strongest sense of the word, consoling.

"Let's do that," I said. "It's only a few weeks off." Then I asked him softly, "Do you remember the night we were married?"

"Sometimes you say the darnedest things." He did not let go of my hand, but I felt his thoughts shift as if they were on

187

a track to which I was sensitive. I did not know their exact direction.

"What'll we buy?" I went on after a while.

"Does it matter? We'll think of something." He released my my hand and reached for his pipe.

In the throes of Saturday marketing I put the fund in the back of my mind. But I got around at lunch to telling Babs and Eileen about it. Already it was burning a hole in my mental pocketbook.

Babs put down her glass of milk. "Isn't that a coincidence." She eyed me speculatively. "There are a couple of matched traveling bags downtown that cost just that. They're some sort of blond leather. You could buy them, chum, and I could borrow them for my honeymoon."

I smiled. "I think Daddy wants it to be something for him and me."

"Pardon *me!*" Babs pursed her lips. "Of course I wouldn't know about love; I'm only engaged. Then what *are* you going to do with the money?"

I hesitated. My plans did not sound glamorous. "I *was* thinking of reupholstering the big couch in the living room."

Babs's hands fell from the table. "A pretty summer day and all that dough to spend and you're going to repair a horrible old piece of furniture. I give up." She shook the catsup bottle vigorously, eliciting a few berry-colored drops. "How about a little imagination; how about a knockout clip, with earrings to match? Or a big yummy alligator purse with globs of tortoise shell on it? Then, at least, you'd *have* something."

"I'd grab this chance to redo the couch." Eileen understands how I feel about the house.

"Don't worry," I assured her, "that's just what I'm going to do."

The main job that afternoon was getting some used clothing for the destitute of Europe down to the collection center. I put it in the car and drove to the unrented shop. It was just across the street from our one big sporting-goods store. As I came out of the center, I saw Ed standing just inside the door over there. I joined him.

"Hello," he said. Then, "Why, hello!"

188

I told him why I had come down and went on, "What are we doing in here?"

"We're looking at things."

An elderly clerk came forward. I felt it wasn't the first time Ed had been in that day. The clerk preceded us at once to the back. Standing on its edge, like a wheel, was a big octagonal affair. Its rim was a trough of dark wood, its hub a plane of green felt. It was, in short, a de luxe poker table.

"Pretty nice, isn't it?" Ed asked. "There are some chairs that go with it too. I don't suppose it's mahogany, but it looks like it."

I stared in silence at this enormous gadget.

"Nobody's got anything like it." Ed was talking happily. He went on, "I bet Fred Beard and Ben Smith will get a kick out of this; and so will Bill."

So that was it. Our anniversary present to each other was to be this thing that Fred and Ben and Bill would get a kick out of. Where I came in I did not see. I stood without speaking.

Now Ed glanced at me. Something gay in his face went slowly out. He turned to the clerk. "Well ... we'll think this over."

"Just as you say, Mr. Breton. But it's the last one." The man moved off, his interest in us slackening like a loosened rope.

We drove home in silence. Ed concentrated on the road and I was engaged in building up something which already was big enough to cast a shadow.

It wasn't as if Ed really cared about poker; bridge is his game. If he got this table the children, instead of bringing their friends around, would go out, all of them. Who wants to sit around a living room in which seven men are seated all back-to? Worst of all, it meant my hopes were blighted. My plans had enlarged. This money was going to treat the couch and a couple of the big chairs as well to really good-looking slip covers. It would simply make over the room. Well, I could just forget all that in favor of something for the boys!

Once at home, I went up to our room and stood looking out as from a cage. Beyond the sleeping porch the leaves of the pear tree were a dark and confused pattern. I felt confused and dark too.

The door behind me opened and Ed came in. He stopped short in the middle of the room. "What's the matter with you?" he asked.

I was careful about my voice. "Well, it's nice we're going to spend that money on a poker table for Fred and Ben and Bill."

"You'll like it too, you know you will." His tone was light. "We might even let you play once in a while, if you're good. Anyway, you can sit there with us all the time."

I swung about. My eyes felt hot and heavy as I lifted them. "I don't have to leave the room?"

He chose to treat this as a joke. "Only to get us ice."

For an instant our glances locked. Then to my horror the muscles of my face went out of control pulling it awry. Ed turned to his dresser and stood lifting the brushes up and down.

As if it was someone else, I heard myself saying, "Pushing the children out of the house and their friends too; and nobody for me to talk to. I don't want to be married to somebody who plays poker every night."

"Who said I was going to play every night?" Ed strode back and faced me. "I never heard anything so silly in my life. I wish you could be married to a couple of other men I know."

"One is enough!" Almost, I laughed.

But Ed did not laugh. As the tide of my anger ebbed a little it began to fill him. He walked nervously to the window, then turned and went quickly out of the room. I was alone until I went down to supper.

The evening was oddly quiet. Everyone was out, everyone but Ed, that is, and he busied himself with the radio and a magazine.

After a late news program he put down his magazine and getting up came and stood next to me. "It's all right about the poker table." His hand cupped the back of my head. "It was just an idea I had."

The bright wool fell to my lap. I studied his face anxiously. "But it isn't all right! You wanted it!"

"Well, I don't now; not any more." He looked down at me without smiling.

"I was awfully mean," I told him. "Somehow it all hit me the wrong way."

190

"No, you weren't mean." He hesitated. "You just ... you just put it kind of strong."

"I react kind of strongly." I burrowed my head back into his hand. "Sometimes I can't help it."

"I like people who react strongly. Maybe that's how you got me in the first place, Mrs. B." He indicated my knitting. "Do something with all that stuff." He pulled me up by the hand.

The wind blowing through the sleeping porch, when we reached it, passed like a living thing through the pear tree between us and the stars.

Next morning, it being Sunday, I slept late. The birds had already gone about the business of their day, whatever that is. Babs came out and sat on the foot of the bed.

"Where's Daddy?" Her expression was serious.

"Daddy?" I yawned. "Driving off the first tee by now, I suppose."

"You mean you let him go to the golf club?" Babs's eyes were glued on me.

"I don't have much choice about that," I answered cheerfully.

Eileen's voice came up from the lawn below. "Want some coffee? I'll bring you a cup."

"Mother!" Babs's voice dropped. "Before she comes; I know about yesterday afternoon."

"Yesterday afternoon?" I repeated hazily.

"Mother! Don't act as if you didn't remember! Eileen and I were going along the hall. We heard you tell Daddy you didn't want to be married to that kind of man."

"Oh, that," I said. Then, suddenly, "Oh, *that!*"

"Mother, don't be so dead-pan! And now he's gone off to the club and you lie there as if nothing had happened."

I sat up abruptly, very wide awake indeed. This was taking on unexpected proportions. Eileen came out with the coffee. I motioned her to sit down too; I swallowed the drink slowly, fighting for time.

Making them understand was terribly important. Babs, with marriage ahead—well, Babs was hothearted but hotheaded too. Eileen would have a very tired husband due home before long, we hoped, from Italy. She would need all her good sense. With the hot coffee giving me courage, I began.

"Listen, you two little half-wits, you don't seriously think I'd quarrel with Daddy, do you? I mean you don't think I'd be serious?"

Babs came right back, "Maybe you weren't, but Daddy was. I can tell."

"Look." I leaned forward. "People differ; married people most of all. They differ over things like 'What'll we do tonight?' 'Who'll we ask in?' 'Are we going to have that radio program on or off?' It's all awfully irritating, and it's terribly unimportant."

"People should be considerate," Babs said. "I don't think it's unimportant." Eileen, who's reserved, made no comment.

"But you've got to be yourself in marriage," I explained. "Otherwise the foundation isn't real. The catch is you ought to be polite about it and I guess I wasn't. I got personal which Daddy never does and there's no excuse for that."

Babs's eyes met mine. There was a kind of defiance in them. I had no wish to lay my heart out for her to walk on, yet I was under a kind of compulsion to tell her the truth.

"Look," I began again. "I adore Daddy. I always have and I always will. I shall also fight with him over certain things until the end of time. That's what I—that's what family life is; it's peace at the heart of everything and commotion on top. When you get married you're a family."

"You took the words right out of George's mouth." Babs bounced on the bed. "He thinks people that get married are a family, and that's that. But gosh, when I heard you talk that way to Daddy, well, it was kind of like the end of the world."

"I know." I huddled back in the pillow. "Don't say that again. I can't bear it."

"There's a bright side!" Suddenly Babs gave us a pleased smile. "Now you can have the money for your old furniture, can't you?"

I nodded. "No doubt about that. Daddy's fed up with the whole business. I'll order the covers and surprise him with them on the night of our anniversary party. So don't forget they're a secret."

192

"You won after all," Babs said. "Good old Moms!"

Accordingly Eileen and I set out the following day to find the slip-cover material. It seemed unbelievable how little there was to be had; a few yards of this, a remnant of that. When we finally found something, we realized we did not know how much we needed. The store agreed to hold it pending the time when their operator could come up to measure the pieces in the living room.

He arrived a couple of days later; a dark man, vital as an eel. As he measured, I tried to impress upon him the fact that the work must be completed before the great event. Babs joined in, feeling he had not even heard me.

He straightened up, looking peculiarly at Babs. "We wouldn't want Mother disappointed, would we?" he said in an oily voice.

Babs swallowed. I had feared the reverse. Things like that affect her unfavorably. But there was no incident. He left agreeing to go to the department and pick up the material the following afternoon.

"What a guy! Never mind, now you're going to get your big wish, and in time too." Babs patted me on the head as she passed.

That night I stood alone once more in the center of our living room. It was late and I was on my way to bed. I stopped just to indulge myself in a little game of imagination.

I scrutinized the furniture; its drab tapestries; the impression they gave of hard facts; facts about wear and tear, neglect.

Funny how as you grow older emphasis shifts, I thought. Babs, at twenty, seems to want nothing that she cannot wear or carry. I think in terms of my home, my surroundings. That is where my pride operates. I thought of the lovely material that Eileen and I had found; the intricate pattern, the cool, widely spaced background, the brilliant yet subtle effect. At last the living room would have an air. The room would suggest gaiety; people off stage just coming in, friends for tea, for cocktails. I would inaugurate that lighthearted hospitality on our anniversary.

"Hello!" Ed's voice came from close behind me. "Are you

still up?" He put his arms over my shoulders from the back. "Whatcha doing?"

"Planning our anniversary!" I leaned my head back until it was against his face.

Unexpectedly (what Ed says is often unexpected) he asked, "We had an awfully good time up at the Lake last fall, didn't we? Remember how good everything tasted? Remember the quail somebody shot and gave us?"

Almost with a jerk I brought my mind to them. I nodded.

I remembered having heard shots, earlier that same afternoon, as I had gone down to the lake. I remembered how startled I had been by them because I am terrified of guns.

Ed squeezed me closed. "Want to see something?" he asked. "I wasn't going to bring it out until our anniversary; I found it this afternoon. But I think I'll show it to you now, when there's just you and me. It's something we need up at the Lake, you and I."

He went out into the hall. I stood as I had been when hunched within the ring of his arms. Inside me, something was contracting . . . contracting . . .

Ed came back. He stood squarely in front of me.

"Twelve gauge. Twenty-eight-inch barrel. Full choke. Automatic ejector. Scarce as hen's teeth, but I found this one. They say hunters ought to get a hundred rounds of shell this fall; they did last year."

He held the shotgun as carefully as if it were a child. His right hand went delicately over the polished walnut stock, the engraved side lock.

"Isn't that sump'n?" he asked proudly.

I looked blurrily down at the dark barrel of the gun. I saw Ed's hand curved over the walnut.

"It is," I said. "It certainly is."

CHAPTER

22

"WITH ONE BLOW OF HIS AX, the woodcutter killed the wicked old wolf and out jumped Red Ridinghood's grandmother, none the worse. . . ."

Barbara Elizabeth, her curls shining above her pink bathrobe, leaned over the book of nursery tales. I drew her closer. "Did you like that one? We're reading aloud." For now Ed stood at the door of the living room.

"So I see." Ed smiled, but briefly. "Here are the Smiths, dear."

Ben Smith came forward, sank on the arm of the couch, and gave me a friendly pat. "Hello, Elizabeth."

"I snagged these boys downtown." Margery Smith's face was gay and eager under her fluff of blond hair. "You and I are being taken out to dinner, so get ready." She stooped down and smiled at Barbara Elizabeth. "Hi, Barbie!"

"How wonderful!" I disengaged myself from Barbara Elizabeth. She still sat back against the cushions, feet out and book open on her lap. Suddenly I remembered. "But I have to stay with this one. Everybody's out but me."

"How about Eileen?" Ben wanted to know. "It's her child."

"Didn't we tell you? Ed blew her to a holiday. She's just left on a week's vacation with some girls she used to know in New York."

"She's earned it," Ed put in tersely. "She's had to worry right through this war from the beginning; Dick was drafted the first day, you may remember. Now the anxiety is over, the strain of waiting for him to come home is almost worse." He was silent for a moment. He was thinking of Dick somewhere

195

in Italy, hoping to be shipped home. Then he went on lightly, "Elizabeth, here, has nothing to do but take care of the house, anyway. She might as well take on the small fry, too."

"She'll collapse on you." Margery's manner was serious. "You've no idea how gruesome it is taking care of a three-year-old. Washing, lugging them to the bathroom, picking up after them." She paused for breath. "What you ought to do, Elizabeth, is pop her into a good nursery school. I know one."

I smiled. Margery is my best friend; she's also pretty hard-boiled in a nice way. "It isn't just a question of my being able to care for Barbara Elizabeth," I told them seriously; "I *want* to. We're going to have a lovely time together; aren't we?" I put my arm around Barbara Elizabeth again. "We think a little girl who isn't even four years old yet is just as well off in her own home. Better!"

Margery eyed me curiously. "Come on, Ben," she said at last. "Good-by, Ed. If Grandma ever comes up for air, let me know." She walked out, her husband after her.

It was five-thirty the following morning. Like one drugged I heard, as from a great distance, little noises, close at hand. And now a small knee groped at the edge of the mattress. Barbara Elizabeth, in thin pajamas, inched herself up caterpillarwise onto the bed. Sleepily, I made room for her. She would be fun to have snuggled down beside me. But nothing came near me. The air was dim and cool this early in the morning, though it was summer. Duty, the most uneasy of bedfellows, prodded me. What was she doing? Was she catching cold? I twisted my head around to see.

This was a tactical error. At once she leaped, fitting herself into the small of my back. "This is the way the farmers ride." She jounced all breath from me.

There was nothing for it but to find something to keep her quiet and off my spinal column. I got up and brought a magazine, crayons, a pair of blunt scissors, and slipping a light bathrobe on her set her between me and the lump of blankets that was Ed. Then I closed my eyes again.

At seven or so he rolled over. We both awoke and watched.

Barbara Elizabeth was busy with the scissors. The spread was strewn with paper.

"I'm cutting. I'm cutting a picture." She held it up. It was a reproduction of one of those pen-and-ink drawings of a woman with pouter-pigeon lines, a prissy little V of a mouth, small (although kindly) eyes peering through glasses. The hair was dressed high with curls on the forehead somewhat as I do mine. "I cut a picture of you, Grandmother," she announced.

"It does look something like you, at that." Ed grinned.

Barbara Elizabeth knew when she had scored, if not why. She repeated her success. "That's a picture of you, Grandmother." She leaned her head back and ho-hoed at the ceiling.

"All right for both of you." I got up with a sniff. "And just for that," I told Ed, "you can dress her."

He didn't, of course. He brought her down as she was. I set a chair for her between us at the big table. (One of the odd things Eileen does is to feed her alone. "The family's too distracting," she tells us. "Threes can't concentrate.") I came behind her with a bib.

Barbara Elizabeth glanced up and down the table. "I don't want a bib. I want a napkin like you."

"But you always wear a bib." I slid it under her chin.

"But *you* have a napkin. I want a napkin like *you*."

Was she going to cry? "All right, dear." Hastily, I gave her mine.

"Well, that all blew over!" Ed observed.

"Eat your cereal, Barbie." I avoided his eye.

"I will, Grandmother." Barbara Elizabeth lifted her spoon. Then she put it down. "Are you having your coffee, Grandmother?" she asked interestedly. Now her glance fell on a china elephant used to hold matches. She reached for it, her eyes brightening.

"No, no, dear." I took it from her. "Eat your cereal."

Ed came around and kissed me. "Let me know how it comes out, because I've got to go to the office."

"I've got to go to my office, too." Barbie slid down from her chair. With a sigh, I went after her.

What with one thing and another, it was at least an hour from starting time when I got the last spoonful of egg into her mouth. But never mind how it had been done; she was fed. I said as much to Margery, who called up just as I finished clearing the table.

"You and Mary Lee," Margery said. Mary Lee stays with babies evenings as a "sitter." "The other night she had to give a bottle. It seems this infant was a spitter-upper. 'Only one thing to do,' Mary Lee informed us. 'You ram the nipple down into the baby's mouth and simply *hold* it there.'"

"*You* try to feed someone else's child," I came back.

"Not me." Margery's voice was repellently cheerful. "To take care of small children you've got to be going nowhere and doing nothing. Well, run along, Grandma!" She hung up.

I did; upstairs, to a closed bathroom. I waited; then, "Unlock the door," I ordered.

"I'm very busy." A soft voice spoke from the other side.

I stood uneasily on the landing. It was silly to be nervous, of course. The medicines were high up; Ed's shaving things were out of reach, I hoped. But I began to tighten inside. "Open the door, dear," I said, as compellingly as I knew how.

This time there was no response at all. I stood, uncertain. I *could* climb out, go across a sharply sloping bit of roof, and force the screen. I started.

Suddenly the door was opened from within. Barbara Elizabeth stood holding a cake of soap and Ed's toothbrush. "I cleaned the floor for you, Grandmother."

I spoke more sharply than I meant to. "That's Grandfather's and he doesn't want you to have it."

"Yes, he does want me to have it." She was going to cry. "Grandfather would be glad to give it to me."

I knew I had been ungracious, not appreciating her work. But so many issues were involved now that I didn't try to unravel them. Instead I took her by the hand. "Come, dear. Grandmother has a lot to do."

"I have a lot to do, too."

I resorted to bribery; "We'll go to the store, later, and buy some candy," I promised. "Now come play on the back porch while Grandmother does the breakfast dishes."

"I don't want to go later." I paid no attention to this remark, which seemed childishly vague. I put her out on the sunny veranda and I went into the pantry. When the glasses and silver were polished and put away I glanced out the door. She was not there, not even in the garden. "Barbara Elizabeth!" Again I felt that rising lump of alarm in my throat.

I overtook her, two blocks away. She was going to the store to buy the candy. She took my hand but she did not and would not turn back.

I stood looking down at her determined little figure. I was beginning to see that for someone minus four to live happily with someone minus fifty was hard. It was a matter of tempo. Thus far we had not meshed. We had slid past each other like people dancing on a different beat. Where I was fast, she was slow. I was always pressing, riding roughshod over the present toward the future. Barbara Elizabeth did not anticipate the next hour or enjoy pleasures ahead. She did not recall the past, wistfully or otherwise. She lived in the here and now. She was immediate. Understanding this, quite suddenly, I reached for her hand and together we started for the shopping district.

Like all the other children, Barbie ranged the market. We came forth, at last, with only one unintended purchase; her choice this time was animal crackers. I hugged to myself a huge brown paper bag with three lemons precariously topping the contents.

"Come, dear," I said as I managed to hold the door open. "Grandmother wants to go home."

She was before me on the sidewalk. "Grandmother wants to go home," she chanted. "Rum and Coca-cola! Rum and Coca-cola!' Grandmother wants to go home."

A passing dowager eyed me until I shrank away. In so doing I squeezed the lemons out. They rolled into the street, Barbara Elizabeth after them.

A car swerved sharply. The driver gave me a bitter glance. Then as I spilled the contents of the bag in reaching for Barbara Elizabeth's arm his mood changed and he grinned. "Watch it, Grandma," he called.

Grimly, I gathered up my packages. We resumed our journey, pausing from time to time to pat cats, say hello to doggies, and go up and down other peoples' steps. It was lunchtime when we reached home.

I put Barbara Elizabeth at her own little table but I did not leave it bare and cheerless as her mother would have done. Instead, I covered it with one of my new flowered mats. While I was taking up her food she tore the flowers off in long, lovely strips. "Oh, Barbie, dear, how could you?" I began. But I did not launch any further reproaches; I saw they would strike harmlessly all about her thoughts without touching them. I gave up the struggle. At last I took her up for her nap. Now I would have an uninterrupted hour or two.

The fourth time I went up the stairs to put her back into bed I decided to stay up there until she had dropped off. "I'm right here!" I told her. I sat down in the hall. Every few moments the door opened very softly and her head peeked around it. "Are you right there?" she asked.

I followed her into the room. "I'm going to be really angry."

She scrambled onto the bed and lay down. From her pillow she looked me interestedly in the face. "Are you going to be really angry? Come here; I want to give you a big hug."

The situation was rapidly deteriorating. I considered it. "How would you like to nap in Grandmother's room?" I asked at last. "If you will go right to sleep, I'll let you lie on my bed."

She agreed, all smiles. At least, she was quiet. I went downstairs to the laundry. "You'll find it easier to do her washing every other day," Eileen had said. As long as we had had a washing machine, we had also had Norah. She was on a semi-annual vacation of a week. I was not too familiar with the workings of this large gadget. However, at last everything was washed. On the main floor someone called, "Who-hoo!"

I ran up to the front hall, pushing back my hair and wiping my forehead with the back of my wrist. It was Margery, dressed for town in a cool gray rayon suit and hat to match. She looked pityingly at me. "How's about getting a sitter and coming downtown with me? We'll buy something, a hat perhaps, and then have some tea."

"I'd like to." I hesitated. "But I'm not nearly through and really," I added earnestly, "while Eileen is away, my place is here."

"Taking it hard, eh?" Margery patted my damp cheek. "Well, don't get a complex about being the indispensable woman!" She consulted her jeweled wrist watch and once again walked out on me.

I watched her trim little figure go down the street. I smoothed my own wet dress and went thoughtfully upstairs.

Suddenly, I was terribly tired. I would take a few minutes off to lie down. I stepped through the low hall window to my sleeping porch. Nothing must waken Barbara Elizabeth. I fell on the pillow dead to the world and then, opening my eyes for a conscientiously careful glance, I saw her. And I saw something else as well; something flat, curved, green, and shining that she was turning in her hand. It was the shine of polished jade surrounded by gold. I got up and rushed in. It lay on the blanket cover; a lone link out of the bracelet Ed had given me on our first Christmas. The stones, each about as large as a dime, were set in flat rings of gold, each heavily linked to the next.

"Oh, *Barbie!* You've broken Grandmother's lovely bracelet!" I stood aghast.

"I didn't break it," she said. "I took it every bit apart." She touched the curved surface with loving fingers.

"Darling! Where are the other pieces?" I must be careful now; careful not to make her nervous or she would forget. "Try to remember," I urged.

"I'll find them. I'll get them for you, Grandmother." And now indeed she did find a second one hanging on the nail where Ed puts his watch. Another was on the window ledge. A fourth we discovered together in the drawer of the night table. The fifth apparently defied us both.

I was close to tears. There was no use trying to make her understand the value of this bright, shiny object. She knew, of course, that some things were mine and others hers; but it was too late for that to do any good. The issue open was to keep her concentrating on the whereabouts of the still missing piece; to help her remember. A few moments, and it would be too late. She would really have forgotten.

"Barbara Elizabeth!" I sank exasperatedly onto the bed. Then, "Open your mouth!"

It slid from her cheek; the precious link. "I found it for you,

Grandmother!" She giggled happily. We had reached the climax of a great joke. "It was there all the time!" she said.

Had she been my own child instead of my grandchild my reactions would probably have been quick; as it was, I didn't know exactly how to deal with this.

I dressed her in silence, trying as I did so not to dwell on how narrowly she had escaped swallowing the hard disc; on how it might have blocked her insides, perhaps even killed her. "From now on," I told her firmly, "you are going to stay with me where I can see you every single minute."

Accordingly, I took her along as I went wearily back to the laundry where her small dresses, overalls, and nightclothes lay in a sodden heap, waiting to be hung out to dry. I drew out a chair and lifted her onto it. (Eileen would have let her climb up herself.) With the unaccustomed weight of the basket pulling on all my back muscles, I went out into the yard. The sun was now heading downward. This was not at all the way washday was pictured over the radio and in the lovely colored ads. It must be that I was inefficient. Tomorrow, I really must organize. . . . I thrust the pins firmly onto the line.

Suddenly, the piece in my hand fell to the grass. A loud scream was issuing from the basement; one scream, then utter silence. For just a second everything stood still, including me. I could not move; I simply could not go inside . . . and then I raced for the door.

It would be the wringer, of course. She would have started it and caught her little hands, her soft arms. I did not know the mechanism was practically foolproof and childproof. I went in almost physically sick.

She was standing up on the chair leaning over the sudsy water. Her arms and hands thrashed through it, scooping it up. Her shout had been a cry of sheer delight. With another scream of pleasure, she splashed the foam toward me. To my undying credit let it be said I had just enough of something left to lean down and throw a handful of foam back; I played her game. After which I dropped on the bottom stair and closed my eyes in tired thankfulness. I'm too old for this sort of thing, I said to myself. I'm not sure I have the strength left to finish this dawn-to-dark, up-and-down day. There are times when even love is not enough—

I might have gone on sacrificing myself and to no purpose had not several things occurred. In the first place, while bathing her, I did one of the senseless things you do at my age. I lifted her into the water and slipped on the tiled floor. The curved rim of the tub struck me just under the lowest rib and seemed to stay there. I drew up, gasping for breath as Barbie went bounding into the water. "Did we go whoops, Grandmother?" she asked.

"We did! We certainly did!" Now the welt in my side felt like the track of a heavy car wheel and something like rubble moved above my heart. I managed, however, to go down and fix her supper, and, when she was through thrashing about, to dress and feed her. With a promise of toys I took her up to bed. Ed would want to play with her as he always did on coming home. Too bad, but tonight she would, I hoped, be fast asleep.

I put her, freshly scrubbed and shining, into her small bed and drew up a chair near by. Nothing, not even weariness, was going to cheat me of this moment. "And now let's say your prayers," I urged.

She looked me gravely up and down. "I don't want my prayers," she told me. "I'd rather have my scissors. And no more kisses," she added as I rose disappointed and prepared to say good night. "My kisses are all wore out."

But when I started out of the room, she was quick to stop me. "Grandmother, can you read me the nursery tales?" Ed walked in to find me finishing, aloud, the tale of the wolf and the grandmother who emerged none the worse.

He did not kiss me. Instead he leaned down to the small, shiny cheek. "Hello, sister." Then he turned and stood in front of me, his eyes on my dress. "What's that; chocolate?" He pulled an immaculate handkerchief from his breast pocket and began to dab at me. "This grandmother looks a good deal the worse," he said.

Then suddenly, quite suddenly, the wheels of my imagination began to turn over. I saw Barbara Elizabeth followed by a person who constantly said, "Don't!" or, "Hurry, dear," or simply, "No, *no*." I saw this woman, old enough to be Barbara Elizabeth's grandmother (I smiled involuntarily at that one), trying to be her playmate. I saw what all this was doing to me; I saw what it was failing to do for her. I saw her in a grownup's house, so wrongly equipped for one her age; so full of actual dangers. There must be a better solution.

There was. Margery had been right; I saw it now. I swept past Ed, scooping my lipstick off the dressing table on my way to the telephone. As the mechanism set up a buzzing at the Smiths' I made up my lips; a lovely scarlet.

"Margery?" I asked. "Listen, dear, what's the address of that nursery school? You were right, Barbie is ready for it."

Besides, I told myself as I wrote the street and number down, out jumps Grandmother, here and now.

AT FIFTEEN OR FORTY one intends to do a thing and looks for the tools with which to do it. At three, one explores, one experiments with objects to find out what they will do; the many objects of an ordinary household. And there isn't much a family can do about it; or is there?

From the direction of the kitchen, I heard a soft scraping sound. I was out in the pantry getting myself a late cup of coffee. I knew Norah was upstairs. There was another scraping sound, prolonged this time, but after that came silence. The noise was forgotten.

Later I carried my empty cup out to the kitchen. It was then I found Barbara Elizabeth. She stood on a small stepladder, her three-year-old person in pink denim overalls pressed against the sink. Her curly-topped head was bent intently and she was stirring with a spoon.

"What are you doing?" I asked interestedly.

"I'm *doing* something." Her voice was even; sweet. She did not look up.

On the shelf beside her were seven or eight empty pasteboard pudding boxes. The powders they had held lay in glittering mounds of yellow, rose, and lime green. She was spooning the green gelatine into a bowl of water.

"I'm making something." She enlarged this. "I'm making something for you."

Before I could answer her mother appeared. "Oh, Barbie," she leaned horrified over the child, "I've told you not to take things down. I had to shop all over for those puddings and now look what you've done!" Eileen's voice was distressed and

205

she went rapidly on, "You *know* you're not allowed to play with water and I *said* you weren't to climb—" She set Barbara Elizabeth on the floor with a thump.

A look of confusion clouded Barbara Elizabeth's face but she got back to the main issue. "I'm *doing* something." She stepped onto the ladder.

"Not here, you're not!" Eileen pulled the ladder back. She turned on the water and the brilliant streaky liquid gurgled down the drain. She took Barbara Elizabeth to the foot of the stairs. "Run up and play with your own things," she said.

Barbara Elizabeth's face tightened like a monkey's but she did not cry. Instead, she plodded obediently up the stairs. When a road is closed one goes another way.

That afternoon I was attracted to the living room by the sound of Ed's and Babs's voices. It being Saturday, my husband was home early and had dropped into his big chair optimistically holding the evening paper.

Babs leaned over him. "Here, I'll show you." She riffled past the war news and stopped short of sports. "See those two people? See what it' says? 'Married today at the St. Bernard.' Come on in!" She had seen me. "I'm only telling Daddy people do have wedding receptions in hotels." She crossed over and sat down beside me.

"Who's getting married and when?" I asked.

"George and I are, I hope, I hope. George doesn't have to report back every whipstitch now to that old Navy hospital. And anyway, it's fun to talk about it," she finished realistically.

"I like a wedding reception in one's own home." I was entering into the spirit of the thing, or so I thought.

"I'm sure you do. I suppose it doesn't cost as much." Babs attempted a disdainful look at me, an economical streak, being, to her, about the same as a criminal tendency.

"What's the matter with receptions at home?" Ed wanted to know. He was feeling big expenses coming on like a cold spell.

"The home." Babs came back promptly. "Especially the front hall. You ought to see the way George's mother has done theirs. The walls are soft turquoise striped with gray. The console has a dull mirror top and the chairs are Swedish modern." She sighed. "But of course Madelaine has super-super taste."

I sighed too. What had once been a pretty green paper in our hall had faded to gray and not uniformly. The once apricot-colored flowers had sickened, and where Freddie and his crowd had raced hundreds of times over the stairs they looked what they were, kicked. "I suppose," I said, "we really should do the hall over."

"I don't." Ed's tone was short. "And now how about letting me read my paper?"

There was a suspicion of tears in Babs's eyes. She got up to hunt a cigarette. Williamsburg blue, I thought. "It would refine that old mahogany clock. I'll paint the woodwork white and put a touch of American beauty somewhere and a hint of chartreuse—"

A noise diverted me. Barbara Elizabeth was coming down the stairs. With her right hand she clutched the banisters. With her left she held a wad of material to the top of her head. She was saying something to herself in a loud tone. "Lammer girl, lammer girl." Her voice was loud and doleful like a street crier's, yet there was a note of satisfaction in it.

"She's copying the twins." Babs screwed her face around toward me as she put a light to her cigarette. "They hang kerchiefs on their heads like the high-school kids and call themselves glamour girls."

Barbara Elizabeth swept into the room ahead of a train of scarlet and white stripes. "That child has your color sense," I observed.

"She has my blouse! Hey, have a heart! I just bought that." She pried it out from under the baby's fingers.

And now Eileen came down the stairs breathless and apologetic for her child. "Oh, your lovely waist! I hope she didn't hurt it. I've *told* her not to climb up and take things."

Babs swung down like a bear. "So you climbed up, did you?"

Barbara Elizabeth hesitated a moment between her mother and Babs and chose Babs. She giggled, prolonging a ho-ho-ho just to hear it. "I can climb," she announced. "I can climb up you." She grabbed Babs by the skirt. In the scramble that followed the matter of the hall was forgotten.

It was very late in the afternoon when I re-entered our house or, as Ed calls it, the Occupied Territory. I came in the back way. Babs heard me. "Guess who's here?"

I dropped my drugstore purchases on the kitchen table and hurried out into the hall.

George came forward to meet me. Sick or well, George steps up life for everybody, and he now was well again. Something, perfect metabolism or perhaps a happy childhood, makes George the sunniest of men. As Eileen put it once, "George is wonderful to have around even if you aren't in love with him."

His right arm was around Babs, more or less permanently it seemed, but he withdrew it to put his hand out to me. As suddenly he dropped it. "What goes on? Look out!" He pushed past us toward the dining room. We followed. I covered the space between the table and me almost in a jump.

On the table stood a little brown bottle of powerful disinfectant—open. Blimp cowered into a corner. Barbara Elizabeth stood in front of him holding a spoonful of the dark liquid up to his jaws.

The dog twisted his head aside. Babs seized the spoon and the bottle. I held my breath so suddenly it hurt my heart. Suppose she had tried it herself? Was it possible she had? The first thing to do was call up the doctor—I fled to the telephone while George put his head out in the pantry and asked Norah for the white of an egg.

Luckily Fred Beard was in his office. "I don't believe she took any herself," he said reassuringly. "She wouldn't like the taste—and there would be burns on her mouth. It isn't so easy to tell about an animal." He stopped short, his professional pride rising like a gorge. "Hey, Elizabeth, I'm not a vet, you know."

"Listen, Fred, don't be that way." I was ready to cry. "We're giving the dog white of egg."

"Well, keep right on giving it." Fred hung up.

We had just finished treating Blimp and trying to impress on Barbie the untouchableness of disinfectant in a bottle, when Eileen arrived. She had been out all afternoon at a movie. She found us exhausted and relaxed as she picked up the whole story.

Eileen's eyes were clear and angry. "I suppose the boys left the package where she could open it," she remarked.

"I left it," I told her. "And don't let that keep you from saying what you think."

"Too bad it was Mother," Ed intervened evenly, "because you can't pick on her." I shot him a glance of gratitude.

Eileen's alarm, transmuted into anger, had to find another vent. "Why didn't you spank her," she said. "I would have."

"I considered it," Babs admitted. "But she—she looked at me."

"You can't beat up on a kid like Barbie," George put in.

"I could." Eileen was coldly firm. "She's my child and I'd rather have her alive and spanked than—" She hesitated. "Much rather, thank you," she finished. "Besides," she hurried on to cover up her feelings, "she's got to be taught not to touch everything she sees. The next time she takes things she shouldn't I'm really going to punish her. She's got to learn."

Ed eyed her curiously. So did George. "May I come and see her in the brig?" George asked. He grinned at her warmly. He was very sorry for Eileen.

It seemed terribly early next morning that I heard sounds from the room next to ours. It is a small room over the front hall. We had converted it into an unmodern but very comfortable bath, large enough to hold a bureau and a rocker. It was the creak of the rocker I was hearing. I tried to pretend I needn't investigate, that it wasn't Barbara Elizabeth. There is a time of day, about six in the morning, in the summer, when rabbits and birds and children and that sort of people are at their best. I am not. Maybe Eileen would wake up—

During a pause in the creaking, I realized the water was running—running and running. I jumped for my bathrobe and flew in.

Barbara Elizabeth sat back, feet out, rocking happily. She had had a busy morning and now she was resting. Her pink pajamas, the ones with the blue lambs on them, were water-splashed. She said, pleased, "You woke up!"

"Good morning, sweetie." I kissed her and glanced hurriedly about. Spilling off the bureau was a strip of ink-blue paper—

209

the wrapping of a large roll of absorbent cotton. From a few woolly bits in the bowl it was evident she had been trying to float the stuff. A trail of water across the room led to a conveniently low piece of plumbing down which she had put it, finally, pressing the release for the water. Plugged up, it had stayed released and now the far side of the uneven old floor stood under half an inch of water. I began with a towel and a cry for help.

It brought the whole family in assorted costumes and tousled from sleep. Investigation convinced Ed this was no job for him. He went down to phone the plumber. At the foot of the stairs he paused. Then, "Come here, dear, a minute, will you?" he asked.

I ran down, the others after me. And now I saw it too; a widening patch of wetness that darkened the wall above the hall table and slid slowly downward. The water must have been running a long time; it had loosened the paper from the wall. Now, before our very eyes, it curled slowly, like a plume.

Eileen, last on the scene, was the first to speak. She came down holding Barbara Elizabeth tightly by the hand. "*Look* what you did," she told her. "*You* did that."

Barbara Elizabeth's glance followed the direction of her mother's. She was surprised but most of all she was interested. ("I know just how she felt," Babs commented later. "Like in chemistry lab; you fool with a test tube, and what do you know, it fizzes!") It would have been an important moment even for an older person, to stand there with a crowd around, the author of all this commotion. This was really something. "I did that," she repeated admiringly. "I wetted the wall."

Eileen moved swiftly. She is thin as a stick but she put Barbara Elizabeth over her hip and started up the stairs. "You were a bad, bad girl to spoil Grandmother's wall," she said severely. The arms and legs began to flail.

"I'm *not*. I'm *not* a bad girl!" Barbara Elizabeth was shouting in her own defense.

Eileen's nerves were too fine. The muscles of her mouth grew stiff as her lips closed in a straight line. Her arm tightened like a vise. She disappeared in the upper hall and a door closed sharply behind her.

Rather silently, the rest of us straggled back upstairs to dress. From the baby's room came the sound of loud protesting cries and then of persistent, unrhythmic weeping. Incredibly to us and probably most of all to her mother, Barbara Elizabeth was taking a spanking.

I dropped on the edge of the bed while Ed walked nervously to and fro. I felt physically sick, yet at Eileen's age, though I couldn't remember doing it, I might have done the same thing. Babs came in with the air she has of being the third partner in our marriage and curled up on the quilt beside me. "Gosh," she said. "Golly!"

There was a long pause during which Ed studied Babs absent-mindedly, yet critically; I knew he was wondering why she didn't go and let him get ready for breakfast. But she did not go. She was inching up mentally on the subject next to her heart. After a time she said, conversationally, "Well, it looks like we'll have to repaper, doesn't it? I figure it'll be just in time or didn't I tell you? George wants us to be married the first minute he doesn't have to live in a hospital ward, when they stop swirling his leg in warm water. He told me, last night."

I too studied Babs, sitting there in this tense moment when we were all upset over the baby, completely concerned with her own affairs. Maybe you can't cure people of being their age, I thought. Maybe at three a person has to get into things and at twenty a person has to fall in love and be blind to everything else. Can a family do much but to protect them and wait for them to grow older? I wondered.

As if to answer me, Eileen poked her head through the door. "I'm terribly sorry, Mother B.," she said slowly, "about everything. But I can tell you one thing, she won't do it again. She'll think twice before she meddles with anything that doesn't belong to her."

She stood there irresolutely, her face a sallow gray from what she had been through. Ed sauntered across the room and put a warm hand on her thin shoulder. I saw her tremble. She was close to sobbing herself. He leaned over and kissed her in the hollow of her temple, respectfully, shyly, as a man kisses a child. "It's all right."

Babs was right about the paper; it had to be replaced. We succeeded in finding a grim, hard-pressed boss "decorator" who would do the work at once. We located a copy of an old French paper with little ships and palaces and men in faint rose and turquoise against a background of delicate gray. By the noon of the following Saturday it was on and the boss and his elderly helper had gone their way.

Ed had been giving us as wide a berth as possible to avoid the confusion and the smell of fresh paint. He came home so late now that George was practically behind him. He found Babs and me in the hall admiring our achievement.

"It's all right." He studied it. "It's all right, I like it."

"Doesn't it make the house seem entirely different? Aren't you very pleased?" Babs peered at me as if I might say no, I wasn't.

I stood taking it all in, this immaculate loveliness in my house usually so battered by family life; I drank in the soft colors, the cleanness, the effect of depth in the hall. I sighed with pleasure. "It's perfect; simply perfect."

"Let's go somewhere and sit down." Ed turned toward the living room.

It was then Babs said very quietly, "Don't look now but isn't that somebody we know? Up there, at the top of the stairs?"

Ed swung around in the doorway. We glanced up. On the landing we saw the back of a small figure; Barbara Elizabeth in clean white underwaist and pants. She was concentrating on something we could not see.

"What are you doing, dear?" I asked.

"I'm *doing* something." She did not move.

Babs loped over the stairs. "Let's see."

She drew the baby aside. And now indeed we could see. There were broad smears of red along the wall; great disfiguring scrawls, made with a scarlet lipstick, defacing the dove-gray paper.

"I drawed. I drawed the little houses." Barbara Elizabeth studied with astonished interest the highly satisfactory effects of her work. "I did. I did it."

"You certainly did." Ed's voice came from very close to my

ear. I felt his fingers push through mine holding them tightly. I was near to tears and he knew it.

That night, Babs came into our room. It was just after ten o'clock and we were both in bed, reading.

"I just heard from George." Babs spoke very slowly, circling the bed. "We don't have to get houses ready for weddings. He just called up. He's leaving right away for the west coast."

"What's all this?" Ed put down his magazine. His voice was harsh with sudden emotion.

"He's going out as a replacement. They'll be in San Diego first and then go to the South Pacific."

Ed fumbled for words. "That's too bad," he said at last.

Babs stopped at the foot of the bed; her hand went aimlessly over the pineapple top of the bedpost. Her face was drained of all color. Her eyes were shining. They had the exceptional brilliance you notice in the stars on a night preceding rain. She went on. "Yes, he's probably on his way by now." Then, suddenly, she put into words the lesson of all wars for women. "I didn't used to think that I could wait. I wanted things to go my way and be quick about it, too. It's queer," she hesitated, "but I know he'll come back; and I'll be right here waiting for him. No, I never thought I could, but now I can." She came around and kissed her father with an oddly gentle gesture and then went out.

"Well, there's nothing we can do about that, I'm afraid." Ed picked up his magazine but he could not see the print. The hand that held it sank to the bed. It shook so he could no longer hold it.

ON A COOL GREEN August morning I came downstairs to find everyone at breakfast. "Sorry I'm late," I said. "I sleep too well."

Ed lowered his paper. "Happy anniversary!"

"Is it really your wedding day?" Babs relinquished a doughnut to stare at us each in turn. "How many this time?"

"It's Dick's age plus three, as usual," I told her. "If you recall, Daddy and I were married during World War One after which he went overseas and left me for two whole years."

"And how it rained that day," Ed said. "Four of us were playing bridge (Uncle Bill was our best man, you know), and we certainly hated to stop just to go to an old wedding." He put his head on one side and looked across at me. "No rise?" he asked.

Freddie's curiosity went further into the past. He bent forward, eying his father shrewdly. "How did you propose to Mom?"

Babs gave him a withering glance. "I suppose you'd like him to re-enact the whole scene?"

"Would you really like to know? Well, I'll show you." Ed came around and stood beside me. "First, I got down on one knee, like this."

"Did it creak, like this?" Babs wanted to know.

Ed ignored her. "Then I lifted her lily hand to my lips, like this, and asked her to be mine. It was a very moving scene."

"Look out, Ed, you'll tip over the whole table." I helped him, for now he was pulling on the corner for support.

214

He got up and dusted his knees. "That gives you a general idea how the thing's done," he told Freddie.

"Daddy, you're such a fool." Babs sank back in her chair. "Personally, I'd be willing to bet Mom proposed to *you*. That's the way really good men are had."

"Aren't we going to celebrate?" Eileen asked, going around to administer the last two bites of cereal to Barbara Elizabeth.

"We *had* planned a party," I admitted. "But somehow, it went out like a light."

"Let's have it." Ed sat down. "But let's not go to a lot of fuss and bother; just ask the people we like. I'll drive downtown and buy everything. Only tell me what you want."

"Can Charlie and I have Bingo and Harold and Ears Summers—"

"You can ask Bingo," I said, "but stop right there." I stood up. "Come on, everybody, let's get going."

The thing that had extinguished our personal plans was the news of peace. Perhaps it would be wrong to say extinguished and certainly overshadowed would be too dark a word; rather, it outshone them and made them seem insignificant. The omen of peace, the news of the atomic bomb, had come with the suddenness of lightning. Slowly we had tried to imagine what this liberated force meant. Did it mark our world for destruction, as a death squad taps a man condemned to die? Or had it dealt to a mad civilization the profound shock that might bring it back to sanity? One did not know. All one was sure of was that the scientists would never get what they had loosed back into the wizard's bottle. Under the terrific shade of this new knowledge we clung to what we knew.

An incident at the close of V-J Day showed that in this we were not alone. We were sitting on the porch. It was getting dark. Across the meadows back of our garden and up a little hill we could see the lights in the big room at the golf club. Cars continued to go up to it, to twist, turn, and park.

"We could go up too, I suppose," Ed said. "Everybody we know will be there. I'll bet there'll be a lot of good liquor poured down tonight." We both sat silent, remembering the hysterical celebrations in 1918. "But I'd rather sit right here," he finished.

It was quite dark now. Someone was warming up the club piano. "I'd rather stay quietly with the children." I agreed.

Then it came. I could not have imagined it. It could only be that it was so. Up the hill the casual young and the careless-seeming older people were singing. To some spiritual force, vaster in its impact on savage human history than the impact of the atomic bomb on the New Mexico desert, they were turning to steady themselves. The sound traveled across the fields, simple as a little wind. "Abide with me," they sang through the clear darkness. "Help of the helpless, Lord with me abide."

"Well, I'll be damned." Ed spoke from a dim corner of the porch. "And I thought I was the only one."

That was how we came to forget our anniversary until the very morning.

Gathered by phone calls, guests came; the Smiths, including Mary Lee, and a score or more of our contemporaries, not to mention various friends of the children.

The preparations had been quickly and easily made. Babs had come in with flowers and candles. "I couldn't get foliage green," she had said anxiously. "These are a kind of sage; will they do?" And suddenly we had looked at each other and burst out laughing. It seemed very long ago, the time when the coloring of a lump of wax was important.

And as the guests came they also went, leaving us just a family again.

One by one the children, too, said good night. Freddie even passed on a compliment. "Bingo says he bets you were real good-looking, once."

"He does, does he?" Ed began indignantly, but I motioned him to silence. "That was nice of him," I told Freddie. It meant a lot from Bingo, who I did not suppose had ever particularly noticed me in all his fifteen years.

Eileen carried Barbie in to be told good night; Ed had insisted she be allowed to stay up. "A little fun won't hurt her," he had said. Now he kissed her softly on either side of her eyes. "Good night, little girl."

216

Babs was the last. She ran her hand over her father's hair. "Some parent I have! I can't imagine how you ever landed him." She followed the others upstairs.

I remained curled up on the couch while Ed settled in his armchair and packed his pipe. "Well, dear, this time next summer, we'll have been married thirty years."

"You sound like Freddie, when he was six. Remember? Somebody asked him how old he was and he said, 'Do you mean now? Because I *was* five.'"

Ed smiled. "Thirty years is a long time."

I resisted the temptation to make something of this remark. "And the last few years seem the longest," I said. "Such a lot has happened. Why, even five years ago, there wasn't any Barbara Elizabeth."

"I've been wondering." Ed puffed slowly. "I suppose Dick will be back soon and getting out of the Army."

"And looking for a place for Eileen and Barbie and it won't be in this house," I warned him.

"That's what I mean," Ed said slowly. "First, he has to find a job. Well, I think I can give him one, down at the plant. In fact, I'm making a place for him, as my assistant."

"Oh, Ed!" I hugged the pillow. "That would be wonderful, just wonderful."

"He may not want it, of course; you can't tell." He looked seriously at me. Then he smiled. "But I kind of think he will."

"Too bad you haven't a job for George, too," I said tentatively.

"He's a different boy." Ed spoke with conviction. "It's not that he hasn't just as stable a character or isn't as steady underneath; but I think there's a strong streak of adventure in him. Dick will want security; George won't care about that."

"It's because with money behind him, he *has* it," I remarked.

Ed came back promptly, "You underestimate him. What I mean is, a strong sense of adventure is part of his nature. It wouldn't surprise me to see George dream up something entirely new and all his own, and put it over, too."

"Funny how different your own children can be. Well, there can't be too much excitement in life to suit Babs," I said, "so I guess she's got the right man."

"George is really crazy about her," Ed said simply. "That's the all-important thing."

"She adores *him,* and personally, I think that's even *more* important." I turned my engagement diamond on my finger, looking back. "A woman's life after she marries is so largely her husband—she's *got* to love him to death, to be happy. When Freddie grows up, I'm going to warn him to be sure the girl he proposes to is all overboard for him first."

"You can save your breath," Ed said comfortably. "He won't take anybody's advice on that."

I sat up suddenly. "Ed! What about Charles! Do you think he'll have to go home to England now the war's over?"

Ed spoke thoughtfully. "I suppose he will."

I lay back, for a time, in silence. Then, "It's funny, but England doesn't seem so far away now. No place does, not any more. Not even those tiny little islands, 'way out in the Pacific; it's as if they'd been brought up close by a mirage and we could almost see the people on them."

Ed nodded. "I know."

"And as for countries across the Atlantic," I went on, "they seem just across the street. I was in a shop today, trying to replace some of our everyday china, when all of a sudden it came back to me, something I'd heard over the radio. It was a woman, being interviewed in London. I could imagine how she looked, sort of little and tired, yet cheerful too. They asked her what she did after her home was ruined, without even dishes to eat from. She said, 'We went to an aunt of mine. She had eleven whole teacups left, and we managed.'" I paused. Then I went on, "War is so dreadful, yet it makes you aware of human beings all over the world; it makes you know how they must feel. So in a way, it's kind of wonderful, too. I can't figure it out."

"You're funny, the way you try to figure it all out." Ed's voice was slow. "But then, you were a funny little thing when I married you."

He watched me for a time in silence. His eyes were very steady. Suddenly he leaned forward and held out both his hands. "Come here!" he said.